KU-126-502

Acknowledgements

I am deeply grateful to Tess Wixted, who was there from the beginning. Many thanks to my readers for sharing their valuable insights – Joan Blakeley, Kathy Bridges, Fell Cheston, Stephen Cocconi, Peggy Hennessey, Jay Hinchey, Linda Kim, Bill McElroy, Katie Nelson, Lew Walker, Dawn Zervas, and Audrey Mackaman, copy editor.

Hand over my heart, I extend my eternal gratitude to my literary angel for believing in *The Last Supper Catering Company*.

The Last Supper
Catering Company

—◆—

Michaelene McElroy

The Last Supper Catering Company

Copyright 2012 by Michaelene McElroy

United States Copyright Office

Registration Number TXu 1-783-953

E-Book ISBN: 978-0-9853593-8-6

ISBN-10: 0-985359-32-3

EAN-13: 978-0-9853593-2-4

Library of Congress Control Number: 2012907324

Michaelene McElroy, Coupeville, Washington

Printed in the United States of America

The Last Supper Catering Company is a work of fiction. Names, characters, places and incidents are either the product of the author's imagination or are used fictitiously, and any resemblance to actual persons, living or dead, business establishments, events, or locales is entirely coincidental.

www.michaelenemcelroy.com

Cover design by Natasha Brown, www.futureimpressions.com

For my son, Nathan

One

———◆———

My momma died on a hot August afternoon in 1950, right before I was born. My grandma, Little G, was out picking blackberries for pie making, and my momma-to-be was out hanging sheets on the line, when Little G heard a scream from across the yard. She looked up from her bucket of berries just in time to watch Momma begin a lazy fall, as if overcome by some long held tiredness. The wooden clothespins flew from Momma's hands, snapping at the air on the way down, looking for something to hold onto. Momma was dead by the time she hit the ground, her head resting on the damp pillowcase in her hand, her *why* questioning eyes looking up to God.

Little G said I could probably see daylight when Momma squatted down–that's how close to being born I was. So, despite her motherly anguish at the sight of her dead daughter lying in the tinder dry grass, Little G reached into her baby girl's womb and pulled me into this life. Little G swore she heard a thousand voices follow me into the world, but not a single one was able to comfort her that day.

I listened to Little G tell of that day so many times her words became the marrow of my bones. And I always took delight when she turned boldly dramatic in acting out the part where she held me upside down and slapped my behind again and again, not because she was angry with me, but because she needed me to live.

"Be thankful for life! Be thankful for life!" she called out then and with every retelling.

When I let out my first baby cry, Little G cut the cord connecting me to Momma's tragedy, wrapped me in a pillowcase, and clutched me to her old woman breasts. What with life coming and going in the same moment, Little G's tears were no doubt confused as to why they were called upon.

Poor Little G had no time to consider the why of it all, for the sun was so white hot it made the air too lazy to move, and my dead momma was beginning to sunburn. For the life of me, I could not imagine Little G holding me in one arm as she dragged her broken daughter into the shade of the old red oak. To add to her troubles, I was longing loud for a breast to suckle. Like those old clothespins, I, too, was looking for something to hold onto.

Though it might sound a bit more than strange to some, I believe every mother will understand why Little G did what she did next. Sitting with her back against the old red oak, she took her daughter into her arms, Momma's head resting childlike in the crook of Little G's elbow. One-by-one, she unbuttoned her baby girl's pink rosebud blouse, pulled back Momma's brassiere, and laid me to her milk filled breasts.

"Pretty Childe, this is your daughter, B. Thankful Childe. B. Thankful, this is your momma, Pretty Childe."

2

There she stayed, rocking her baby girl and me until the sun set and Tyler Lucknow came calling, as he did most every night to make sure everything was right and in its place.

According to Little G, Momma walked with an empty spot on her right shoulder where her guardian angel should have been. Without a guardian angel to protect her, and blind to the love of the one who truly cared for her, Pretty Childe fell into the arms of every junkyard dog of a man. When the dark water washed away what goodness lay deep within Momma and sent her lost soul wandering, looking for some kind of hurtful love for the night, Tyler would come along and find her banged up body outside some booze joint. Setting the threats to his own life aside, he'd take her home, where Little G cleaned her up and put her daughter to bed. Shotgun in hand, and Tyler by her side, Little G would stand watch on the porch until the morning light rose over the hills, and the threat of no-account cowards who slithered in the night, passed.

After I heard Little G tell that story, I was certain Momma did have a guardian angel watching out for her. And that angel's name was Tyler Lucknow.

The day after Momma died, Tyler dug her grave out in the back forty where all who had gone before were waiting. No one but baby me, Little G, Big G (my great grandma), and Tyler were there to say goodbye.

My Little G's refusal to see the world in black or white, preferring to embrace all the colors God created, set tongues to waggin' when she placed Tyler Lucknow's name on my birth certificate in the box where a daddy's name would show up proud. It was such a nice thing for him to allow, trying to save me from being looked upon as a bastard. But to town folk, having Tyler Lucknow's name on on my birth certificate made being born a bastard appear saint-like.

Years later, but still with nothing better to do, those graceless folks made sure their hurtful stories traveled all the way down our road. One day, Little G found me down by the river, my tears bubbling up and over onto the latest spiteful notes I found nailed to our mail box post. Little G took my face into her calloused hands, wiped away my tears, and brushed back my unruly hair.

"B. Thankful, you are a blessing from God that just happened to ride in on a cursed highway. Those fools are just jealous because God brought you into this world to do Him a big favor one day."

Whenever I tugged on Little G's patience with my questions around what that favor might be, she would name a chore to be done and send me on my way. While I waited for God to call upon me and ask His favor, I lived an isolated childhood in the woods between Beauty and the land of Majestic with three of His finest.

Two

Since the day I was born, I've heard whispers of the departed settle into the curve of my ear, cooing and sweet talk in my baby years, but as I got older and learned to write, I was called upon to bear witness to the lives and loved ones they left behind. As they shared their stories, my right thumb tapped an Earth-to-Heaven code to let them know I received their message, then put pen to paper so I'd never forget their names or the stories that spiraled down from the curve of my ear and rested in my heart. Sometimes I would share their stories with Little G and there were moments when she laughed so hard, or was brought so near to tears by the retelling of a departed's story, a twinge of guilt ran up my spine for claiming it as my own.

One night, when the need to wash away my guilt overtook me, I snuck down to the river running through our property and handed myself over to the river, chill and fresh, its edges disappearing into nothingness. A shimmer of stars floated alongside me as if they had fallen from the sky, and the Big Dipper looked close enough to ladle me up and carry me away. With God's handiwork all around me, the idea that maybe Little G was right about God having a favor to ask of me cropped up. Maybe it was God talking to me all along. You know, using different voices and stories to warm me up for the day He called upon me with that favor of His in mind. Just as I was beginning to feel good about being chosen, the way the outside world looked down on me yanked on my leg, pulling my shiny, bobbing imagination under water, and taking with it the notion that God would choose me for anything special.

The next day, I fessed up and told Little G the truth: that the stories came from heavenly strangers passing through. Fearful of the consequence she might inflict on me for making claim on another's story, I was tempted to sidetrack her by telling about the things Momma whispered in my ear. But in the end, I never tattled that on more than one spiteful occasion Pretty Childe told me that Tyler Lucknow wasn't my daddy.

For the life of me, I didn't know why Momma wanted to take away such a small comfort. Wasn't it painful enough for me to know I wasn't conceived in love? Didn't the fact that I had to float around for nine months in a sea of resentment, Momma looking upon me like an unwelcome relative who dropped in unannounced and then overstayed their welcome, count for anything?

And it wasn't as if I couldn't tell Tyler Lucknow wasn't my real daddy. Tyler was tall, dark, and handsome. I was turned out with red corkscrew hair, one green eye, the other brown; and I heard voices of the departed. Wasn't it bad enough an entire town, filled with notions of bad luck and evil spirits, was so boldly ignorant they'd have nothing to do with me?

Some girls (I was one of them for a time) pine away for their mother's love when it's out of reach. Trying to make things right with Momma, which is hard when you can't look a person in the eye, or them you, to see how true your apology is, I tapped out my bid for forgiveness so many times one summer, I formed a callous on my thumb. I hate to say it, but Momma's spitefulness made me wonder if she was in Heaven.

It was a heart wrenching decision, but when I had all I could take of Momma's hurtful whispers, my thumb sent a final message her way: G-o-o-d-b-y-e. Just because you love somebody, you don't have to let them hurt you. My motto is—Love doesn't hurt.

And mark my words, nobody, not even Momma, was ever gonna say anything bad about Tyler Lucknow in my presence. My heart still goes soft with the recollection of his generosity of spirit. My seventh birthday was a testament to the man's deep rooted goodness.

There I stood on the porch, uncomfortable as sand in my butt crack, in a plaid party dress Little G stitched up for me that was so heavily starched I couldn't put my arms full to my sides, and appeared to be an upward pointing arrow. My feet were crying and sweating fierce in a pair of too tight Mary Janes, and though Little G did her best to tame my unruly hair by braiding it, it had a mind of its own, tight curls expressing themselves by springing to freedom.

Even though I appeared to be coming apart at the seams, my heart still raced when Tyler, after such a long time gone, finally drove down our dirt road in his old, rusty orange pickup—one that moved more sideways than straight ahead. It was easy to see Tyler had gone to great strains to look especially handsome for my birthday, decked out as he was in an ironed white shirt that looked sorta new, and dark brown trousers pressed with such resolve they held a crease so sharp it cut through the air as he walked my way. And he seemed a mite nervous, acting as stiff as my overly starched party dress, when he pressed his cheek to mine. Heck, it was only me and Little G, and I didn't care what he looked like as long as there was a Banner Bar hidden somewhere under all his sorta new fanciness. I loved Banner Bars so much that just two weeks prior, while kneeling by the side of my bed, I offered up this brand new prayer to God. *"Now I lay me down to sleep, I pray the Lord my soul to keep, but if the Lord my soul would take, send me off with a Banner Bar for goodness sake."* It's true, if I only had one last supper before I died, I'd ask for a Banner Bar.

Tyler did put a hair of a scare in me when he handed me an envelope instead of the answer to my prayer. My Little G acted as confused as I was, but I saw a wink pass from Tyler in her direction. Inside the envelope, I found official papers making me his lawful daughter—B. Thankful Childe-Lucknow. I was too young to understand the importance of the paper, but I really liked the fancy look of my two last names on the parchment. Better yet, at the very bottom of the envelope, I found a Banner Bar—dark, bittersweet chocolate, wrapped in gold foil, and tied with a lavender ribbon.

Little G and Tyler, I mean, Daddy, sipped a little 'shine she uncorked to celebrate the occasion while I enjoyed some of her homemade root beer. The three of us laughed and lingered over my birthday dinner for a good while. Such a glow of love filled the room, I was unaware night had fallen around us, time to set out to the porch so I could make a birthday wish on the first star. Little G believed making wishes on birthday candles was for fools, said if you wanted a wish to come true, you had to look God directly in the eye, and you were less likely to make a careless wish if God was looking back at you. Had I known the turn of events my life would take so soon down the road with Little G and Daddy, I surely would have made a different wish.

Thrice blessed that day with my Banner Bar, and a brand new last name that came with Tyler as my Daddy, I wanted to give him something in return.

"Daddy," I said, a grateful tear appearing in the corner of Daddy's eye when I called him by his new name, "tonight I'm going to teach you the Ritual of the Five Senses."

Real careful, I turned the Banner Bar over and over in my hands (touch). I untied the lavender ribbon and wove it through my unruly hair, then opened the gold foil slowly, pressing out the creases with reverence. My eyes consumed the dark, bittersweet chocolate, so glossy I swear I saw my reflection smiling back at me (sight). I shut my eyes so nothing could mess about with my concentration, raised the chocolate to my nose, and inhaled its earthiness (smell).

Daddy laughed and teased I was going to sniff the letters right off the bar, and he wasn't too far off. The glorious fragrance alone made me so dizzy, the words *Banner Bar* jumbled up in my head until I finally exhaled, and the letters scrambled to their proper order.

Yoo-hoo, over here, my taste buds called out (hearing).

With a crisp snap I held the *B* in my hand. I always ate the *B* first, being a part of my name and all, but that night I offered it to Daddy. Understanding its worth, he accepted it with the respect due. I broke off the *R, Remember,* for myself. I closed my eyes and let the bittersweet taste rest on my tongue, its dark richness coating the inside of my mouth, and lingering holy like at the back of my throat, until it flowed into my belly and warmed me with primal fire (taste).

"Why?" my Daddy asked when he saw a tear roll down my cheek. I knew the why, but just didn't know how to explain to Daddy that I tasted my life—bittersweet, yet joyful. From that night into forever, Daddy and I would be bound together for the sharing of eternal Love found in a Banner Bar. *Remember me, for I will remember you.*

———◆———

Three

When I was seventeen, Daddy took up with the sickness that's got no cure. As Daddy had no people of his own to care for him, Little G had me move him from his cabin across the river into our house. Though the times had somewhat changed, some folks still saw the world in either black or white, and those same folks didn't take to Little G swirling the colors together. From the day we moved Daddy in, she made sure her shotgun was always loaded and near the front door. That's how much she loved Daddy.

I, too, would have done anything for my Daddy, and there must have been some part of him that knew it to be true. One morning, when I finished telling Daddy one of my stories, he rested his tired hand on mine. He watched the curtains lazily rising and falling with the breeze; his tapered breath, best it could, doing the same. Daddy's speech came out slow, the space between each word giving thoughtful consideration to the next.

"You know what would make me happy before I die, B.?"

Daddy had never before mentioned the absolute, and I was so taken aback by his matter-of-fact way, I lost my reply, could only shake my head. Truth be told, I wasn't sure I wanted to know, fearful if he leaned toward suffering, he might ask me to help him cross over before the hour God intended.

Between breaths as light as the flutter of a butterfly's wings, Daddy said his wish wasn't for himself, but for Little G, who seemed as near as Daddy to calling an eternal time out. My heart started beating fast because I knew what Little G was longing for, and had been longing for it ever since Big G's passing, seven years prior.

It was all I could do not to call out my own wish: *Please don't say it, Daddy. Please don't say it.* And then the three words never meant to line up one behind the other did just that: jellied pig's feet. I grew up spying that nasty concoction in the icebox, and no matter how many times I saw it, it turned me shrill. Tired of my shrieks, Big G hid the jellied pig's feet under a plastic shower cap, but it was a useless cover up. And, try as I might, I couldn't hide my disgust when Big G spooned the whole wobbly mess onto a plate and Little G slathered horseradish mustard over each nasty bite. The way it quivered up to Little G's mouth made it look as if the pig's feet were making one last attempt at a getaway.

But here's the thing I'll never forget—the sound of pleasure coming from deep within Little G, the pure joy lighting up her face, and that same joy resting on Big G's face as she watched her girl. A kind of holy communion took place between the two of them, like Daddy and me sharing a Banner Bar.

If I could bring a final joy to Daddy by fixing jellied pig's feet for Little G, I would just have to pull on my big girl boots and make Big G's god-awful dish. I owed them both that much.

Slowly and gingerly, so as not to cause Daddy any discomfort, I climbed onto his bed, my head finding its way to his shoulder. Through his nightshirt, I felt Daddy's bones where strong muscles once resided, muscles he used to lift me up and free me from whatever trap of trouble had caught hold of me. I opened my Daddy's hand and rested my fist in his palm. He wrapped his long fingers around it until my world and his became one. Daddy hadn't done that since my first day of school when I got kicked out for punching Onida Bossier, who was at least three of me in size, in the stomach for calling me the devil's child, my momma a drunken whore, and my Daddy even worse. Say what you will about me, but suffer the consequences when you name call my family. I struck Onida with so much force all of her soft belly flesh wrapped around my fist and wouldn't let go. When a bawlin' Onida went running to tell on me, I was still dangling from her midsection like a belly button cord.

Truth be told, I really didn't mind getting kicked out of school. It's too hard to make believe everything's right and good when people are spitting on you and name calling. When I refused to tell Little G why I punched Onida, unable to repeat such dreadful words for the pain they would cause those I loved, she sent me down to the river to think about what I had done. I did as told and thought about it for awhile, but sometimes the outside world's unkindness is too hot to the touch for me to hold. Besides, another truth be told, the fish were biting.

When I came up from the river with a string of fish I hoped would be salve for Little G's irritation, Daddy was standing at the screen door, his wide shoulders filling the space. Maybe it was the hard coal dust covering him that erased the good man I loved, for it was the only time in my life I was scared Daddy was gonna whip me. Finally, after a hellish eternity, Daddy came out on the porch and sat down on the top step. With a whirligig of fear spinning inside, I had mixed feelings when he patted the empty space next to him, but did as I was told.

"Give me your fist, child." Daddy took the fist I used to punch Onida and placed it in the palm of his coal dirty hand. He wrapped his long fingers around my fist until it was out of sight, my anger cloaked in his unswerving kindness. Daddy looked inside me with his soulful, hazel eyes. Shame brushed up against me. If anyone had the right to be angry, it was Daddy, but never in my life did I see his gentle way turn hard.

"Fists never solve anything, B. They're used to break a body's spirit. God didn't send you here to fight ignorance with your fists, daughter. God sent you into this world with a gift to share. Never forget, you're B. Thankful Childe-Lucknow and you are loved."

We sat on the porch for a long while in silence until Daddy kissed my forehead, leaving a coal smudged 0 in the center. He climbed into his truck, and though I usually ran alongside calling my goodbyes, I stayed put on the porch that day. I didn't want Daddy to know I had peed my pants.

That fateful day was over ten years ago, and I was no closer to knowing what gift Daddy was talking about than I was to having straight hair.

Lying next to Daddy, I could feel my time with him racing by, the finish line only an arm's reach away. Truly, I did want to do something great, if not for the world, for Daddy. But I'll be honest, even with the fresh memory of Little G's pleasure filled face when she ate Big G's dish, I tried one more time to get out of making those vile jellied pig's feet.

Awkward as I was born to be, when I worked on Daddy to get my way, I'd try to go all girly. "Daddy," I said in a dreamy voice, "wouldn't you rather I fix *you* a special supper instead?"

Daddy looked right through me and gave me a weak grin. "B. Thankful Childe-Lucknow, the thought of you fixing up a pot of jellied pig's feet for Little G will surely get me from here to Heaven with my own belly filled with delight."

And then Daddy laughed as hard as a body could whose coal tarred lungs have turned to angry fists.

Four

―――――――◆―――――――

Next morning, on the sly, I thumbed through Little G's recipe box, where I found a worn-out piece of paper with the ingredients for jellied pig's feet. I recognized Big G's stiff letter-by-letter way, but she didn't spell out how much of this or how much of that to use. Deep down in her belly know-how, Big G understood numbers had nothing to do with the righteous power of food; a person's loving intention was the main ingredient necessary for an eternal soul-to-soul union.

If still alive, Big G could have taught me how she made her jellied pig's feet with so much love it had reached right in and took hold of Little G's senses for all of time. Without Big G's help, my Daddy's final wish, the only thing he ever asked of me, wouldn't come true. I couldn't let that happen. Hard pressed to make Daddy's wish come to pass, I gave birth to the most far-fetched plan I ever hatched.

I went searching for Little G's old wooden picture box and found it in the sideboard. If you put Little G in an angry state of mind around you, she took your picture out of the box and placed it in an old medical book under *diseases*. When things went right again between you, back to the box you'd go. That is, everyone but Little G's ex-husband, Useless, who ran out on her when she was pregnant with Momma. His picture was permanently glued in the old medical book under *warts*. And when Little G had enough of everybody, only pictures of dead relatives could be found in the box. When I say dead, I don't mean it was an old photo of an uncle or aunt from better days, I mean close up pictures of them right after they died. I never took the time to look at those pictures because, quite frankly, I found the very idea unflattering.

Thumbing through pictures of long gone strangers, looking for a picture of Big G, I discovered there were notes on the back of each picture. The back of a picture of Daddy standing proud by his truck when it was as new as it was ever gonna be, told me he was partial to fresh caught trout fried with a cornmeal crust, and surprise, surprise–Banner Bars.

There were pictures of folks who loved stews; cornbread (some the way those up north ate it, and those who were staunch in the way of the south); ice cream in every flavor imaginable; barbecued ribs; thick slices of ham with their eggs–sunny side up, scrambled, poached, wrecked on a raft; mustard pickles on buttered rye bread; potatoes–fried, hash browned, boiled, baked; you name it. And some folks yearned all the cold winter long for cobblers filled with the fat berries and juicy peaches only found in the heat of summer.

When the next picture I turned over held Momma's image, I grew first day of school nervous. Pretty Childe appeared picture perfect lovely from a time before she was worn down by her daily argument with life, before the years had done irreparable harm. Even though it seemed a little unfair to learn something so particular about Momma that she'd never know about me, I was just too curious not to turn her picture over—when the season was right, she ate nothing but wild strawberries. Maybe that's why my hair turned out so red and untamable.

Finally, I found what I was looking for and sat down at the kitchen table with a picture of Big G. Unlike Little G, who was about as big as a minute—but don't let that fool you, that woman was strong—Big G was a tall woman with broad shoulders, large hands, and a vestigial third tit. I kid you not. And she wore a look in her eyes that told you she didn't have the time for much more than a postcard conversation.

The photograph had Big G forever sitting in a rocking chair on the very porch just outside our kitchen window, and I could see the shine of newness on the house. A large earthenware bowl sat in her lap, and I could almost hear the snap of the fresh picked sweet peas Big G was shelling. According to the back of her picture, Big G took delight in rabbit stew with rutabagas, and tapioca pudding with a shot of 'shine poured over the top.

We didn't mind Big G taking a nip now and then, for it always put the music in her. She had one heck of a time re-calling words, so she mostly hummed, and she was so pow-erful in expression, Big G's humming had once drowned out a hive of buzzing bees.

Like I said before, the departed had been sharing their stories with me for as long as I can remember, but Big G had never dropped so much as a single word anywhere close to my ear. I closed my eyes, rested my hand on Big G's pic-ture, and put my plan to the test. My thumb tapped out:

I-n-e-e-d-t-o-t-a-l-k-t-o-y-o-u-a-b-o-u-t-y-o-u-r-j-e-l-l-i-e-d-p-i-g-s-f-e-e-t-B-i-g-G.

Since only Big G had the answer I needed, I couldn't give up hope. I tapped and tapped. Waited and waited. If by some miracle I reached her, I figured Big G might start with a "Howdy, B. Thankful," or "Isn't this a hoot!" But when Big G suddenly came through, she got right to the point, like a postcard. Fortunately, without *Wish you were here!*

"Ask when the pig was slaughtered, and to see the blood. It should be deep red, not rusty in color. Look for meaty feet. Peel the skin back to see the flesh."

Somewhere around "peel back," all of my insides started churning. I was glad for the chair beneath me, for my own feet turned jellylike and would have left me lying in a pool of quiver.

A quick rap to the side of my head brought me back to attention. I rubbed my eyes to prove I was seeing things with my daytime mind and not dreaming. As if she hadn't dropped dead seven years back, there sat Big G at our kitchen table, just as nonchalant as could be.

I had never actually thought about, or, for that matter, desired to talk face-to-face with the departed; hearing their voices was quite enough. As was its job in the past, my thumb was busy tapping away, but it wasn't spelling anything. While I was gawkin', Big G went on talkin', not giving me one iota of a chance to ponder how this wonder of wonders was possible. As always, Big G's manner was direct, her words lean.

"You won't find the soul of this dish in words or numbers. You've got to go beyond what you see, into what you feel. I can show you how. Let's fetch supplies and get to work." Well, so much for pleasantries.

Before leaving for town, I set Little G and Daddy up on the porch with some sweet iced tea, hoping an afternoon in each other's company, recalling old times, would be potent enough medicine to cure what ailed them. I whispered my plan to Daddy and he smiled wide, but ever so slowly. Little G hated secrets being told in her company and turned her head away when I tried to give her a goodbye kiss.

Until that day, I had never been off the property by myself, and, certainly, I never went into town, even with somebody by my side. Hard stares, and harsher judgment that didn't know when to keep quiet, were just too much for me to bear. But Daddy had one last wish, and I was going to make sure it came true.

What a day Big G and I had together. Ever the boss, she rode along beside me telling me how to drive. "Slow down! Where's the fire? Watch out for that critter!" Finally, my nervous brow as shiny wet as a soaked slicker, I had enough. "Big G, what are you worried about? You're already dead!" Big G let out one of her big woman laughs.

Out at the Stillwater place, Preston Stillwater was about to wrap up some pig's feet when Big G whispered in my ear there was a fresher kill in the meat locker he wasn't showing me. When I called on Preston to answer to that fact, his head dropped south and turned east a bit, coming back to me with an excuse that held forgetfulness. Wasn't a minute later, Preston Stillwater was wrapping up his finest goods.

Our final destination led us down an unmarked dirt road where wild vines intricately woven above and across the road created a canopy that was choking the life out of the trees, and untamed bushes and brambles scratched their watchdog warning along the side of the truck as they tried to climb through the open windows. I didn't want to be scared, but I was.

"Honk your horn," Big G said.

"Why?"

"One: because I said so. Two: because Harmonia Pennywhistle doesn't like surprises. I know you might be tempted, but do not pick her up or treat her like a child."

Filled of late with my own share of surprises, I respected how the unexpected might disturb Harmonia Pennywhistle's composure, and pushed on the horn as we rounded a curve that led to the most curious place I had ever seen. Harmonia Pennywhistle's home, though spread out to a good size, wasn't much taller at its peak than a playhouse, and when she came galloping around the corner of an undersized barn on the tiniest Shetland pony I had ever seen, it was all I could do to stay respectful. I stopped short of laughing out loud when I noticed Harmonia was wearing a child like holster, but with a gun I took for real. She pulled up on the reins and lowered herself to the ground. I'd swear on a stack of bibles if I had put a yardstick next to Harmonia Pennywhistle, numbers 32 to 36 would have gone unused.

Miniature as she was, but fearing that gun to be loaded, I made right smart sure she knew I was Etta Childe's great granddaughter when I introduced myself. Harmonia didn't look up, so, in turn, I had to bow down to meet the gaze of her blue-milk eyes. Once I got low, I saw the hair sticking out from her cowgirl hat was as white as a sharp sun. Harmonia offered her hand, no bigger than a brand new patty pan squash on the vine, and shook my own with the strength of a woman who was no stranger to hard work.

"You must be looking for herbs and spices." Harmonia's voice turned those simple words into a melody that floated through the air like cottonwood.

"Yes'm. I'm here for..."

I had no idea why I was calling on Harmonia Pennywhistle, and turned from the littlest woman I had ever met to Big G. Standing between a dead woman and another I could fit into my knapsack made me so nervous my armpits started to leak, sopping crescent moons soaking my t-shirt.

"Black peppercorns and bay leaves," Big G said.

"Black acorns with big leaves." Criminy, that didn't even make sense to me. I tried to appear as if rethinking my order by creasing my forehead and tapping my brain temple.

"Not black acorns with big leaves; black peppercorns and bay leaves," Big G said.

"I mean, black peppercorns and bay leaves."

Not on purpose, my words came out slow and snooty sounding, and I feared Harmonia might think I was talking down to her, but she ignored my frazzled state and led me around to a room at the back of her house. Near bent in half, I crossed the threshold. Once inside, I was overcome by the exotic fragrances of the herbs and spices that hung from the ceiling and lined the walls, the glass jars crowding up against each other on the shelves, their insides introduced by names taped to their front side.

"You must be making jellied pig's feet."

"How'd you know?"

"Etta Childe always came to me when she needed spices and herbs. Black peppercorns and bay leaves meant she was fixing up jellied pig's feet for Corina, and everything had to be just so."

Harmonia snapped a bay leaf in half and put it to my nose, then had me bite the leaf. It was pungent, sharp tasting.

"Once cooked, the fragrance of the leaf will be more noticeable than the flesh."

A quick rap with the back of her knife shattered several black peppercorns into fiery mosaic pieces. "Taste." The bold personality of the pepper changed as it found its way from the front of my mouth to the back.

As if handling the bones of a sanctified saint, Harmonia placed four bay leaves in a glassine bag and filled another with enough spicy black peppercorns to serve my purpose. She handed me the bags along with a helping of sage advice.

"Remember, food made with love feeds not only the bodily appetite, but the spiritual appetite as well. It takes an understanding you'll never find on a piece of paper or in a book. And keep in mind—spices and herbs are like good looks, they don't last forever."

Harmonia Pennywhistle touched my arm. "I'm glad Etta's passing her knowledge down to you, one-on-one."

As soon as Harmonia mentioned Big G as if still alive, the melody I heard before in her voice turned sharp in my head. That little lady had a way about her that made me feel safe, but nervous at the same time. The jitters took over and I jumped up, bumped my head on the ceiling where a bundle of dried lavender and thyme grabbed onto my crazy hair, and ran outside where Big G was waiting.

There came that second in time that gets caught between the blink of your eyes, when I swear I saw Harmonia wink in Big G's direction. If Harmonia Pennywhistle could see her, I did not want to know. With my Daddy and Little G nearing the end, and Big G visiting from the great beyond, my plate was already overflowing, and I had no need for another side dish of strange.

I offered Harmonia Pennywhistle fifty cents from the money Daddy gave me, but she wouldn't take it, said no money ever changed hands between her and Big G, and then predicted I would come back some day with an offer equal in worth. As I drove away, the sight of Harmonia Pennywhistle standing next to her miniature pony was one I longed to see again real soon.

On the way home, Big G told me she was proud I wore my manners where they could be seen and didn't treat Harmonia like a sideshow circus act. For some reason, Big G being proud of me seemed as necessary as my thumbs.

"Big G," I said.

"What?" Big G had a way about her that could stop a conversation with a question.

"Nothin'."

"Must be somethin'."

"Nah."

"What?" Her question was a demand.

"Well, I was wondering what you're doing here?"

Big G sighed like she was dealing with a slow learner. "B. Thankful Childe-Lucknow, you called on me for help and here I am. Besides, you didn't really think I'd let you fix my jellied pig's feet for Corina by yourself, did you?"

Big G had a point, for I claimed no fame when it came to cooking.

"I sure as hell don't want to spend eternity with Corina Childe pissin' and moanin' about being served up some low-down-dead-man-walkin' last supper."

I hit the brakes hard with both feet. Daddy's truck skidded to a sideways halt in the road.

"Hold on a minute, Big G. What do you mean by 'last supper'?"

Big G stared out over the meadow at that time of day when the soft glow of light along the horizon makes a harsh world seem dreamlike.

"Why, I'm here to take your Little G home with me."

I laid my head on the steering wheel and cried. I cried for Little G. I cried for my Daddy. And I cried for the pig whose feet were sitting next to me in a brown paper bag. But most of all, I cried for me.

Death had softened Big G's heart, and she didn't shame me with a *tsk, tsk*. Instead, she moved toward me like music. Music can't touch you directly, but you can feel it on your skin all the same.

"Can I go home with you, too?"

"No, B. Thankful. Your work here is just beginning, and Little G is your first customer."

"Customer" was an odd way to describe my Little G, but I wasn't about to quibble with Big G while the music played.

Five

———◆———

It was getting late by the time I got home from my day with Big G, and I found Daddy and Little G in full slumber exactly where I had left them. After I fixed them a simple supper of collard greens and cornbread, which they mostly just poked at, I tucked them into their beds and, as if they were my own children, told each a special story I made up just for them. When I was certain they were asleep, I went about my business in the kitchen with Big G. We had no more than started when Little G called out, "Who are you talking to?"

Big G gave me the hush signal, as if I might tell Little G her dead momma was visiting, and maybe she'd like to put on her chenille robe, come out, and chew the fat with her. I waved Big G off.

"Nobody, Little G. I'm just singing. Are you all right? Do you need anything?"

When she didn't answer, I hurried down the hall. Frail as a baby bird, Little G was perched on the edge of her bed, her skinny legs dangling over the side. Little G stared down at the very close veins on her hands, and then into my eyes.

"You sure there's nobody else in the house but your daddy?"

I didn't think myself lying when I nodded my head. Really, there was no other *body* in the house.

"Have you checked in on your daddy?"

"Yes'm. The elixir you had me brew up last week took the edge off his pain, and his breath is rising and falling in a comfortable way. He's sleeping soundly, like you should be."

I really needed Little G to call it a day so I could get back to work, but you didn't cut Little G short.

"I forgot to ask if you fed the chickens this morning. Did you milk Beautiful Beulah? If you forget, she's gonna hold it against you and put you through udder stutter."

Little G was right about that. If I forgot to milk Beautiful Beulah right on time, she punished me by making me work twice as hard. I'd nuzzle my head up against her side, and with an apologetic hand, I'd pull on her teats, but she'd only give up a drop, drop, drop into the milk bucket, then a short stream, and then back to drop, drop, drop. Udder stutter.

Before I could declare all the chores had been seen to, Little G kept right on. The urgency in her voice shoved each word up behind the other, crowding them together.

"Did you pick the fruit and vegetables that were ripe? You've got to stay on top of the garden, B. Thankful. If you're mindless about it, your food supply will be spare in the winter months. And you'll be mighty sorry come Christmas when you don't have any spiced peaches to serve alongside gingerbread."

I tried to make light of what Little G was saying, but I'm pretty sure my trembling voice gave me up as scared.

"Little G, I've taken care of everything. And, old lady, I expect you to get your tired butt out of this bed and can spiced peaches like you do every year. You and Daddy and I are gonna open them together come Christmas morning, like always." That's what I said, but in truth, I knew our house was lined with departure schedules, because my heart was as empty as the station they were leaving, and try as I might, I couldn't pray it away.

I was near to making a clean getaway when Little G remembered she hadn't brushed her teeth, which was how she signaled the end of her day. I helped her to the bathroom and sat on the edge of the tub while she scrubbed her teeth, then smoothed some Cameo Cold Cream over her face and removed the eyebrows she still penciled on every day. Some days her right brow curved higher than the left, her look appearing doubtful. On those days, a lie was hard to form when face-to-face with Little G.

I tucked Little G back into bed, spooned behind her, and stroked her hair while I took her back to the time I told her a story she found particularly funny and laughed so hard the cider she was sipping shot out her nose. Little G remembered the day and told me that's when she knew I was a fine storyteller.

In the middle of my latest story, I heard the familiar sound of Little G's sleep whistle calling to the crickets down by the river, and eased myself away from her frailness. I opened the bedroom window wide in case a breeze decided to come a calling and put an end to the summer night's stifling heat.

Back in the kitchen, Big G ordered me to pour half a shot of 'shine in a glass. I never partook of Little G's 'shine, worried if I took a sip I'd go down the same dark road as

Momma, but I did as told. I put the glass to my nose and sniffed, the potent smell causing me to cough and my eyes to water.

"Go on now. It won't hurt you," Big G said.

I put the glass to my lips and tilted my head back, all the 'shine rushing down my throat in a stream of liquid fire that exploded in my belly, and sent me running around the kitchen with my hands waving in the air. To end my suffering, I stuck my head under the faucet and baptized my burning throat with cool water.

Dizzy from all that waving and running around, I sat down at the table and rested my head on my arms. The fire in my belly turned to a soft glow that traveled up my spine and came to rest in my mind. Once my mind turned aglow, I felt good. Real good. I was as ready as I was ever gonna be to make my Daddy's wish come true.

For old time's sake, we kept one of Big G's aprons on a hook near the pantry. When I slipped it over my head, an unfamiliar sensation moved through my body. My insides grew fuller and my skin turned as tight as a ready to burst watermelon left too long on the vine. Couldn't be the 'shine, for my thinking was clear.

Please don't think me crazy, but I got the feeling I wasn't alone in my own body, someone else working from inside me, tying the apron strings. I looked over to where Big G had been sitting, but the chair was empty; only her picture remained, leaned up against the honey jar. I panicked.

"Big G, where are you?"

"I'm right here, B. Thankful."

Oh, mercy! Saints preserve me! I swear what happened is not one of my stories. I wouldn't know how to make this up. If I'm lyin', let me be dyin'. When Big G's voice sat in the curve of my ear, I was fine with that, recognized it for what it was. I was even getting used to having her come back for a visit. What I was not ready for was Big G *inside* of me.

"Get out! Get out!"

"Now, don't go all haywire on me, B. I'm new to this, too. We don't wanna get stuck in some oddball way that would be hard to explain, do we? Shouldn't we give God's handiwork a try?"

Soon as Big G mentioned God, I recalled Little G saying God had chosen me to do Him a favor one day, and then Daddy telling me God sent me here to do something great. Just in case this was it, peculiar as the setting was, I handed myself over.

"Okay," I said, same as if Big G told me she was going outside—no mind about it, really. But I had a question I needed answered. "Do I have to talk out loud to you, or can you hear me through my thoughts?"

"Good question. Let's find out."

I screwed up my forehead and concentrated, then asked with my mind, *"What do I do first?"*

"Put all the ingredients on the counter," Big G answered. It worked! Big G heard my thoughts.

I laid out the ingredients on the kitchen counter: pig's feet, celery, carrots, garlic, black peppercorns, and bay leaves. My movements were Big G's movements—quick and sure; my hand, her hand that knew her old knife, had lived all the stories held in its handle. We had become woven into a tapestry of good cookin' know-how. Together we trimmed the feet, plucking out a bristly stray hair, and then christened the pig's parts under cold water and scrubbed away anything unholy.

"Good job, B. Now, one more time in clear water, honey, then light the stove."

Once the fire got going and we put the pot on the stove, Big G started humming *Down by the Riverside*. My own vocal chords strummed along with her until we were humming in fine harmony.

"I'm like a ventriloquist who swallowed her dummy," popped into my head.

"Not funny!" But Big G was laughing when she said it.

When the water came to a boil, I carefully set the feet to cooking.

"Now's the time to add a little salt. Salt now will enter the meat in a slow way; salt at the end will simply sit on top. You don't want that. And not too much now, you want to add a little more when the time comes to add the vegetables. Okay, B., take some of those peppercorns, about the size of a blackberry not quite ready to pick, and set them down on the board for cracking."

I gave them a whack and some of the peppercorns turned buckshot, flying out from under the knife.

"Now add the peppercorns and two bay leaves to the pot. Wait." Big G had me taste a bay leaf. *"No, make that two and a half bay leaves."*

Once the liquid came to a boil, I turned it down to a simmer. For the next two hours, the pig's feet simmered in a relaxed way, the pointed hooves floating to the top and bouncing up and down in a circle like fishing bobbers.

In their own time, the bay leaves gave themselves up to the broth and the peppercorns released their fiery oils. A meaty, yet delicate fragrance tinged with sharpness rose from the pot and found its way into my lungs. A burst of aliveness sent me spinning through the kitchen, where the temperature was no less than a hundred and ten degrees.

But I was cool as a cucumber as we sliced through carrots without effort, orange coins stacking up neatly, then chopped sweet celery, and garlic, sticky and sure of itself.

One time, when I was a smidge of a girl, my Daddy woke me from a sound sleep in the middle of the night and carried me outside, where the cold air of winter stung my face, and rain rushed from the sky, as if late for a reunion. Daddy pointed up, and I was put out he woke me just to show me a full moon. Before I had a chance to start squawking, Daddy turned me around to the sky opposite the moon and I witnessed a most rare and mysterious sight—a moonbow. Mystifying as that moonbow was, it paled in comparison to the sanctified magic spinning around Big G and me in our kitchen.

It was around midnight when Big G gave me the go ahead to add the vegetables. I watched as the carrots, celery, and garlic took a slip slide from the board and joined the bobbing hooves.

"Now's the time to see if a little more salt is needed."

Oh, jeez, I knew that meant I was gonna have to taste the broth. You'd a thought I was about to take a dose of cod liver oil the way my face squeezed up. With more than an ounce of queasiness, I dipped the spoon into the broth, tiny rafts of pepper floating on the surface. Trying to buy time, I blew on it and blew on it until Big G cleared her annoyed throat.

When my lips touched the edge of the spoon, I tasted how the pork had turned the broth meaty and salty; the fat was smooth on the inside of my mouth. The pepper and bay leaves didn't bite back; they laced the broth with their spicy perfume. None of the ingredients stood in front of the other; they worked together in harmony.

Big G let out a little sigh, as if she had sampled the broth and found it just right. It was then I knew it had all come together, and I quickly doused the flame beneath it.

"Nice call, B. You recognized the moment of perfection all on your own. Now you need to strain it off. Set the colander over my big earthenware bowl and run some cold water alongside it. The cool water will keep the steam from taking over. Go slow so you don't burn yourself."

I watched the broth fill the colander, with fall-off-the-bone tender meat, and vegetables right behind. With the flesh shrinking up some during cooking and the bones of the pig laid bare, a deep and abiding respect for the animal rose within me.

The next part of my job took some getting used to, but with Big G's expert hand I learned how to crack the joints to extract all the meat. Once the vegetables had been added and the strained broth poured over the meat, I looked upon my very first batch of jellied pig's feet. By the grace of God, and Big G's help, I had been shown how to recreate the meal that, even across the great divide, forever linked two souls together.

The most important ingredient not found in the words or numbers was Love. *Remember me, for I will remember you.*

That ready to pop feeling I had when Big G entered my body was plucked from me, and a big sigh went along with it. I opened my eyes and there sat Big G wearing a blue ribbon smile.

"Well, that was different. I gotta say, B. Thankful, traveling light is a lot better than being stuck in a body. I forgot how tight they feel. And, double G-daughter of mine, I am so proud of you. You accepted your calling with willingness and grace."

"What calling is that, Big G?"

Big G puffed up as if ready to recite a script she had rehearsed over and over again, her manner of speech, preacher flavored.

"B. Thankful Childe-Lucknow, God has chosen you to walk among the dy —"

An urgent call from Little G sent me running to her room before Big G could finish her sermon. When I got there, Little G was sitting up in bed, crying. Little G's face was so wrinkled, when she cried, which was as rare as fat legs on a bat, her tender tears never fell in a straightforward way; they turned her story folds into sad tributaries flowing into her heart. I brushed her wilted hair away from her empty eyebrow forehead.

"What is it, Little G? Why are you crying?"

Little G's voice was hiccupy, her words bobbing up and down like the simmering pig's feet. "I've been dreamin' all night that my momma is in the kitchen. I swear I can hear her humming, and I smell her jellied pig's feet cooking."

Boy, I didn't see that coming. To cover up the truth, I talked fast while tucking Little G back into bed. "What a wonderful dream, Little G. You close your eyes and go back to dreaming. You need your rest. The sun won't be up for a couple more hours. Sleep now."

I was almost through the door when Little G caught sight of Big G's apron and asked about it. Even without her eyebrows, Little G's look had the power to question my intention.

"I couldn't sleep so I thought I'd get up and get an early start on my chores. Hope you don't mind me borrowing Big G's apron." I hurried out of her room before Little G's stare whittled me down to the truth.

While down the hall, I peeked in on my Daddy. I found his forehead hot when I kissed it, but his breathing came easy. "I love you, Daddy."

When I got back to the kitchen, Big G was missing. I tapped out a message, but she didn't answer. I looked and looked, and finally found her on the porch, sitting in Little G's rocking chair. There wasn't enough of Big G to make it rock anymore, so I set my foot on the back rung and gave it a press down. I found comfort in the back and forth motion.

I figured Big G would finish her pitch for God that she started in the kitchen, but she pointed to a cardboard box with my name scrawled on the side. Inside the box, there were all sorts of keepsake bits and pieces, but it was the top two items Big G wanted me to see. The first was my paint-by-number picture of The Last Supper. Little G bought it for me when I had the measles, hoping it would keep my hands from scratching myself. I still have the tiny scar on the tip of my tongue from biting down so as not to go out of the lines or mix up the paint numbers. I did a pretty good job, except for Jesus's eyes. I was so nervous, what with Jesus looking upon me, they turned out a bit cockeyed. I told Little G I planned it that way so Jesus could keep one eye on that Judas fella. My thinking made Little G laugh.

Beneath the painting, I found a scrapbook I had never seen before, and that surprised me. Whenever I had the house to myself, I went snooping for answers to questions I didn't have the nerve to ask, but I never came across it. The cover was shiny black and *B. Thankful Childe* was printed in gold by a professional hand. It must have been sometime after Daddy adopted me when Little G took it upon herself to scratch in *Lucknow*. No way could she match the perfect gold script, but her go at it made it all the more special.

Completely staggered is the only way I can describe my reaction to what I found inside the scrapbook. There were nearly naked pictures of me as a baby, a diaper the only thing keeping me proper, and several of me later on when I had the measles. Why anyone would take a picture of a pockmarked child was beyond me. But here's the tender part: next to every photograph up to the age of four, Little G made note of *my* favorite foods—from mashed peaches and cream of rice in my baby stage; peas and carrots when I sprouted a few teeth (which loomed large in a close up picture); and cinnamon toast in my third year.

The next page held a picture of me and Daddy on my fourth birthday. I'm sitting on Daddy's lap and we're sharing the very first Banner Bar he ever gave me. I had chocolate spread from ear-to-ear, and my smile appeared to wrap all the way around, so big it was. Little G taped the lavender ribbon and gold foil wrapper next to the picture, but, over the years, the tape had dried up and now they hung loose and lopsided.

Big G leaned near to me. "Little G has so much love for you, B. Thankful, she couldn't contain it in that picture box of hers. She had to make a picture book just for you."

I can't say I remember the occasion of the last photo in the album, but Big G must have taken it. I'm nestled between my Daddy and Little G, and they're planting kisses on my cheeks; Daddy's profile is strong on the one side, while the side view of Little G is surface soft. I am the only one looking straight into the camera and not even my two-color eyes, nor my crazy hair, could dull the shine of my smile that day.

I went back to pumping the rocking chair for Big G as I watched the sun come up, the leaves on the trees turning pink and orange, then gold. When I turned around, Big G was gone, the rocking chair empty, and her sermon left unfinished.

Six

———◆———

Whatever sickness had settled into Little G made her so very weak and tired that there were times when I feared she wouldn't wake from a nap. But weak and tired as Little G was, keeping her out of *her* kitchen wasn't easy, so I came up with a plan. Let me be clear, I am not a deceitful person; however, a small white lie is acceptable when told for a good cause.

My idea came from a moving picture that flickered in my mind the night before where Little G, Daddy, and I enjoyed a lazy day picnic down by the river. That morning I called up the image again to make sure I had everything right. Just as I saw myself snap the picnic blanket in the breeze, I heard Little G's frail footsteps coming down the hall. I left the picnic blanket floating in midair and made a swift beeline in her direction.

Before Little G reached the kitchen to snoop around, I scooted her into the dining room where breakfast was waiting—hot coffee, biscuits and peppered bacon. Daddy was so convincing when he asked if the three of us might take a ride down to the river, as if it was about him, something he needed. No way could Little G deny her Tyler.

After breakfast, I asked Little G if she needed any help getting ready for our outing. She waved me off the way a child does when she no longer needs her momma's help, and I was glad, for it gave me time to fill the ice chest and hide Little G's surprise.

When I set my hand on a jar of horseradish mustard, a sudden worry came over me. I hadn't prepared anything else to go with the jellied pig's feet. How had I failed to recognize there should be something more on the plate? My ear buzzed and Big G came in loud and clear and to the point.

"Stay to purpose, B. Corina only had eyes for jellied pig's feet when they were served, blind to everything else on the table. Don't fuss it up with side dishes and the like. Keep it simple."

T-h-a-n-k-s-B-i-g-G. W-h-e-r-e-d-i-d-y-o-u-r-u-n-o-f-f-t-o?

"I had to get back before the Pearly Gates closed."

I couldn't tell if Big G was pulling my leg or not, but the vision of her knocking on the Pearly Gates handed me a hard laugh. Maybe I would make up a story for Little G around that idea. Little G loved stories about all things sacred laced with a bit of irreverence.

It was almost noon by the time I loaded Daddy and Little G into the truck, the bed of it covered with blankets to keep her surprise under wraps. I climbed in and took hold of the wheel. Next to me, Daddy looked small, Little G even smaller—and like a girl child who had messed around with her momma's make up. She was wearing way too much powder and had penciled on her eyebrows so high they seemed to ask the question I posed every day. *Why, lord? Why?*

I drove the bumpy road leading down to the river slow and easy, precious cargo riding by my side. Before they took ill, we hiked down to the river, Daddy and me carrying the ice chest between us, Little G on the lookout for birds partial to our fields. She loved to call a warning to the young, gangly turkeys roaming the fields in the summer that they'd be on her supper table come Thanksgiving. Daddy nudged me, tilted his head to the right, his eyes focused about ten yards ahead. I honked the horn and a young flock of turkeys took to fluttering and flying across the road. Like old times, Little G called her warning, but her voice was so weak it got caught in the side mirror.

When we reached the bend in the river where we used to picnic, I held the wheel tight as tight could be as I brought the truck to a halt, but it still shimmied sideways. With a hefty helping of *because I said so* in my voice, I told Little G and Daddy to stay put until I got everything set up under our grove of white ash. They obliged without making fun of my bossiness, but I saw Little G take more than one curious peek in the side mirror.

The recollection of better days laid its kind hand on Little G and Daddy when they saw our picnic set up like old times. I walked between them, supporting their frailness, and it was good to feel their arms around me again. Once I got Little G situated, I sat Daddy right next to her, both leaning up against the mother tree for support. Little G slipped her blue-veined hand into my Daddy's hand; sunlight filtered through the trees and leaf shadows danced across their friendship. Little G sighed and closed her eyes—not quite here, not quite there—somewhere between for the moment. Daddy smiled at me and nodded his head, his wordless way of telling me I had made him proud. Sometimes a look presses right up against your heart and says it all.

If Big G was right, this was to be Little G's last supper. Like Jesus's last supper with his friends, I wanted our final time together to be extra special, too, so I packed the cloth napkins we used at Christmas (the ones I painted pine cones on with my left over paint-by-number paints), and Little G's best jelly jars for our drinks. My gut feeling told me it wouldn't harm them, so I even brought along some 'shine for Daddy and Little G to enjoy with their lunch. So nervous I do everything perfect, my heart pounded hard and fast, my head ready to explode same as Little G's pressure cooker last summer, her strawberry jam covering every inch of the kitchen.

When I opened the ice chest, Little G turned bloodhound curious, head rising from her in-between state, coming full into the present, her poorly drawn eyebrows bobbing up and down. Not even Daddy's coal soaked laugh could break Little G's concentration. I decided to string Little G along for a while.

"Daddy, are you all right? Maybe we should pack up and go home. You think?" I closed up the ice chest, folded up the napkins, and stacked the plates. If I moved any slower, I'd've been moving backwards. Little G couldn't take it any longer.

"B. Thankful Childe-Lucknow, what's that I smell in the ice chest?"

My antics might come across unkind to some, but if this was the last time I was to sit with my Little G, I wanted her to remember our time all the way to heaven. Daddy shook his head, but he knew my mischief was laced with love. I lifted the lid again and stuck my head down in the chest so she couldn't see my grin as I called out foods that made her mouth pucker sour at their very mention.

"Oh, I've got some fried bologna sandwiches, deviled eggs, and bread and butter pickles."

Like a hound dog hot on a scent, Little G sniffed the air one more time and, for a minute, I thought sure she was gonna howl.

"Like hell, you say."

The minute Little G saw the old plastic shower cap and the earthenware bowl her momma always used for jellied pig's feet, she began to clap her hands the way a happy child, who has yet to find her way with words, will do. Before I could set the bowl down and get the horseradish mustard out of the ice chest, Little G had her napkin tucked under her chin and held her fork and knife *ready, set, go*.

"What made you go and do a thing like this?"

"My Daddy asked me to."

"Ah, Tyler, that was kind of you; course, you know, nobody can make jellied pig's feet the way my momma made them."

We'll see about that.

What happened next was finer than any Christmas present I ever received. With her first bite, Little G untied the ribbon. A *How could this be so?* look settled on her face, her eyes closing, as if readying for a kiss. The wrapping paper fell away with the second bite when a moan escaped her lips, and the gift revealed itself when she opened her eyes and looked directly at me.

"I don't know how, not certain I care to, but as sure as I'm sitting here, these jellied pig's feet were made by my momma. Ain't another body alive could make them with such pure Love." *Remember me, for I will remember you.*

Little G's damn questioning eyebrows honed in on me, and I turned fearful I'd crack under the pressure.

"I've got to pee," I said and took off running down to the river. I had just pulled my pants down and formed a sizeable squat, when Big G started yapping in my ear.

C-o-u-l-d-y-o-u-g-i-v-e-m-e-j-u-s-t-a-m-i-n-u-t-e-t-o-d-o-m-y-b-u-s-i-n-e-s-s? I tapped.

Big G's voice followed me down to the river.

"Eweeee! Did you see the look on Little G's face when she took her first bite? I could feel the Love all the way up here. B. Thankful, you have a powerful gift."

I wasn't sure how I felt about this "gift," seeing that when I used it, it meant my Little G was going to die, and, well, where did that leave me? In case Big G didn't know the answer, I asked my question out loud, just in case God was listening in.

"I'm happy for you and Little G, but how am I supposed to keep my heart from breaking when God takes her away from me?"

"B. Thankful, your heart is supposed to break when you lose someone you love. There's no gettin' around it. That's how we know we've loved deep as deep can be. But in the spirit of mercy, God gave us hearts that mend again and again. Cry all your tears and then cry some more. But leave the door to your heart open. Love will walk in and find you once again."

I did cry, right there at the water's edge. A school of minnows, shining silver in the sun, darted away to avoid my fat tears plopping on the surface. I stripped off my clothes and dove into the water. An eagle soaring overhead dove swiftly, accurately, and pulled an unsuspecting trout from the water, carrying it up and away. An understanding buried deep inside me rose up with the trout: time is precious. We never know when death will come, or how we will greet each other. Strangely, I felt more alive than ever, as if I held the secret of secrets inside me.

When I got back, Daddy was napping and Little G was resting on her side, watching the leaves on the trees flutter. My Daddy took me to his church one time, and when I see leaves flutter, I'm reminded of those beautiful, plump, berry-brown women fanning themselves from the summer heat and the fire of bible quotes. Unfortunately, there wasn't a quote in the good book to convince the congregation to embrace the girl with red corkscrew hair, two-toned eyes, the one who heard dead people. No sir. And since the Fellowship of Christ didn't want a fellow like my Daddy attending their services, we decided to hold our own Sunday worship down by the river, where Daddy baptized me in God's holy water the summer of my seventh year.

My Gs and Daddy didn't believe in thumping bibles or preaching fire and damnation; they lived simply in upright truth. And before my Little G fired off a round, she was charitable enough to warn trespassers up to no good by calling out a Christian warning. "I believe in Jesus and God Almighty, but I'll shoot you in the eye first and ask their forgiveness later if you take another step on my property."

I shook the river water from my hair, sprinkling Little G until she giggled and waved me off. Like all our nap time together, I laid down in front of her so we appeared spoons in a drawer. I reached behind and pulled her wilted arm over my shoulder and rested her hand on my heart while I told her the story of how Big G showed up in our kitchen, our ride out to the Stillwater place, and meeting Harmonia Pennywhistle. I went on and on about how I spent all night in the kitchen making jellied pig's feet with Big G right under my skin. Little G was right, I told her, it *was* her momma's Love she tasted. I offered a polite excuse for Big G, how she wanted to be there for the picnic, but had to punch in at the Pearly Gates before the sun came up full over the mountains. I didn't tell Little G what Big G said about the last supper business, because I was hoping Big G got it wrong.

"B. Thankful, that was your finest story to date. I believed every single word you spoke, even the line about Big G jumpin' in under your skin. That was my very favorite part. And Harmonia Pennywhistle! What a great make believe character. How does your mind make that stuff up?"

Maybe it was just a good tall tale. I mean, Little G was of the mind I made up Harmonia Pennywhistle, but she was a live person. Wasn't she? Lord, had my imagination run away with me and Big G showing up was all in my head? As crazy minded as that would make me, if it meant my Little G wouldn't leave me, I'd've been happy to wear a warning sign saying as much.

"But you know what?" Little G said.

Fearful I'd tear up if I looked for words, I shook my head, drops of river water riding down my cheeks.

"There are even greater stories inside you, yet to be told, B. Thankful." Before a blanket of hush covered Little G, she dove right into the pool of my heart.

"B. Thankful Childe-Lucknow, in case I forget to thank you when we get home, you gotta know you have made this the best day of my life. I love you, B. Thankful. Forever and ever."

Little G held me soft the way you hold a peach, 'cuz everybody knows a peach is so tender you can bruise it just by staring at it too long.

The sound of the loons that take to the river as the sun begins its fall brought me around from our afternoon nap. From the shady forest of trees on the other side of the river an eager whippoorwill called out his name over and over again. *Whip-poor-will, Whip-poor-will.*

My Daddy so loved to sit by the edge of the water in the twilight hour, I thought it worth the gamble to take the short walk down to his favorite spot. I reached out, tapped his boney knee, and he slowly opened his eyes.

"Walk with me to the river?"

Daddy nodded.

"I'm gonna take Daddy down to the river for a look see. I love you, Little G."

I kissed her powdered cheek and slid from her spoon embrace. Little G pulled in her arm, tucking all of herself safe inside. Maybe things would have turned out different if we hadn't gone down to the river, but I'll never know.

The trail leading to the river was flat, but I heard Daddy's breathing fold up, felt the burden of his weight leaning on me. Halfway down the trail, I suggested we turn back, but Daddy was determined to look upon the water. When we arrived, there was just enough light riding the river to see the manmade barrier of rocks separating shallow water from deep. It had been a long, long time since I stood in the wading pool Daddy had fashioned to protect me from the current. I wanted to stand in that safe place and never leave, even when my skin turned wrinkly like a prune, but Daddy couldn't protect me any longer. Life was about to throw me into the current.

Daddy sat down on his favorite boulder and kicked off his shoes—shoes that had grown too large, leaving an empty space that flipped and flopped when he walked. I sidled up next to Daddy and wrapped my arm around his waist, our heads resting one against the other, teepee-like. My Daddy believed a river's current carried silt covered stories, more ancient than the land itself, downstream, but you had to be quiet and still for them to speak to you. We dangled our feet in the river, the upstream stories licking at our toes on their way downstream. Before we left, I wrapped my own story around a stone and tossed it into the water, the last light of the falling sun rippling across to the other side as my story fell to the bottom of the river.

Maybe an upstream story that held promise had healed Daddy, for the walk back down the trail didn't tear at his lungs near as bad, though, I've always found when headed in the direction of home, the road always seems easier to travel. Maybe it was that way for Daddy, too, a bit of his old self rising up one last time.

Too dark to see all of what needed to be done when we got back, I turned on the truck's single headlight. That's when I saw her. Big G was sitting up against the great white ash wearing a smile that spoke neither happy nor sad. My hands let go of the ice chest and it slammed to the ground. All of the birds that had found homes for the night took flight, the sky filling with fearful wings.

"What is it, B.?" Daddy asked.

"Little G's dead, Daddy."

I didn't mean for it to come out so matter of fact. If I had it to do over, I would speak in the manner of Harmonia Pennywhistle, who had the perfect voice for delivering such dreadful news.

Daddy was unbelieving at first, but when I wrapped the blanket around Little G like a newborn baby and her body went limp as I lifted her, her head falling back into

48

the crook of my arm, he couldn't deny the truth. I carried Little G over to where Big G sat and leaned against the great white ash, its hardwood used to make a Louisville Slugger bat. Wouldn't you know my Little G would hit one out of the park when we weren't looking. I pictured her rounding third base, headed for home, a stadium full of angels cheering her on. I moved gently to and fro, the way I imagined she rocked me and my momma the day I was born. I turned her face up to mine and kissed her lips, traced her crazy eyebrows with my fingertips, told her how much I loved her, and how much I would miss her. My tears landed on Little G's own cheeks as I scolded her for not being around to can those damn spiced peaches. Real close to her ear, so Daddy couldn't hear me, I asked Little G how I'd take care of Daddy without her help when his time came. By the look of Daddy as he hung on to the truck for dear life, I could see his own last supper was next on the menu.

From the trees along the bank, a wise old owl called *hoo, hoo, hoo*.

"Corina Childe, Corina Childe, Corina Childe," I cried out, my answer riding the light of the moon.

"Time to take Little G's body home, B.," said Big G.

I didn't answer Big G, cross with her for acting like Little G's passing was so trouble free. I heard the cry of an eagle flying home for the night. If God could take hold of us without warning, the same way that eagle plucked up the unsuspecting trout, well, I didn't want to fritter away my between time mad at Big G.

O-k-a-y, I tapped. O-k-a-y.

With Daddy too drained to help settle Little G in the bed of the truck, I did my best to make her comfortable by swaddling her nice and tight, and using the extra blanket as a pillow for her head to rest upon. Scared she might roll out of the truck's bed, I braced her in place with the ice chest and the spare tire.

I sat behind the steering wheel, my body so still, my mind somewhere outside itself. Daddy moved up next to me and placed his trembling arm around me. I waited for some wise words to flow from him, maybe one of those ancient stories had found its way up through the river bottom and spoke to him. But with the Great Divide riding along with us—Little G on one side, me on the other, and Daddy straddling the divide in between—well, not even my Daddy owned a story long enough to cross over that kind of gap. I turned the key.

Driving down the road, I felt a toad-sized lump of woe in my throat kicking to get out, so fierce it was, my hands gave up on the steering wheel and covered my face, the smell of cool, green river water lingering in my palms. With a voice as fine in texture as the wings of a damselfly, Daddy told me to step on the brake. I hit the brake too hard and two thumps hit the road behind us. I prayed it was the ice chest and the spare tire, and not one or the other along with Little G. A quick look in the rearview mirror and Daddy assured me Little G was just fine.

"I didn't kill her, did I, Daddy? Tell me I didn't kill my Little G with my cooking," I cried.

"No, of course not. Oh, baby girl, you know what I believe?" Daddy removed my hands from my eyes. "Look at me, B. Thankful." I raised my eyes to Daddy's own.

"Somewhere inside us all there is a time marker, and sooner or later it surfaces and calls us home. You filled Little G up with so much love and comfort through your food, awoke such a potent memory of Big G's love for her, any notion of fear she had toward her time marker rising to the top fell away. You helped set Little G free. That's a powerful medicine you got there, B. Thankful. Powerful indeed. Now, let's get Little G home." Daddy was so spent by the time he finished talking, his breaths were hard to come by.

As I drove, I thought about what Daddy said—the part about powerful medicine. All my life Little G told me God made me special because He was gonna ask a favor of me one day, but she never named the favor. That very morning, even Big G told me God had chosen me, but she never finished telling me what I had been chosen for. I was more befuddled than ever.

As I turned up the drive, the solitary headlight shined over the vegetable garden and I made note its bounty was bursting to be harvested. Two deer, trying to find a way in through the wire mesh to do their own gathering, fled when the light gave them up as prowlers. The night seemed too quiet around the house, none of the usual calls crossing the river back and forth. The frogs weren't singing their croaky songs; the coyotes' howls, silent. But, oh, the moon and stars were loud that night.

Before Daddy could offer to help with Little G, I walked him up to the house, the flip and flop of his big old shoes making me cry all the harder. I sat Daddy in Little G's rocking chair, where he stared into the dark of night. Something vital inside my Daddy broke with Little G's passing and it scared me. Scared as I was, I had no time for it; Little G was waiting on me.

During our drive home, Little G had rolled all the way to the front of the truck bed near the cab, so I had to climb in and crawl to get her. Little G would have liked that. I tugged on the blanket until I had inched her up to the back of the truck. I sat down and propped Little G against my side. By the time I remembered to close Little G's eyes, it was too late, and they were permanently set in a *here's lookin' at you* kind of way. With Little G's head leaned back and turned up to the sky, a stranger passing by could have mistaken us for stargazers.

Like Daddy, my own breath came in spurts the farther I carried Little G, and I was thankful only a handful of steps up to the porch remained. I rested Little G across Daddy's lap, and he held her the way a new daddy might hold his first baby: a little uncomfortable in the beginning, but then coming into the how and why of it. Once they were settled in with each other, I went inside the house to give Daddy some alone time with Little G.

It was the summer of 1968, but we lived over the hills and way behind the times. We didn't have a phone and we didn't own a television, but we had an old radio Daddy found at the dump and fixed up best he could. When we were lucky, we could pull in the occasional radio hour story, but most of the time there was too much static. One night I convinced Little G if she placed a crown of tinfoil on her head and held the cord to the radio, it would cut through the static and she might be able to hear her favorite program, *Cisco Kid*. Little G was about ten minutes into twisting her tinfoiled head to the right and left before she finally caught on. When Little G went running for her broom, I hightailed it outside, Big G and Daddy not far behind when they couldn't keep a lid on their laughter.

But our nights were not sorry ones for lack of a television or radio. Most nights Little G played fiddle, Big G her mandolin, and Daddy sang songs that could raise you up from your deepest despair. Some evenings I told stories, and other nights we played pinochle or canasta until Little G got mad and threw down her cards. She did it more for fun than spite. I think. On sweltering summer evenings, when more than a few words could wear you out, we'd sit on the porch and listen to the music of God, my Gs fanning themselves and Daddy cooling my forehead with an iced cloth.

We owned a washer, but the washer was so old it came with a ringer and a warning for large breasted women. Our oven was even older than the washer, the temperature never true, and two of the stove's burners were as useless as bare gums trying to bite into an apple. But we did own one big ticket item: a Sears and Roebuck freezer, and not the kind over the ice box, the kind that took up most of our pantry. It was seven feet long and wide enough to hold all the game my Gs hunted.

On the hottest days of summer, when I knew for certain my Gs would be out hunting for most of the day, I'd open the freezer, climb in, and cover myself with frozen animal parts. One day, Little G came back unexpected and caught me climbing out of the freezer, my mouth chockfull of homemade strawberry ice cream. Like the wildlife she hunted, I stood stock still, hoping she'd overlook me. Little G pulled me out by my ear and warned if she ever found me wasting electricity by cooling off in the freezer again, she'd close the lid and lock it tight. From then on, every time I went to fetch something from the freezer, I called out my intentions, just to be safe.

To know my Gs is to know that *Waste not, want not,* was their creed. Among the many items they considered a waste of money (and, in this case, wood) was a coffin.

They preferred to make what they called sleeping bags. One Christmas Little G gifted her momma with a sleeping bag she quilted from meaningful scraps of fabric. There were zippers, one at the top and one at the bottom, and Little G even embroidered some of Big G's favorite things in the squares: flowers, blackberries, her shotgun. Being only ten years old that Christmas, and ignorant to a sleeping bag's purpose, I figured the zippers were at the top and bottom in case Big G wanted some fresh air, or her feet got too hot while she was sleeping. All in all, I thought it was a so-so gift. When Big G died a short time thereafter, and I saw her resting in that sleeping bag, from then on, I opened my Christmas presents from Little G with a handful of hesitation.

While Daddy spent his final moments with Little G, I searched her dresser for her best underwear. I picked out my favorite Little G dress—summer sky blue with a scoop neck collar trimmed with lace; capped sleeves, perfect for the hot weather; and a white belt to accentuate her tiny waist. Next to the dress, as if planned, I found another quilted sleeping bag with a note pinned to it. *Happy Birthday, Corina—Love, Momma.* Sorry to say, Big G never got to give Little G her birthday gift in person, for that was the same day Big G dropped dead after shooting a 12-point buck. Little G and I had that in common—we both lost our mommas on our birthdays.

As I closed the door, I heard something at the back of the closet fall to the floor. I found another sleeping bag inside, but this one was much longer and made from fine navy blue wool, and *Tyler Lucknow* was embroidered in the right-hand corner. I shoved the sleeping bag, along with my fear, inside the closet, slammed the door, and ran from the room.

Michaelene McElroy

While the basin filled with warm water, I laid out Little G's clothes and her cosmetics on the sideboard, then dressed the dining room table with a plastic cloth. When all was ready, I waited by the door for Daddy to finish his goodbye.

My poor Daddy rocked and cried over Little G as if she was his own momma, and in a way she was. Mother fierce in her loyalty to him when his own momma died shortly after he was born, Little G gave up an old way of life for Daddy that really never fit her; still, there were harsh prices to be paid. Feeling she had sufficiently paid her dues a long time back, and bone tired of ignorance, Little G took it upon herself to educate the local yokels who came around to put down new property line markers, knowing their snooping had more to do with Daddy than land squabbles. Once they looked through their spyglasses and saw Little G's shotgun pointed at them, and heard her call out her Christian warning, the smart ones never came back. No one was ever going to hurt her Tyler.

I opened the squeaky screen door. Daddy's hazel eyes glistened under the porch light and I noticed the too soon flecks of grey in his hair.

"Daddy, I have to take Little G from you. It's so very late, and I need to bathe her one last time." Daddy cried so hard his lungs seized up, his breathing so labored he was unable to rise up from the chair.

Perhaps my weariness was a blessing, for it put the hurry out of me, and I waltzed with Little G in my arms, gliding across the porch and into the house. I rested her atop the dining room table and went back for Daddy.

I ended up having to carry Daddy to his room. Every fiber of his being was so weak, I had to use an eye dropper to place some of Little G's elixir on his tongue to calm his lungs. Daddy sucked on the dropper.

"I never thought I'd be like a wounded bird," he said. Along with my hand, Daddy took a broken breath; his words to follow chopped into little bits.

"B. Thankful Childe-Lucknow, you are an angel from God."

I kissed Daddy's fevered forehead and thanked him for loving me in the way of no other. Daddy's eyes closed and his hand slipped away. It tore at me to leave him alone, but there was so much left to do for Little G.

The heat in the dining room was stifling and cramped. I opened all the windows and switched on the fan, the hem of Little G's dress fluttering every time the electric breeze passed over her. Preferring to work by the glow of light from the rooms surrounding us, I turned off the overhead light. The truth seemed less harsh that way, but no less real, especially with Little G staring up at me. After I removed Little G's house dress and undergarments, I laid a sheet over her body in honor of her modest ways. The know-how to perform the ritual that lay before me must have been passed down soul-to-soul from my family of women, for I knew what to do next, and no fear of the task churned within me.

I dipped the cloth in warm water dressed with lavender oil, then washed across my Little G's shoulder blades, and down her arms to the tips of her fingers. I kissed her calloused palms that had known such hard work and clipped her nails of their jaggedness. I washed under her arms and over her breasts, where I laid my head on her still heart. Since I may run into Little G again someday, I'm gonna skip over the washing of her private places. As much as she enjoyed my stories, I know she would tell me I went too far.

Once Little G's body was sparkling clean and rubbed down with lilac lotion, I labored over her hair. Since the back of Little G's head wouldn't be seen, I put my best effort into making the front of her hair look special occasion pretty. I even used a dab of glue to keep the curls on her forehead in place, and a bit more between her lips to keep her mouth from going slack. Little G loved her Cameo Cold Cream, so I spread it as liberally as butter on a biscuit over her face, removed her childlike makeup, and tucked her suspicious eyebrows in a tissue. I licked the tip of the eyebrow pencil the way Little G did, and drew on her right eyebrow, then the left. I tell you, it's much harder to do than it looks when watching. I wiped her brows off and tried again, but now she looked angry, so off they came. Finally, with the help of a half-pint jelly jar, I was able to create a perfect arch over each eye, and Little G didn't look suspicious at all; maybe a little surprised, but who wouldn't? There was so much more I could've done to make Little G look even lovelier, but something inside told me I could overdo this sort of thing real easy.

Getting Little G's underwear and dress on her didn't cause me much trouble, but I had gotten so lost in my final hours with her that I didn't take notice she was turning stiff so quickly. So stiff, that when it came time to put Little G's shoes on, her feet refused to bend to their form. The unwelcome memory of the pig's feet cracking as I picked off the meat floated to the surface of my mind. No way I was gonna crack my Little G's toes just so she could wear shoes. I tossed them aside, and placed a nice pair of wool socks over her feet, and told her she was ready for all kinds of weather.

Normally, I would have placed two silver coins over Little G's eyes as payment for her crossing, but Little G refused to close them. To be safe, I attached a note to one of her socks telling the ferryman who would row Little G to the other side, he'd find two silver dollars tucked inside. Without such payment, Little G might ghost wander for the next hundred years, and that notion gave me the willies.

Just as I was getting ready to slip Little G into her sleeping bag, a crash came from Daddy's room. Like a wobbly top, I ran down the hall to Daddy and found another baby bird had fallen from the nest.

"Daddy," I screamed, when I saw him lying on the floor.

Daddy's breath was shallow, quick, his head tilted to the side; a slow, jerky motion tied to the rhythm of his breathing. His nightshirt was twisted around, betraying his privacy. I reached over and pulled it down. So afraid I might harm Daddy, I pretended my hands to be clouds as I lifted him from the floor and placed him back in his bed.

A cry of anguish escaped Daddy, a sad song falling from his mouth. The same mouth that sang me to sleep for as long as I could remember, the same mouth that chose its words with a wise heart when he was the only one who could comfort me in times of sorrow, doubt. Daddy gasped for air. Again. And again.

My trembling hands tried to serve up some of Little G's elixir to calm his lungs and help him breathe, but Daddy wasn't right in his mind, didn't know I was trying to help. He struggled with me, kept pushing my hand away.

"Please, Daddy," I begged. "Please take this medicine."

And then Daddy went calm. He sat up in bed and looked out the window, where three mourning doves called to him in their sweet, melancholy way. Light as cottonwood fluff, Daddy seemed to float off to a place in the distance only he could see. He reached in for another breath, but his wounded lungs said *no*. Daddy shrugged his left shoulder in a *give up* kind of way. *All right*, his shoulder said. *All right.*

"Daddy, don't you leave me!"

Daddy closed his eyes and made a feather soft landing into my waiting arms. His final sigh filled the whole room with emptiness. One minute my Daddy was here; in the next he became a memory.

The world was spinning in the wrong direction, everything wrong side up. Two of the mourning doves flew the wire, but the lonesome dove that stayed behind kept flying into the window pane, frantically looking for a way in, while I was looking for any way out.

My fear's scythe sharp voice severed me from my familiar roots. *You're all alone now. There's no one to love and care for you; no one to kiss you goodnight and bid you sweet dreams; no Daddy with whom to share your Banner Bar.* My chest went tight, as if someone had placed a belt around my heart and cinched it up a thousand sorrowful notches.

I fluffed Daddy's pillows and laid him to rest there while I searched inside myself for a thread of common sense. Facts: Little G was growing riper by the minute. I wasn't able to perform the ritual Daddy deserved. I needed help. I ran back to the dining room.

"Little G, Daddy's dead," I cried, but Little G just stared up at me. I tried my hardest to remain as strong as my Gs had raised me to be, but I *felt* my heart break again, like delicate bone china falling onto hard tiles, shattering into a million pieces. Caught in a weak spot, I zipped up Little G in her sleeping bag, but just to her shoulders, and put her in a safe place.

I jumped in Daddy's truck and headed toward the highway. The same wild sounds I heard running through the fields at night, empty and in need of sustenance, came from the deepest part of me as I drove away from the only safe place I had ever known.

The truck's solitary headlight bobbed fiercely up and down. I made a sharp turn off the highway and then another, until I was driving under the familiar canopy of brambles, their scrapes along the side of the car as screechy as the piercing cries inside my head. I laid my hand on the horn and honked, again and again. When I reached the clearing, I slammed on the brakes and skidded sideways, the truck's headlight forcing its way into Harmonia Pennywhistle's home.

I shoved the truck door open and made a feeble attempt to run to the house. My exhaustion felled me somewhere short of the front porch, bits of gravel stripping the skin from my knees. I woke to the sun coming over the mountain to find myself in the arms of a stranger.

Seven

———◆———

"Hold on! Hold on! No harm intended," he said as I thrashed about.

The stranger held me tenderly; the remedy to my misfortune stretched between his hands and shoulders, if I would just surrender. But only three pairs of arms had ever held me close for comfort; one was in the ground and two were at home waiting to be buried alongside her, so I kept up my struggle.

"B. Thankful, it's all right. Pride means you no harm, child. Stay still now. It'll hurt less if you do."

Harmonia Pennywhistle's comforting voice covered me with a blanket of calmness, and I surrendered to the stranger as Harmonia gently picked the gravel from my torn up knees. The sting of eucalyptus on my wounds made me flinch, the sting of my loss made me weep. Raised by two strong women who kept their emotions tucked deep in the pockets of aprons and the wooden handles of hard work and perseverance, I was embarrassed my emotion had fallen out of my pocket, my tears proof of failing my Gs' values.

Harmonia rested her hand on my heart, waltzed right in, and took hold of my sorrow. Her eyes welled with grief.

"Oh, B. Thankful, I am so sorry for your loss." She turned to the stranger holding me. "Pride, B. Thankful needs our help. You drive the truck and we'll ride in the back."

Sure I hadn't spoke of my circumstance or the need for help, I was taken aback as to how Harmonia knew about my Daddy and Little G. In the last twenty-four hours, I had walked out of my everyday life through one mysterious door after another. And through the last door, in walked a stranger who would see me through my sorrow and forever change my life.

"I'm sorry for your troubles, B. Thankful." Pride's throat apple bobbed up and down, setting free each word once stored inside with a cadence I had never heard before, one that marched in a straight line. My people spoke in patterns that rose and fell like the hills around us, and stretched their words out afternoon shadow long. Through the shimmer of my tears, I looked upon the young man holding me. As Harmonia was short in stature, he was tall. My Daddy stood well over six feet when barefoot, but the man Harmonia called Pride could easily touch the sky. Pride lifted me from my fallen place and carried me to Daddy's truck.

Overcome by exhaustion, my head nodded up and down as if in agreement with the way things were. I wasn't. When Harmonia shouted out her final direction that led up our road, my eyes flashed open, and my spine went ax handle straight. In the distance, our lonesome porch caused the woeful ache in my heart and lungs to swell, taking them prisoner.

Coming around the truck to help me, I signaled Pride I could walk on my own, and he stepped away with regard for my resolve. Grim expectation filled my every step as I climbed the porch, the pain in my skinned knees reminding me I was alone. Unable to cross the threshold into my empty house, I sat down in Little G's rocking chair where just hours ago my Daddy had been rocking her. It was the first I ever felt the passing of time to be unfriendly.

"B. Thankful, you stay right there. Pride and I will get your Daddy set up for dressing and then we'll come get you."

Before the screen door stopped squeaking, Harmonia was back on the porch. "B. Thankful, we found Tyler, but where's Corina?"

I pushed myself up from the chair and took Harmonia by the hand. You'd think with her being so small it would be like holding the hand of a child, but it wasn't. Her hand was so ample in its motherliness, I never wanted to let go. I led Harmonia to the kitchen, the scent of bay leaves and peppercorns still lingering in the air along with Big G's humming. I pointed to the pantry.

"I didn't know what else to do," I said.

Harmonia pushed her way through the pantry door with the flair of the unflappable to find the door to our Kenmore freezer propped open with a frozen turkey leg, the icy fog drifting just above her head. Harmonia dragged the stepstool to the freezer, lifted the lid, and looked in. Anyone else would have cried out at the very least, what with Little G staring up at them, but not Harmonia Pennywhistle.

"I don't think I've ever seen Corina Childe look so lovely." Harmonia slowly closed the lid.

Since I didn't want Little G to think I was getting back at her for threatening to lock me in the freezer with all those animal parts, I asked if we might leave the lid ajar. Harmonia agreed with me one hundred percent and wedged the turkey leg back in place.

By the time we came back through the dining room, Pride had already moved Daddy to the dining table, where he lay covered with a bed sheet; his razor, shaving soap, and brush lined up nearby. Standing in the middle of the unthinkable, it seemed an overlooked custom hung in the air, thick as the heat, and then I came by my missing manners.

"Pride, I'd like you to meet my Daddy, Tyler Lucknow. Daddy, this is Pride."

"Pleased to meet you, Mr. Lucknow," Pride said, as if he and Daddy were standing man-to-man, his slow bow trading places with a handshake.

Once the introduction had been seen to, Pride placed Daddy's shaving soap at the bottom of his mug, lathered up the brush, and, with a marked gentleness, covered Daddy's cheeks and neck with soap—its scent, lime sharp. With concentration as honed as mine when I created my paint-by-number Last Supper, Pride carefully shaved Daddy's cheeks and neck. When it came time to bathe and dress Daddy, Harmonia and I took our leave to the kitchen and shared a cup of her herbal brew.

"How are you feeling, B. Thankful?"

I wanted to honor my Gs and keep my emotions on the back burner as taught, so I did my best to put the lid on my feelings bubbling up in the kitchen that day by changing the subject. Sorry to say, my weary brain passed out, my mouth yammering without forethought.

"My dead Big G visited me yesterday; came all the way down from Heaven to help me prepare Little G's last supper; told me I had answered God's call with willingness and grace, and right before she left, she turned preacher and said, 'You have been chosen to walk among the'..."

The light in my brain suddenly switched on and snapped my trap shut. I bit my lip when I realized the truth and my tea had spilled onto the tablecloth.

"Did I say Big G visited me? Boy, that's just crazy talk, isn't it? I mean, how could that be? She's been dead seven years now. May I please have some more tea?"

Harmonia smiled at me, a ruby-studded, gold tooth flashing to the right of her front teeth. Her blue-milk eyes pierced my own. *Child, you can't fool me. I see you.*

"Harmonia, how will I know if I'm doing what God intends me to do? How will I recognize what's pure and true?"

"Well, how did you feel while fixing jellied pig's feet for Little G's last supper?"

I was hoping for an answer rather than a comeback question, and was at a complete loss as how to reply, not sure how to say it wasn't exactly *me* who fixed the jellied pig's feet—more like *us*. I hemmed and hawed, and picked at the tablecloth's red roosters as if I could pluck the answer from under their feathers. Harmonia studied my face with such intensity, beads of sweat formed over my upper lip, and my throat turned as dry as overcooked stuffing.

"Promise you won't think me daft?"

"I promise."

"Well, when Big G —"

"Sorry to interrupt," Pride said, as he walked in. "B. Thankful, your Daddy's ready for you now."

Harmonia patted my hand. "We'll visit this matter another time."

Pride had dressed Daddy in the same shirt and pants he wore the night of my seventh birthday. Though frayed around the edges, and too large on him, Daddy still looked handsome. I ran my hand over Daddy's forehead, his pain creases finally erased. I lifted the silver dollars Pride placed over Daddy's eyes to pay for his crossing, kissed his eyelids, and bid him safe passage. I placed my fist in my Daddy's palm and wrapped his long fingers around it until our worlds became one for the last time.

I kept a box of treasures, small items that meant nothing to anyone but me—the feather of an eagle, stones that spoke to me in wordless ways, a button from the blouse my momma wore the day I was born, and a stack of Banner Bar gold foil wrappers tied with lavender ribbons. I reached in my pocket and took one of the folded wrappers I had taken from the box and tucked it inside the shirt pocket resting over Daddy's heart. It may seem a small gesture, but my Daddy knew our eternal love for each other was wrapped inside. Any other day I would have turned minutes into hours telling stories, Daddy listening as if every word I uttered was special, but the words I wanted to say to him were as lost as I was. Unable to commit to the truth of the situation when we placed Daddy in his sleeping bag, I left the top unzipped.

With kindness equal to his stature, Pride covered the hard surface of the truck's bed with the same blankets we used on our picnic and laid Daddy and Little G side-by-side. *Napping*, I told myself. *That's all, B. They're just napping.*

Frozen in place, I could only watch as Pride gathered the necessary tools while Harmonia filled the water jug and loaded up the garden basket with bundles of Little G's cabbage roses. My arms and legs knew they should be helping out, but my brain couldn't tell them what to do. I shoved my hands into the pockets of my overalls so they'd stop fidgeting with each other.

When everything had been gathered, Pride lifted Harmonia into the cab of the truck, and then he slid behind the wheel, while I remained standing in the middle of the yard, unable to take the next goodbye step. *They must think I'm crazy,* crossed my addled mind, but if they did, they hid it well. For my sake, Pride pretended his own mind was muddled, and offered up an apology for leaving me behind. My hand in his, he led me to the truck.

We must have looked a sight—Harmonia, so small; me with my red corkscrew hair and swollen two-toned eyes; and Pride, so tall, even with the seat pushed all the way back, his legs were scrunched up, knees riding higher than my shoulders. And then there was Little G riding in the back, staring up at the sky.

Clouds, pregnant with rain, crowded out the sun, but the humidity's scorn for dry sleeves and seams didn't stop Pride. He picked and shoveled the hard ground as if fertile soil, his long, raven hair and t-shirt drenched with hard work. When the graves reached a good six feet deep, I tell you no lie when I say almost two feet of Pride remained above ground. My face flushed when Pride looked up and found me staring at him. Pride regarded me, but without statement, and I liked that. Right then and there, I decided to heed Big G's advice and keep the door to my heart open. I wanted Pride to walk in and be my first friend.

The sun had moved far west by the time we were ready to lay Daddy and Little G to rest. When my shaking hands were unable to seal their fate, Harmonia was kind enough to zip up their sleeping bags for me. Pride lifted Little G from the truck and carried her to the gravesite. I looked around for Big G, but she was nowhere in sight, and the curve of my ear remained as silent as an unanswered prayer. My sorrow paced to the right, to the left, like a caged animal longing to be set free, and trying my best not to breakaway or cry out, I bit my lip so hard blood trickled into my mouth.

Pride laid Daddy next to his grave, climbed in, and did something I will never forget. Pride placed one of his large hands under Daddy's head, the other under his feet, and raised Daddy up, offering him to God. A story buried beneath the riverbed climbed up and wove itself into the song Pride offered. The language was unfamiliar, but the sound gave birth to a quiet stillness inside me that recognized the song of man, his call earthborn of water, wind, and fire. When his song came to an end, Pride, as if handing a newborn to its mother, gently laid Daddy at the bottom of his grave.

With great care, Pride raised Little G in the same manner, but it was Harmonia who called up to Heaven. Her voice, like a bird that flies into your dream, rose higher and higher. I wanted to ride on the wings of her song over the mountains, beyond the horizon where my Gs, Daddy, and I would fly together forever. But when I opened my eyes, I saw the undeniable truth as Pride handed Little G back to the earth.

Harmonia came to me with an armload of plump cabbage roses, their scent, spicy and proud. We tossed lavender, pink, white, and yellow velvet petals over Daddy and Little G until their sleeping bags looked like a beautiful paint-by-number flower patch. But when the sight of Pride lifting the shovel from the ground brought me full into my body, all the bright colors turned to gray.

There are times in your life when you've got to do a thing so you know it's real. Though my tiredness weighed heavy on my legs, I staggered toward Pride, took the shovel from his hand and pushed it into the mound of earth next to the graves. I shoveled the soil on Daddy first, and then did the same for Little G. The sound of the dull, heavy thuds struck my chest, burying my hope it was all a bad dream. I shoveled dirt again and again, my arms burning from the inside out, my muscles trembling with pain. When I could no longer stand, I fell to my knees, my emptiness bleeding into the soil. I pushed the earth above to the earth below with my hands until my entire body was covered with its musty dampness, while Pride and Harmonia stood by and let me be with what I needed to work out.

By the time I finished burying my Daddy and Little G, the sounds of the night were gathering in the woods. It was time to go home, but I didn't know why.

Eight

———

Upon rising from sleep, it takes a good while before a full-on awake resides in me, and, until it does, I have no recall. Maybe God felt sorry for me after we buried Little G and Daddy and stretched out my *no recall* minutes that morning.

I woke up wearing my favorite cotton nightgown, my body so clean I smelled like spring grass. I jumped from my bed and ran to Daddy's room, my bare feet slapping the already warm wooden floor. Gone to work, I guessed, finding his bed was made, the shades drawn to keep the sun from pushing its way in. I peeked into Little G's room and found it just as tidy. A tempting aroma from the kitchen pulled me from Little G's room and down the hallway. Hallelujah! My eighteenth birthday had finally arrived and Little G was fixing my birthday breakfast. Daddy would come home later, a Banner Bar in hand, and like all my birthdays, we would perform the Ritual of the Five Senses. Until then, I had all day to ponder the perfect birthday wish to make on the first star to appear. True happiness bounded through the kitchen door with me.

"Good morning, Little G. Smells like a birthday break…"

Lingering in the valley of *no recall*, I had fallen into believing everything was like the old days, but before I could finish my salutation, God snatched up my *no recall* minutes and handed me the truth of what the new day held: my life without Little G and Daddy.

Harmonia stopped filling the coffee pot, hopped off the stepstool, and took the same sunny approach she did when she found Little G in the freezer.

"Is the third day of August your birthday, B. Thankful?"

"Yes, ma'am, the third day of August is my birthday."

My announcement sounded more like a sad song, but that didn't deter Harmonia's enthusiasm.

"Why, then today is your day! Happy birthday, B. Thankful!"

I sat down at the kitchen table, stretched my nightgown over my scabby knees to cover them up, and then tucked both under my chin. Pride poured me a cup of coffee and placed a plate of warm, honeyed fry bread in front of me.

"Happy birthday, B. Thankful."

"Thank you," I said, that sad song still tugging at my bottom lip.

Not wanting to step on Pride's feelings, I dipped his fry bread deep into my cup, coffee dripping down my chin when I bit into the crisp puff. Jesus watched me from my paint-by-number Last Supper leaning up against a formal looking envelope, like the one Daddy gave me the night I became his lawful daughter, but this envelope was a good three fingers thick, and B. Thankful Childe-Lucknow was printed by my Daddy's hand across the front.

"What's this?" I asked.

"I found that envelope at the foot of your daddy's bed when I cleaned his room." Harmonia opened the refrigerator and came to the table carrying a box marked *Perishable* on the sides. "And the postman delivered this for you yesterday. He dropped it on the porch and ran back to his truck like a swarm of bees was chasing him." Everybody knew my Gs took their *No Trespassing* sign seriously.

I ran my hand over the first package I had ever received, traced the letters that spelled my name, then peeled the *Perishable* sticker from the side, and stuck it to my nightgown. The box came from the Banner Chocolate Company, Inc., Post Office Box 82350, San Francisco, California. I rested my cheek on the cardboard box.

Always a gentleman, Pride lifted Harmonia onto the chair next to me so she could get a better look. He knelt down on my other side, pulled a knife from his pocket, and sliced through the tape. Inside the box, I found a letter and one hundred Banner Bars, the gold foil sparkling when I held one up.

To my surprise, Harmonia and Pride showed more excitement than I did, encouraging me not to waste any time in opening the letter. Until then, I didn't know you could have more than one feeling moving through you at the same time; in my case, sorrow and mischief. When I saw curiosity had hooked Harmonia and Pride, I bided my time, slowly sipped my coffee, and finished my fry bread. When they finally caught onto my mischievous way, their laughter filled the kitchen and my empty heart cup to the brim.

I slid Pride's pocket knife along the edge of the envelope, careful to keep the line straight and free of jagged edges. Inside, the paper was as white as a brand new handkerchief, the company name standing proud and firm at the top. I began to read the letter to Harmonia and Pride.

"BANNER CHOCOLATE COMPANY, INC.

July 29, 1968

Dear Miss B. Thankful Childe-Lucknow:

CONGRATULATIONS! We have been unable to reach you by phone to inform you that your entry was chosen to be used in the worldwide Banner Bar advertising campaign celebrating the Banner Chocolate Company's 100th Anniversary!"

I checked the address on the box one more time. "There must be some mistake. I never entered a contest."

"Keep reading," Harmonia said, as she tapped the chair with her foot.

"Your entry, 'Now I lay me down to sleep, I pray the Lord my soul to keep, but if the Lord my soul would take, send me off with a Banner Bar for goodness sake,' was chosen over 15,000 entries. Enclosed please find a check in the amount of $25,000.00."

"Twenty-five thousand dollars!" cried Harmonia, plopping down hard on the chair. Pride jumped up with so much enthusiasm, he hit his head on the ceiling. I read on while I still had it in me.

"Sincerely,

Robert Banner, President

BANNER CHOCOLATE COMPANY, INC.

P.S. We hope you'll come and visit our factory in San Francisco."

Attached to the letter was a check for $25,000.00 with my name on it, signed by Robert Banner. Twenty-five thousand dollars! A mind of its own, my breath came fast, and my head went lightweight on me.

"Maybe there's something in the big envelope from your daddy that will help explain it all," Harmonia said.

Scared there might be bad news inside, I asked Pride if he would open the envelope for me and tell me what he found. Pride looked over every page with no giveaway signs on his face. No lines of surprise or dismay crept around his deep-set brown eyes, no purse of his full lips hinted at what lay across the pages. You'd think I'd've been the one to crack under the pressure, but it was Harmonia.

"Well, for goodness sake, Pride. What does it say?"

"These papers were drawn up right after you were born, B. Thankful. Do you have any idea how much land Little G owned?"

"No."

"Well, according to this deed, which is in your name, and free and clear of all debt, you own five hundred and twenty-three acres of land."

"Is that a lot?" I asked.

Harmonia and Pride traded smiles.

"Yeah, honey, that's a lot," Harmonia said.

"It seems your daddy also left a savings account, and a good number of Banner Bar stock certificates in your name. B. Thankful, you're a wealthy young woman."

My old sidekicks, sorrow and mischief, cleared the way for confusion. I was just about to confess my befuddlement when another envelope slipped from the papers in Pride's hand, my name penned across the front by my Daddy.

Whenever Daddy wanted to settle in with me to talk about serious life issues, we would walk down to the river. When I told Pride and Harmonia of my need to be alone with my Daddy's words, they were gracious in their under-standing. I put a Banner Bar in my nightgown pocket and headed down to Daddy's spot.

The sunflowers stood at least ten feet tall, their bowed heads offering their condolences. Day birds called to each other and critters skittered through the brush when I disturbed their homes. The sky was a festival of color, its shafts of light streaming through the spaces between the trees, sliding into the water and piercing the ancient secrets at the bottom. Shading my eyes against the stare of the sun, I saw minnows rise into view, their silvery sympathy written in a swerving pattern. How could the rest of the world still be so alive with Little G and my Daddy dead?

Sitting down on Daddy's favorite rock near the water's edge without him filled me with longing, and my hands shook as I opened his letter. Daddy's handwriting was as wobbly as his legs the last time we walked down to this very spot, wavy letters rising and falling above and below the helpful blue lines. Some words were left unfinished, perhaps a thought come and gone before fully realized, and words that settled into the wrong space were split from top to bottom by a narrow line. How had I come to be blessed with so much painstaking love?

I read my Daddy's letter aloud to the world around me. I wanted his love for me to catch the wings of curious birds, bump up against the trees and spill into the cool water, settle into the silt and ripen there.

"My Dearest Daughter B.," was as far as I got before my tears dropped on the page.

"If you're reading this letter, do not sorrow for me, for I have found my way to the peaceful valley. I'm sorry I missed your birthday and the Ritu". The word left unfinished, Daddy's hand

or mind must have failed him, but there was no doubt he was speaking of the Ritual of the Five Senses. His next few words flipped and flopped like fish caught in a net. Daddy must have taken some time to rest, for his thoughts and writing that followed were determined and bold.

"Oh, my B., I have loved you like no other. The day you were born, a piece of Heaven floated to Earth. When I held you in my arms for the very first time, I knew God sent you to me. Every day that I looked upon your sweet face, I was filled with God Love, the love that has no beginning and no end. I know you carried a burden as heavy as any cross with me as your daddy, but I think it was part of a bigger plan. And now it's time for you to spread your angel wings and fly. I'll be watching you from above.

Love,

Daddy

P.S. I entered your Banner Bar prayer in a contest some time back. You didn't know I was standing outside your door that night so long ago, did you? If you win, B., I hope you'll take the money and travel to San Francisco to see where they make Banner Bars. I'll meet you by the Golden Gate Bridge and we can share a Banner Bar while you tell me one of your stories."

Same as Little G the day I was born, my own tears were confused as to whether happiness or sadness called upon them. I was happy because my Daddy had made his way to the peaceful valley and would love me for all time, sad because my Daddy wasn't sitting next to me on his favorite rock, his love wrapped around my shoulder.

I shoved Daddy's letter into my pocket and ran alongside the river toward the graveyard. Dried shrubs grabbed at the hem of my nightgown, biting into the lace, and my bare feet ignored the stones and thistles that would later cause them to ache as much as my tattered knees and heart.

When I reached their graves, I threw myself down between Little G and Daddy. The fresh mounds of dirt yanked at the quiet stillness that had filled me when Pride and Harmonia sang my Daddy and Little G back to Heaven, and I broke wide open.

"Please don't leave me here alone," I cried. I tore open the gold foil on my Banner Bar, split the chocolate in pieces, and placed the letters one at a time at the mouth of Daddy's grave.

"I won the contest, Daddy, and if you'll come get me, you can have all my Banner Bars. Please come and get me, Daddy. Please." I dug my fingers deep into the earth trying to touch the untouchable.

Black booted clouds kicked their way across the sky, the sun backing down from a fight. A crack of lightning split the sky, severing one of the red oaks along the bank, exposing its heart. Thunder rolled behind the clouds, its sound close and dangerous. Spinning in a circle, arms opened wide, I raised my fist at the sky, called out to the lightning and thunder, and their Creator.

"My family is all I've ever known and you took them away from me! Show me!" I screamed. "Show me where I go from here!"

A pounding rain hammered away at the dirt covering Little G and Daddy. Fearful the mounds would wash away, I fell to the ground to protect them, my face resting on Little G's grave. My fresh cotton nightgown, soaked by the rain and smeared with mud, clung to my body. Though the rain carried no element of cold, my body shivered and I felt as if I was leaving it behind. *Maybe I am dying,* I thought as the world fell away from under me.

Daddy was sitting on his rock, dangling his feet in the water. He patted the space next to him.

"Come sit with me." Daddy wrapped his free arm around me, pulled me in close.

"You're not dying, B."

"I'm not?"

"No, daughter. We die a thousand times before the real thing comes along."

"What does that mean, Daddy?"

"It means little bits of us have to die along the way so the new bits of who we're to become can be born."

Daddy kissed my forehead, rose up from his rock, and walked upon the water to the other side, where he waved goodbye to me.

It was near dark, the sky clear again, by the time Pride found me. Too heartbroken and weak to struggle, I allowed him to carry me home, where the warm glow from inside took the chill off my soul and the smell of a supper simmered in love embraced me. Pride sat down in Little G's rocking chair and rocked back and forth as I leaned into his friendship. It's all I had to hold onto.

I'm not sure how much time passed before Harmonia, holding the promise of a hot bath in her outstretched hand, came to fetch me. Hard as it was to pry myself from the comfort of Pride's arms, I was sure the way Harmonia fixed her eyes upon me, I must look a fright.

The bathroom was warm, the steam laced with the smell of roses. I stripped off my dirty nightgown and slipped into our old tub. My body floated in the shelter of the porcelain womb, my heartbeat the only sound. I slid my entire body underwater and lay in the warm silence where Daddy's words of wisdom floated by. Rising to the surface, a rush of air filled my lungs with expectation. I soaped up the washcloth and scrubbed away the old bits that had to die so the new bits of who I was to become could be born.

After my bath, I took a long while studying my face in the bathroom mirror. Oh, I still saw the two-toned eyes and mop of red tangles, but when I looked real close, my nose almost touching the mirror, I saw a new bit of me that wasn't there yesterday.

I put on my favorite dress—pale butter yellow in color, cut loose and sleeveless for summertime when anything more would wear you down. Without Little G to help, I tied my springy hair as best I could with the lavender ribbons from my treasure box. Barefoot and hobbling, I made my way to the dining room. I lingered there, stroking the memories left on the table.

From across the yard, an unfamiliar music found its way through the still night into the house. Countless candles lit the path down to a table dressed with special occasion dishes and glasses. Flowers from Little G's garden, including my favorite, Black Eyed Susan, graced the table. The openhanded nature needed to create such a setting left me humble.

When I came through the kitchen door, Harmonia and Pride stopped cooking and made a fuss over me. Pride took my hand, raised it over my head, and turned me around and around. I was always shunned by people, and Pride and Harmonia, who really didn't know me from Adam, were loving me up like I was favored shirttail kin. My cheeks flushed to the color of my hair as they wrapped me up in their kind words.

"It smells deeeelicious in here," I said.

A golden corn pudding sat atop the stove, and thick slices of just plucked tomatoes waited patiently for Pride to slide crispy fried trout into the center of the tray. Ready to pitch in, I pulled down Big G's apron, but Pride ushered me out of the kitchen and down the candlelit walk to my seat at the table.

"The stars have been waiting for you," Pride said. "We'll be out soon."

Music played soft and low, the notes riding silver wings outside the circle of candlelight into the darkness where blessings lay all around me. When I looked toward the house, two of those blessings were walking down the path, their arms laden with my birthday dinner. Once seated, Harmonia took hold of my right hand and Pride took my left. We stayed that way until Pride spoke.

"To Mother Earth we give thanks for her bountiful harvest; to Brother Trout, we give thanks for nourishing us."

Harmonia raised her glass of dandelion wine. "To the heavens we offer our gratitude for sending the angel B. Thankful Childe-Lucknow into our lives. Her gift will heal the lives of many. Happy birthday, B. Thankful."

We clinked our glasses together, and I took my first sip of Harmonia's dandelion wine. Tangy as it was, it went down a whole lot smoother than Little G's 'shine. When Pride placed a crispy trout onto my plate, I found a light-hearted memory tucked under its tail.

Whenever the fish were ripe for plucking from the river, Daddy and I would sneak away from the weekend chores Little G handed over to us and spend hours together swapping tall fish tales while casting out our lines. When we came home with a string of a dozen trout, Little G forgot about the overlooked chores, but on less successful outings, when our hooks came up empty, not a single fish suckered into taking our bait, Little G locked the door and made us sleep on the porch.

My first bite of Pride's trout left me yearning for my Daddy and those long summer days spent side-by-side, but now the longing seemed to float rather than sting. And once I tasted the deliciousness of Harmonia's creamy corn pudding, I raised my glass of dandelion wine (which got better tasting with each sip) in her honor. Long into the night, we savored the food and each other's company, until Pride announced it was time for birthday presents. I went shy, for I had never received a gift from anyone outside my small family circle. Harmonia handed me a package wrapped in paper that was painted with stars and moons, some full, some with crescent smiles. Inside the box, I found a pouch holding a braided leather necklace with an eagle carved from a stone I didn't recognize, and asked about.

"Turquoise holds both Heaven and Earth. And the eagle connects one to the Great Spirit."

"Great Spirit?"

"Great Spirit is another name for God," Harmonia explained.

I turned my turquoise eagle over in my hands. When Pride placed it around my neck, a second heartbeat edged up next to my own.

I knelt down by Harmonia's chair and wrapped my arms around her; so small, she disappeared into my love. Sometimes, when I hugged my Gs for too long, they'd pull away. "That's enough of that," they'd say. Outright joy filled me up when Harmonia melted into my arms and let me hug on her until *I* decided when it was time to let go.

"This one is from me, B. Thankful. I made it just for you."

Pride's drawings of eagles, wolves, and bears were magnificent, the paper alone gift enough. I opened the paper slowly to avoid any tears and pressed out the creases, and found the most unusual present—a circle made from willow branches that held a web as intricate as that of any artful spider. In the very center of the web, as if caught by surprise, a see-through stone was tied in place; the feathers hanging from the willow branches, those of an eagle.

"It's a dream catcher. Keep it by your bed and good dreams will filter through and slide down the feathers to you; bad dreams will be caught in the web and disappear come daylight."

"It's extraordinary, Pride. And I could certainly use a good dream. Thank you."

"You're welcome." Pride placed one of his big hands on my cheek and let it linger there.

BABUMP! BABUMP! BABUMP! went my heart. Had my heart gone haywire from all my sorrow of late? I closed my eyes and made a remember notch on my brain to look up heart conditions in Little G's book of diseases first thing in the morning.

"I wish I had something to give to you and Har...I'll be right back." It must have been the second glass of dandelion wine that took the hurt off my bruised feet because I couldn't even feel them as I ran to the house and back.

Being fans of ceremony, I figured Harmonia and Pride would be eager to learn about my Ritual of the Five Senses. I passed the Banner Bar around so they could appreciate its beauty (touch), untied the lavender ribbon, wove it through my hair, and then peeled away the gold foil to let their eyes feast upon the dark chocolate (sight). Once they were awe held, I placed the Banner Bar under my nose to show them how to inhale its sublime earthiness (smell). I asked my new friends to listen closely to their taste buds (hearing). Were they calling out to them?

"Sister, I hear them!" Harmonia cried out in testimony.

Then came my favorite part of the ritual: the communion. I snapped off the first *B* in *Banner* and offered it to Pride, and the second *B* in *Bar* went to Harmonia. I broke the rest into pieces and laid them on the table. We raised the chocolate, dark as a midnight dream, to our mouths. The moment the chocolate touched our tongues, the primal fire was ignited (taste), the eternal soul-to-soul union in place. *Remember me, for I will remember you.*

When the night came to an end, Pride and Harmonia sang happy birthday to me. I tilted my head, and from somewhere beyond the stars, heard the three familiar voices I so loved singing along with them.

Nine

———◆———

By the time we bid each other sweet dreams, the hands of the clock had begun a new day. I hung my dream catcher from the bedpost near the window, and drew back the curtains. The near-to-full moon bathed the pretty crystal in its light, glittering flashes kissing my eyelids as I rested my head on my pillow, and wandered into that place where dreams are made.

I stared long and hard upon my paint-by-number picture of the Last Supper with Jesus and his friends. Jesus's eye (number 4-dark brown), the eye I messed up on, the one looking upon Judas, turned my way, and the eyes of Jesus were upon me.

"Hello, B. Thankful." Jesus's lips (number 17-coral) formed the words, and his cheeks (number 8-flesh tone) lifted up with his smile.

"Hey, Jesus." Oh, good Lord, I just said "hey" to Jesus. I didn't think to call him Mister Jesus, and hoped he didn't think me disrespectful for it.

"B. Thankful, my Father asked me to tell you what a fine job you did preparing your Little G's last supper."

The way I had raised my fist to sky and gave Jesus's Daddy the "what for," I found his compliment generous and forgiving.

Maybe his Daddy didn't see me waving my fist or hear me yelling at Him yesterday after all. A chuckle that spoke otherwise came from Jesus.

"Thank you, Jesus. Mister Jesus. My Big G came down from Heaven to help me, but I guess you already know that. I couldn't have done it without her."

Jesus nodded, a strand of his hair (number 12-sienna brown) falling free. While Jesus broke bread and passed the wine to his friends, the preacher in him picked up where Big G left off.

"B. Thankful Childe-Lucknow, walk in my name among the dying and prepare for them the soul-to-soul communion once shared with a loved one who has departed. In doing so, you will light the way for them on their journey to eternity."

"Who, me?" I asked, my shrill voice slicing the air. Even Jesus tried to pass the cup given to him, so I did my best to talk my way out of such a huge undertaking.

"Oh, Mister Jesus, I don't mean to question you or your Daddy, but with me involved, there's a mighty strong potential for calamity sitting in the center of your idea."

Jesus just smiled as I went on and on, trying to make him understand I was not known for my cooking, how Little G's last supper was a stroke of luck. Jesus was as patient with me as a summer day is long as I prattled on and on, whining my way through never having been away from home, my fear of getting lost, not knowing where I needed to be, who needed my help, not having anyone to guide me.

Just as I was about to unload another stack of weak spots they had failed to notice, the mourning dove that tried to fly into Daddy's room the day he died, soared into my dream and landed on my shoulder. She rested her feathered cheek against my own and cooed. When I turned back to the painting, Jesus was still, and, once again, had one eye on Judas.

A *tap-tap-tap* on my forehead brought me around from my dream. Flashes of brilliant light bounced off the walls as my dream catcher spun round and round, but with no breeze to make sense of it. A small, gray-brown feather floated down and landed on my chest, the call of *coo, coo, coo* coming from the top of my head. I reached up to find a mourning dove had woven a nest out of my crazy hair. I got up slowly and moved toward the kitchen.

Harmonia was sitting at the kitchen table sipping a cup of coffee and studying the very paint-by-number Last Supper I had just seen in my dream. Surely, a bird nesting in my hair would rattle Harmonia's cage.

"Well, that's the cutest hat I've ever seen. My, that bird is lifelike." The mourning dove cooed. Harmonia hopped off the chair and pulled me down to her size for a closer look. Harmonia looked at me, at the dove; me, dove, me, dove, me.

"Oh, you've had a dream, haven't you? I knew Pride's dream catcher was powerful. I wish he was here, but he went to my place to pick up some things."

In my mournful state of late, I completely overlooked the fact Harmonia had her own life to look after. I apologized for taking up so much of her time, but she would have none of it, said people were here to serve each other.

"Tell me about your dream." Had I even mentioned a dream to Harmonia?

The mourning dove flew from my hair and landed next to my paint-by-number Last Supper. She hopped the length of the painting several times, pecking at the bread, the wine goblets, and old Judas. As I studied the painting, my dream slowly came back to me, number-by-number. At the mention of Jesus's name, Harmonia threw her hands up in the air, ready to catch the words to follow; that's how important they were to her. She paced back and forth in the kitchen, and when I got to the part about Jesus and his Daddy wanting me to walk among the dying to fix their last supper, as I had for Little G, Harmonia couldn't hold back any longer.

"Oh, Jesus wants you to go on a road trip!" she cried. "The minute I laid eyes on you, I recognized you as one of the chosen. And don't go thinking too much about all of that 'chosen' business. When you're chosen, you're chosen. Besides, we have ourselves some planning to do for your road trip."

When Harmonia spoke, it was like a beautiful song and I found myself caught up in her lyrics until I took a peach from the fruit bowl and bit into it. The sweet juice running down my chin reminded me I had to can spiced peaches for gingerbread, harvest the garden and orchards, look after the chickens and Beautiful Beulah.

"Harmonia, I can't go on a road trip. Who would take care of our animals, our land? Who would place flowers on the graves of my Gs and Daddy and talk to them?"

The screen door slapped shut.

"Good morning," Pride called out.

"Ask and you shall receive," Harmonia said.

Before I had a chance to return Pride's greeting, Harmonia was tugging on his pant leg.

"Pride, B. Thankful had a dream. No, strike that. She had a visitation. Jesus is sending B. Thankful on a road trip." By the time Harmonia finally took a breath, Pride had heard the whole dream and I had yet to offer up a good morning.

"Well, Jesus inspired or not, everybody should travel the Good Red Road to discover who they are, why they're here. I'd be honored to stay on and take care of your home for you while you're gone, B. Thankful." Pride set his ruler sized hand over mine, and there it was again. The way my heart sizzled and bucked like bacon in a hot skillet, gave me no doubt it was flawed. I didn't have time to look up heart ailments in Little G's medical book because Harmonia was in high gear, and there was no stopping her.

Stacks of blueberry pancakes, as abundant as the story of the loaves and fishes, found their way from stove to table while Harmonia made plans for me. I did my best to ignore all the *what ifs,* but they were stacking up in my head as high as the pancakes.

"Oh, one more thing, Pride. B. Thankful needs to borrow your RV."

"Sure. I'll bring it around tomorrow and teach you how to drive it, B. Thankful. When you're ready, we'll go to town and get you a driver's license."

That old toad-sized lump of worry and woe kicked up in my throat again, my tears hopping all over the pancakes.

"What is it, B. Thankful?" Harmonia's melodious voice did me in and I croaked out my fears.

"I've lived my entire life in this house, in the woods, and down by the river. I've only been as far as town a handful of times, and never alone. I've never been to the movies, I've never sat at a soda fountain, and I've never had a fancy TV dinner while watching television because we don't own a television. I learned everything from schoolbooks Daddy brought home and an old set of the Encyclopedia Britannica. I'd go through those books so fast and always got the answers right when he quizzed me. Daddy said I was smart, and one of the quickest learners he ever met, but he may have said that because he loves me."

As soon as I said "loves," as if Daddy was still alive, my state of mind flipped out of my head and landed on the table. "I mean LOVED me." I didn't mean to shout "loved," but that's how it jumped up my throat.

"I don't know how to be out in the world. I'm afraid I'll get lost and won't be able to find my way home. I don't know which turn to take to find the Good Red Road, or how I'll find the dying folks I'm supposed to cook a last supper for. Besides, I don't know how to cook. And what if no one shows up like Big G did to guide me? If it wasn't for Big G, I could never have made those jellied pig's feet for Little G. And I don't even know what an arvee is."

My head fell forward, my face coming to a halt in a stack of pancakes. Before I suffocated right then and there, Harmonia lifted up my head, blueberries stuck to my forehead, my face covered with maple syrup, tears, and snot. With my emotions flip flopping all over the breakfast table, I was sure my iron-willed Gs were doing the same in their graves.

"You are having a time of it, aren't you?" Harmonia said. She wiped down my face, picked the berries from my forehead, and placed a handkerchief over my nose. "Blow."

My never ending series of breakdowns didn't seem to faze Pride at all. He didn't seem to mind the mess that wore my name, and leaned in close to me.

"B. Thankful, you won't get lost out there. You'll find every person you've been sent to help, and there will be folks along the way sent to help you out, too. That's how you found Harmonia and I found you. I know you're scared, and that's okay. I'll help you get ready for your trip down the Good Red Road. You'll know when it's time to leave."

"Speaking of leaving, I've got to go. I've got some business to tend to." I had never considered Harmonia Pennywhistle might have *business to tend to*, whatever that was.

From the porch I watched Pride pull down a Harmonia-sized motorcycle from the back of Daddy's truck. Harmonia climbed on and called from across the yard, "Care to go for a spin, B. Thankful?" Passing a sly warning off to the side, Pride shook his head.

"Maybe next time, Harmonia. I've got to pick all the fruit and vegetables and start canning. If I don't have spiced peaches for Christmas, Little G will rise up and tan my hide."

"Suit yourself, but you don't know what you're missin'!" Harmonia snapped her goggles in place, and with a kick of the pedal, the motorcycle backfired, chickens flying in all directions. "I'll be back in time to fix supper," Harmonia shouted, through a cloud of dust and noise.

"If I were to know Harmonia Pennywhistle for a hundred years more, everyday would be filled with surprises," I said.

"If she hadn't come along to find me, I'd still be lost and wandering," Pride said

Seeing all we'd been through together, I got my courage up and asked Pride how he and Harmonia came by each other. When Pride didn't answer, I feared I had trespassed onto private property.

"I'm not withholding anything from you, B. Thankful, just looking for the words."

Standing taller than the cornstalks, and they were *get the ladder* high that summer, Pride easily pulled on the cobs at the very top, snapping them free. Six plump ears of corn, perfect for corn relish, dropped from his hand into the basket, and under the next pale green husk, he found the words he had been looking for.

"There was a time when I was broken down on the side of the road. Out of the blue, Harmonia showed up. Her angel voice lifted me up and carried me to her home where she cared for me while my spirit mended. It was there Harmonia taught me to paint what I see."

"Like my painting of the Last Supper?"

"Kind of like that, but I don't use numbers."

Stupid girl, of course he doesn't use numbers. I stared out at the garden, the trees, the sky; anywhere but Pride.

"B. Thankful, look at me," Pride said, but not in a bossy way. I took hold of my courage and turned to him.

"I paint my dreams. I have a painting of you in my RV, one from long before we met."

"Go on now."

"Honest, B. Thankful, I do. And when you showed up at Harmonia's house the other night, my dream came true."

POW! A thump in my chest hit me so hard, my eyes rolled to the back of my head, my legs turned to watery custard, and the earth pulled me down.

"Remember what I said, B. Leave the door open so love can walk in and find you once again," Big G whispered. Heck, I was a stone's throw away from an eternal sleeping bag, and Big G was talking about doors and love.

A gasp for air snatched me back and my eyelids flipped up. I stared at the world through a fuzzy cobweb, Pride looking back at me from the other side. With the possibility death was conning me like a feral cat hoodwinks a cornered mouse, my final words had to stand out and be remembered for all time. My voice was weak, but determined.

"Pride…" Through the fuzzy cobweb I saw the relief on Pride's face turn to amusement.

"What is it, B. Thankful?" Did he just stifle a laugh?

"Pride, make sure you get all the vegetables picked and canned, or food in the winter will be spare. And don't forget to milk Beautiful Beulah…" Hold on a darn minute. This all sounded very familiar to me.

"Who's there?" I called with my mind.

"It's me, B. Thankful. I couldn't help but play a little trick on you, but don't tell Jesus, he thinks I'm out planting flowers in the fields."

My thumb tapped so wildly with excitement, Pride surely thought I was having some kind of fit to go with my heart attack.

L-i-t-t-l-e G! W-h-e-r-e-a-r-e-y-o-u? A-r-e-y-o-u-w-i-t-h-B-i-g-G-a-n-d-D-a-d-d-y?

"Slow down, child!" Little G urged.

I put my thumb on pause and listened.

"B., I'm only here for a minute. I just had to come say thanks for taking such good care of me. Child, your gift helped me cross over with nary a care. But now you have to look ahead and start to live your new life. Promise me you'll set down your sorrow real soon."

There were so many questions I wanted to ask, but like our old radio, static took over. Through the crackles and pops, Little G called out, *"Be thankful for life!"* And then she was gone.

"I will be, Little G. I will be," I called out loud. "That was Little G," I said. "She was playing a practical joke and started reciting her own last wishes through me. Quite the trickster, eh?"

I waited for Pride to run down the road, but he raised me up out of the dirt and walked over to the shade of the old red oak, where he leaned me up against Momma's tree. He turned away and walked toward the house to gather his belongings. Who could blame him? I was acting as peculiar as Wild Mary.

We lived in the woods, but Wild Mary lived so deep in the back woods some people didn't believe she existed; just an imaginary tale born of the ill effects of bad moonshine, they said. But I knew Wild Mary was for real. I met up with her in the woods the day I ran away from home, that day Little G found me cooling off in the freezer. After Little G threatened to lock me in the freezer should she find me misusing it again, I decided to show her a thing or two. I packed up a lunch sack with two hardboiled eggs, fried chicken, a tomato, a piece of fresh-from-the-oven berry pie, and ran away from home in the direction of the deep woods.

So perturbed, I hollered out loud about my hard luck life and gave Little G a piece of my mind. I was stomping out my anger on innocent pinecones and smacking trees with a stick when something came out of nowhere and shoved me down, a jagged rock slicing into me, blood trickling onto the ground. A wounded cry sprang from me when I tried to move my arm, while fearful visions of wild animals picking up my scent and eating me for dinner caused me to cry in earnest.

Wild Mary crouched low to the ground and circled me for a closer look. She sniffed the air and growled at me with teeth that looked like chips of burned wood. Half naked, dirt covered, and her hair matted with leaves and twigs, Wild Mary had the stink on her. Under all the dirt, her skin was as white as fresh washed sheets; her hair the same; her eyes, pink and glowing. Wild Mary reminded me of sweet pea vines tangled under rocks, their true color never taking form. Wild Mary sniffed again, behind me this time. When I reached for my lunch sack, she jumped back and landed on her haunches.

"It's okay," I said. Slow and easy, I pulled out the hard-boiled eggs, chicken and tomato. I wanted to keep the berry pie for myself, but looking into Wild Mary's wanting eyes, I knew giving it up was the right thing to do. Before I could crack a single one of those eggs to share, Wild Mary scooped up all my food and ran to a nearby tree. She didn't even take the time to peel those eggs, eating them shell and all, and she wolfed down the chicken so fast, I couldn't say what she did with the bones. Evidently, Wild Mary didn't take to tomatoes because she threw the one I gave her back at me, but she did away with my berry pie quick as a fox on a chick.

When Wild Mary finished, she crawled over to me, and grabbed me by my wounded arm. Fear and pain cried out from me. Wild Mary reached in between the roots of the tree where I fell and came back with a handful of cobweb. She laid the web over my cut like a bandage, wrapped it with two large leaves, and tied them in place by tearing a strip from my shirt. I didn't want to be rude, but even after eating a heavenly piece of berry pie, her foul breath brought me near to puking.

"Thank you," I said. I'm not sure Wild Mary under-stood, or if she cared to, as she ran howling through the woods.

Later that night I went home, but only because I was near to starvation. Little G caught sight of my bandage. "Her name is Mary Talbert. Don't ever let me hear you call her Wild Mary."

Sometimes I would sneak food we could do without (but no tomatoes) and find my way deep into the woods where Mary Talbert and I met up. One time I even left her a jar of strawberry jam to spread on leftover biscuits. Though I never saw Mary Talbert again, I did find the jam jar on my next visit, a piece of golden honey comb tucked inside.

Now the sun was high and beating on the garden with both fists, and as much as I appreciated the shade of Momma's tree, if I had to tend to the garden and my chores on my own, it was time to pull myself together and get to work. The screen door squeaked open, then slapped shut. Pride moseyed over in my direction and placed a pitcher of ice cold lemonade on the parched grass next to me. He pulled two glasses from his back pocket, one for me, one for him. Pride leaned up against the tree next to me, his legs stretched out twice the length of my own.

"Whenever you're ready, B. Thankful, I'm here to listen to your story."

Like the day I was born and Little G took refuge under the shade of that same tree, or the night I scrubbed myself clean of the old bits that had to die, another new bit of me was born as I told Pride my story. A story in length that took us from the shade of the tree to the sun-drenched garden, where we didn't stop working until our baskets overflowed and the ground lay bare. A story that climbed the orchard ladder steps with me where I picked peaches and handed them, along with my words, to Pride, who held them as gently as he did the soft, ripe fruit. A story that took us clear to the end of our workday and the coming of the twilight hour when Pride grabbed me by the hand.

"Come on!"

Keeping up with Pride's long stride all the way down to the river was hard, but I did. It must have been the magic of the hour, for, as if by myself, I stripped down to my underwear and dove into the river. I heard the splash of water upstream when Pride dove in, and when he didn't surface, a sliver of panic sliced through me. I called out, Pride's name ricocheting off the rocks along the water's edge, skimming the river until he finally broke through the surface in front of me, his wet grin, mischievous.

We floated downstream on our backs, hand-in-hand, Pride's heartbeat coursing through his palm into my own. My heart glowed so bright, its light pushed out from me, and marked our path to home.

At home, we found Harmonia busy in the kitchen, a rosy blush in her cheeks, and a bottle of dandelion wine sitting on the counter. I kissed her right cheek and she turned her left cheek my way for a little more of the same.

"I hope you like chicken and dumplings, B. Thankful." Before I could answer, Harmonia turned lightning quick, her wooden spoon catching Pride's knuckles when he tried to lift the lid.

"Do you want my dumplings to turn to stone, Pride?" she asked, her spoon raised and ready to strike again. Pride raised his hands in surrender and gave me a wink. Wanting to save my own knuckles from Harmonia's spoon, not even the undeniable scent of peach cobbler pressed up against the oven door could tempt me to take a peek. Instead I made myself useful by setting the dining room table so we could enjoy each other's company at a leisurely pace with no mosquitoes nicking our skin.

At suppertime we joined hands and gave thanks for the ordinary moments of the day, each other, and the meal before us. And what a blessing Harmonia's chicken and dumplings turned out to be. I tasted all of her love for us in the tender chicken, the sweet carrots and celery, and the velvety gravy. And her dumplings were as light as feather pillows. No offense to Little G, but it could take days to pass one of her dumplings.

Finishing her last bite, Harmonia wiped at her mouth with her napkin and found an unanswered question from the day Daddy died tucked in its folds. Her voice floated lazily across a pale blue sky and landed next to my plate.

"So, B. Thankful, you never got the chance to tell me what it was like to have Etta Childe's spirit inside you while you fixed jellied pig's feet."

Harmonia's question took me by surprise and turned the dumpling I was taking pleasure in sideways. I pushed the remainder of my dinner from one edge of my plate to the other while I searched for the perfect string of words to explain such a marvel.

"When Big G's spirit settled inside me, my heart took a beat, then Big G's heart took a beat, then mine, then hers, and between the beat of our hearts, by a means I cannot give name to, we became one and the same."

Harmonia dabbed at the corners of her eyes with her napkin, then excused herself from the table, and set out to the porch, where I heard the creak of Little G's rocking chair.

Without any awkwardness, I looked directly into Pride's eyes and heeded Big G's advice: I opened the door to my heart. In the days that followed, I discovered that, just like fixing those jellied pig's feet, what I learned from Pride couldn't be found in any book.

Ten

———————◆———————

Come morning, I drove Pride out to Harmonia's place to pick up his arvee. It was everything Harmonia said it to be. It was a HOUSE on wheels. When I saw Pride's vehicle, which was longer than a boring story, the little bit of courage I had hooked around my road trip for Jesus slipped through a hole in my resolve and landed in the dirt. Just as I was considering whether to pick it up or brush it aside, that doggone mourning dove flew up from behind and landed on my shoulder. *Pick it up,* she cooed.

While I followed Pride home, I tried to imagine me learning to drive a house on wheels, but I just couldn't picture how that could ever come about. Lucky for me, Pride never lost faith, and in the weeks to follow he taught me to drive his arvee without leaving too many irreparable scars upon the land or his nerves. Though he never lost patience with me, every now and then he would suggest we take a break and look to chores.

During chore time, Pride learned the ups and downs of Beautiful Beulah's moods and how to avoid udder stutter. And just in case I didn't make it back before the bitter cold settled in, I shared the story of Big G's hard learned lesson around Beautiful Beulah—one I didn't want Pride to suffer.

It was an icy cold December morn and Big G was headed to the barn to milk Beautiful Beulah, when Little G called out a warning. "Remember to warm up your hands before laying them on Beautiful Beulah's teats." Big G waved her off. "You'd want a body to do the same for you," Little G hollered.

When Big G didn't come back to the house timely, Little G and I went out to the barn where we found Big G laid out in the straw. Evidently, Beautiful Beulah was so surprised by Big G's icy grip, she accidently kicked her in the head and flipped off the switch to Big G's upstairs lights. I could see in poor Beautiful Beulah's big brown cow eyes just how sorry she was. Hard lesson learned, from then on Big G always made sure her hands were toasty warm before milking Beautiful Beulah, but in case warming her hands wasn't enough, Big G fashioned a protective helmet out of an old watering can. *Waste not, want not*.

I was more than happy to turn the job of collecting eggs from the hens over to Pride. No matter how much I clucked and sweet talked each hen before reaching in under a soft, feathered belly, I got pecked. Once Pride took over their care, those same spiteful peckers turned all ladylike and fluffed themselves up whenever Pride walked into the coop. And when he whispered soft and low as he reached under them, those usually ill mannered hens lifted up, eager to offer him their eggs.

While Pride worked his magic on the chickens and took care of the everyday chores, Harmonia and I canned fruits and vegetables, corn relish, pickles, jams and jellies. Every now and then I'd take a sideways glance at my painting of the Last Supper to see if Jesus had anything more to say, but he just watched the goings on. The mourning dove, who I took to calling Livia, watched from the kitchen windowsill as I moved piping hot jars from boiling water to thick layers of towels, the lids pop, pop, popping as they sealed.

In honor of my Little G, I spent one whole day in the kitchen by myself canning spiced peaches. By noon the bubbling pots on the stove and the day's heat had so reduced my brain power I couldn't ponder what needed to be done next. I tapped out a quick message to Little G begging her to take pity on me and listened with both ears for her footsteps as I climbed into the freezer to cool off my brain. It wasn't Little G who found me in the freezer that day, it was Harmonia.

"B. Thankful, I want you to lay out your best dress tonight, because tomorrow morning you and I are going to the Mercantile Bank to take care of business." I had never been inside the Mercantile Bank and told Harmonia as much. "Well, darlin'," she said, "there's a first time for everything. Be ready when I get here in the morning." It's hard to argue with puffy white clouds floating across a pale blue sky, especially with a frozen squirrel resting on your forehead.

Next morning, I skipped over breakfast and went to work on presenting myself as a grown up. I put on clean underwear, my lavender jumper, and polished my work boots. But no matter how I pleaded, my willful hair refused to behave. I finally took it to task by shoving it under my straw hat and pulling the strings up tight under my chin. With my envelope full of documents and my Banner Bar winnings in hand, I was ready to do business.

My knees started knocking against each other when we walked through the bank's door and every eye behind the marble counter turned in our direction. I followed their stares down to Harmonia, who was wearing a red and white checkered blouse with fringe hanging from under the sleeves, and a petticoat puffed, bright red skirt. Her cowgirl boots had bucking broncos stitched on the side and silver spurs that jingle, jangle, jingled when she walked. But it was probably her cowgirl hat that put the envy in their eyes: pure white felt with a brim seven inches broad, the crown wrapped by a band of silver dollars. Harmonia jingle, jangle, jingled all the way up to the window. I borrowed a chair and pushed it over to where she stood, and then helped her up so she could see over the counter. The bank teller snickered as Harmonia climbed onto the chair. The hair on my neck bristled when I looked up and found myself eye-to-eye with Onida Bossier.

"Well, well," Onida said. "Long time no see, B. Thankful Childe-NoLuck." Just as an unsettled grievance reached through the window to grab Onida by her second chin, I heard my Daddy's voice. *"Remember, B. Thankful, you weren't sent to fight ignorant words. You're meant to do something great in your life."* I pulled my hand back to my side of the window, but I kept my eyes snake narrow as a warning to Onida.

When Harmonia asked Onida Bossier to get her boss, Onida grunted her annoyance. "Now, missy," Harmonia said, and there wasn't a single puffy cloud nearby.

The bank's president, Mr. Harper, ushered us into his private office when he saw the amount of my check, but never once did he look me in the eye. No amount of money would ever change the way people in town looked down on me.

"Tell Mr. Harper why you're here, B. Thankful."

What? Why did Harmonia do such a thing? Couldn't she see Mr. Harper wanted nothing to do with me? He heaved a sigh as he stared at his stubby, hairy fingers. I tasted the burnt edge of his hatred, but without Harmonia's help, I had no choice but to spit it out.

"I'm here to open a checking account, deposit my winnings from the Banner Bar Company, and find out how much money is in the savings account my Daddy, Tyler Lucknow, set up for me." Harmonia turned to me and smiled.

Mr. Harper pressed a button on a box and spoke into it. Lickety split, a lady wearing a tight black dress, and shoes with heels so high I was afraid she would fall over, came into his office. She handed Mr. Harper a file with my name on it and turned to leave. I could tell by the way Mr. Harper leaned over the side of his chair and watched that nice lady walk away that he, too, was worried she was going to fall. Without so much as looking at my file, Mr. Harper slid it across the desk to Harmonia, his sweaty fingers leaving smudges on the polished wood.

"Glory be!" Harmonia cried, and hopped on Mr. Harper's desk. She danced in a circle, her petticoats twirling and rising up, showing Mr. Harper her stubby legs.

"Pride was right, B. Thankful," she sang, dancing from one edge of the desk to the other, the spurs on her boots scratching her happiness into the expensive wood. "You are a wealthy young woman."

When I finished doing business, I had a savings account chockfull of money, a checking account with $25,000.00 in it, a credit card coming to me in the mail, and a pen that read *Mercantile Bank–Where the Customer Comes First.*

Unfortunately, for those concerned, Harmonia wasn't finished doing business. The last thing I saw on my way out of the bank was Harmonia Pennywhistle's finger wagging at Mr. Harper and Mr. Harper extending the same about a split hair from Onida's pug nose. Jingle, jangle, jingle, Onida Bossier.

My last week with Harmonia and Pride flew by quicker than a perfect moment. Our days were filled with hard work, our nights with laughter and midnight swims where my spirit dipped and soared. I took some time every day to visit my Gs and Daddy, and as I lay next to them, I promised I wouldn't squander the generosity they had bestowed upon me. I spoke to them of my road trip and, hand over my heart, promised I would use my gift to make them proud of me. When I told them how I would miss my daily visits, I cried.

I was still wiping at my tears when I heard Daddy's truck pull in under the trees. With no hurry in his bones, Pride made his way to the back of the truck and pulled out a large burlap sack. He laid the offering at my feet and a jar of sweet tea in my hand. It was a mystery to me when my painter of dreams found the time to carve tombstones honoring my Daddy and Little G. Under Daddy's name, Pride had carved a wolf—the teacher; and Little G's marker sported two animals—coyote, the trickster, and a pig—for obvious reason. I pulled on Pride's sleeve and he bent down. I hugged his neck tight and inhaled his scent of apples and smoke.

"Thank you for loving my people. They would have loved you the way I do."

Pride lifted me up and held me close, his cheek pressed next to mine, and the word *forever*, tapped my heart.

Back at the house, Pride went about moving his belongings into my home as I moved mine into his. I stood at the stove where Pride fixed his meals, ran my hand across the table that offered up a cozy bed for dreaming when flipped over. I opened cupboards that Harmonia had stocked with dry goods, preserved fruits and vegetables, and found she had packed the small refrigerator and freezer with enough food to see me through a hard winter. In return, I made sure I left them with enough Banner Bars so they could carry on with the Ritual of the Five Senses.

That night's dinner was a beautiful sight to behold, but my nervous stomach kept me from partaking in its goodness. The anxious part of me wanted to go to sleep so the waiting would be over, but the other part of me, the part that couldn't take her eyes off of Pride, wanted the night to last forever so nothing would change. But if the night had no end, there would be no new crop of peaches, no glorious sunrises or magenta sunsets, no new dreams coming true, no new bits of who I was to become would be born.

Ten chimes from the mantle clock told us the time for goodbyes had come. I bowed down to Harmonia the way I had the first time I met her.

"I need to see all of you," she said, and gently pushed my unruly hair away from my face. "Remember, there is no other like you in the whole wide world. Hold everything you see and hear on your journey in your heart. As you serve every person, every person will serve you." She placed her tiny hands on my cheeks, her blue-milk eyes and ruby-studded smile drawing me into the center of all her love.

Harmonia Pennywhistle hopped on her motorcycle and kick started it. "BE FEARLESS!" she called through the night. "BE FEARLESS!"

"Come with me, I want to show you something." Pride led me back to the house and to my room. On the wall facing my bed hung a painting of a girl with red corkscrew hair; one brown eye, one green eye, looking back at me. Barefoot, arms outstretched, and wearing my favorite dress, she floated in the center of a night sky, countless stars surrounding her.

When the air gets thick with the discovery of so much truth and beauty, I find a well-timed joke puts me at ease, so I told Pride I was happy he got my eyes right, unlike the wandering eye of Jesus in my paint-by-number Last Supper. But sometimes truth and beauty will not be denied by a joke, even one well-timed.

"I love you, B. Thankful. I have loved you for a very long time. I will stay here and wait for you until the moon grows dark, until all that is, is no more. Come back to me." Pride kissed me softly and raised me up until Heaven and Earth became one.

Fearful I would turn away from my road trip for Jesus if I looked upon Pride come morning, I climbed the side ladder to the top of the arvee alone. I stared up from Little G's picnic blanket at the stars twinkling above, then to the fireflies below. They seemed brighter, more alive than ever. The river lapped against the shore, crickets and frogs called their goodbyes; coyotes howled farewell, and the call of the loons broke my heart one last time.

I woke up sometime around four in the morning. *Now or never. Now or never.* Before leaving, I peed behind the chicken coop to remind those fickle ladies who was boss, then stood in my yard and looked upon my home and all I had ever known.

In the curve of my ear, I heard the strains of Little G's violin, Big G's mandolin, and my Daddy's sweet voice in song. As Daddy's singing faded away, another voice I hadn't heard in a long time whispered, *"Good luck, little girl."*

T-h-a-n-k-y-o-u-m-o-m-m-a.

My picture of Big G was taped to the glove compartment along with my favorite picture of Little G and Daddy—the one where they're kissing my cheeks. In back, my paint-by-number Last Supper rested on the windowsill, my dream catcher to the right. I touched my hand to the soaring eagle around my neck.

I turned the key, and the motor's vibration ran through me. When I turned on the headlights, from out of nowhere, Livia came flying through my window and landed on the dashboard. Gripping the steering wheel with all my might, I shifted into drive, stepped on the gas, and headed down the road for Jesus.

The last thing I saw in my rearview mirror was Pride standing on the porch, waving goodbye.

My Road Trip for Jesus

Eleven

It was still dark when I drove through town, the sidewalks on either side, hidden. Through the darkness, I called out my goodbye to those hardhearted folks unable to make welcome the girl with two-toned eyes and red corkscrew hair, who heard the voices of the departed. I waved so long to hearts unable to hold dear all God's colors. *So long. So long.*

Riding up high and driving with two headlights was new to me, the road before me all lit up. *This way*, it said. *West*, the compass read. I drove the back roads through small towns with curious names like Mousie, Thousandsticks, and Stab. Hours and miles went by, daylight and hunger coming upon me as I drove through London and entered the Daniel Boone National Forest. Off the side of Mr. Boone's road, I spied picnic tables, a perfect place for my first stop. To my good fortune, I was able to pull onto a nice patch of dirt where I wouldn't have to back up. I didn't fare well during my lessons, nearly taking out the chicken coop.

No sooner had my door opened when Livia flew from the dashboard into the forest. I called out her name, but she didn't look back. I put out a goodly amount of sunflower seeds on the hood of the arvee to coax her around again, but a flock of birds and a number of feisty squirrels scattered the seeds everywhere. And hungry as I was, I couldn't wait for Livia to make up her mind about staying or going.

To hush up my hunger I had a go at frying two eggs the way my Little G made them for me—sunny side up, the bright orange-yellow yolks looking back at me—but by the time I was through fiddling with them, they were pretty messed up. I turned to my paint-by-number Jesus. "Are you sure I'm the one to handle this last supper business?" Jesus just stared at me with his one eye while his other remained on Judas.

Sitting at one of Mr. Boone's picnic tables, I unwrapped the cornbread Pride put together for me and found a tiny piece of waxed paper, no bigger than a postage stamp, holding the heart of a pressed rose petal the color of love. I touched the petal to my lips, and the memory of Pride's kiss sent a shiver and a shake running through me. I folded the paper around the petal and put it into the pocket of my t-shirt for safe keeping.

While I ate breakfast, I read the names of strangers carved into the picnic table. Someone named Francine loved Corny so much she drew a big heart around their names to keep them together forever. At one time, Justine loved Terence, but on a return trip must have decided he wasn't the one, his name scratched out, and Donny written above it. The carving of Donny's name was fresh and I had a hunch he might go the way of Terence. I considered carving Pride's name next to mine inside a heart, but it seemed such an ordinary thing to do. I favored having a rose petal next to my heart that no one else knew about.

A rusty, old car drove by and a little girl waved to me from the back window as if we had known each other forever. Taken by surprise, and my hands full of cornbread, I wasn't able to return her friendliness. So disappointed, I vowed the next time a car passed by and somebody waved, I'd make sure I was able to pay back the kindness. My stomach full, I lay down on the bench, my legs swinging back and forth on either side, and listened to the sounds bounce off the sandstone cliffs. Nature's calls weren't so very different from home, but the number of people and cars zooming by left me feeling like a drowsy bee in a bustling hive until a voice I dared not question came through, calling me to task.

"Time's a wastin'!"

O-k-a-y-L-i-t-t-l-e-G.

With no sign of Livia after calling out her name a number of times, I tied one of my lavender ribbons around a low branch on Mr. Boone's tree as a marker for her. You'd think with all the goodbyes I had said of late, her leave-taking wouldn't have stung me, but it did. Though the flavor of my road trip would be less sweet without her, I had to carry on.

Studying the map Harmonia taped to the refrigerator door, if I did as well on the next leg of my journey, I could make it to the Mammoth Cave National Park where I'd spend the night. I climbed behind the wheel, started up the engine, checked my mirrors, signaled with my blinker, and eased my way down the road.

The next stretch of road wasn't as kind to me as the first. Why, there were times when the curves appeared shaped like Big G's hairpins, and I was certain the back end of Pride's arvee was going to meet up with the front. In the side mirror, I saw a stream of cars slithering up behind me like a snake in the river. Nervous sweat gathered at the roots of my crazy hair and dripped down the sides of my face, and my hands gripped the steering wheel so tight my knuckles turned milk white. And that made me think of Beautiful Beulah, how Pride had milked her that morning, and how the chickens were so in love with Pr... HONK! HONK! AHHOOGA! AHHOOGA! HONK!

The blaring of those horns nearly turned me inside out, my scared-out-of-my-wits voice calling into the side mirror, "Criminy sakes, I'm doing the best I can." In the rear-view mirror, I caught a glimpse of Jesus and his friends riding carefree. If I hadn't been so scared, I'd've given them a serious talking to.

After a few more twists and turns, I pulled over to the side of the road, dust flying everywhere, gravel popping like corn under the tires. Turned out those honkin' folks weren't as angry as I had imagined, waving at me as they drove past. Determined not to overlook another friendly gesture, I smiled and waved my middle finger right back at them, then leaned out the window and threw up my cornbread and eggs.

By the time I pulled up to the ranger's booth at Mammoth Cave National Park, my shoulders were locked up right under my ears. When the ranger looked up from under his Smokey the Bear hat, his manner wasn't lined with restraint.

"You look like you've been through the ringer. That's quite a rig for a little girl like you. Think you can make it up that road to campsite 19? It's about half a mile in." Smokey the Bear's buddy pointed toward a narrow, crooked dirt road.

I nodded my sweaty head.

"That'll be three dollars."

Unable to pry my tortured hands from the steering wheel, I asked if I could pay him once I settled in. He dropped his head, but I saw his smirk sitting at the edge of the hat's brim.

"Sure, you can pay me later. Drive careful."

It took almost twenty minutes to go what turned out to be the same distance from my house to the river. Even in a sticky heat, I could walk that distance in half the time, and with less sweat dripping from my brow. When I finally reached the campsite, I had to free the grip of my hands on the steering wheel finger-by-finger, and that was the easy part. After I opened the door, and eased my legs over the driver's seat, I fell to the ground when they refused to hold me up. As if hitting the dirt had been my intention all along, I lay there staring skyward, whistling notes that didn't amount to a song. A very nice couple came over to see if I was okay, and as much as I wanted to be friendly, I couldn't extend my arm, turned useless as a wet noodle from driving, to shake hands.

"Been driving all day?" the man asked. A single puffy cloud shaded the bright sky behind him. His round, meaty face came close to my own, his fluff of in-then-out nose hairs mesmerizing me, as it appeared my eyes did him.

"Yes, sir, I have been. All day."

"For goodness sake, Winthrow, pick her up," the woman said.

"Nadine, mind yourself," Winthrow warned.

Nadine tilted her head, her long yellow hair hanging free to the side. She pressed her bright red lips together, forming a thin, straight line, pulled down her pointy, gold sunglasses, and challenged Winthrow with her stare.

"Really, I'm okay." I shook out my arms and legs, threw caution to the wind, and stood up. The outcome was new calf wobbly, but I was standing.

"What's your name, sweetheart?" Nadine asked.

"B. Thankful Childe-Lucknow." I tried to keep my eyes lowered so she wouldn't judge me, but Nadine was the most vivid person I had ever met, and I just couldn't take my eyes off her.

Right off, Nadine put her arm around my shoulder, her gesture taking me so by surprise, it was all I could do not to shy away. But Nadine didn't seem to notice, pulling me even closer, and telling me how Winthrow was going to take care of all the "man things" that needed doing to set up the arvee while we shared a glass of sweet tea. Winthrow stood behind Nadine, his hand signing, *yak, yak, yak.*

"Don't think I don't know what you're doing behind me, Winthrow Wainwright," Nadine warned.

I recognized their scrapping was in fun, a way of loving each other without saying as much. Big G and Little G used to scrap the very same way, Big G throwing me a wink and a nod when she got Little G riled up, and Little G doing the same when she got the best of her momma. If you listen closely, you'll hear love expressed in the strangest ways. While they carried on, Winthrow set the blocks in place and hitched up everything that needed hitching while Nadine and I sipped our iced tea. When Winthrow finished with the manly things, I thanked them both for their kindness and told them I'd love to stay and chew the fat with them, but I had to go pay the ranger for my campsite.

"Oh, good, you can pick me up some graham crackers while you're down there. The general store isn't far from the entrance." My foundation quivered at the idea of going into the general store, but Nadine had been so kind to me, I couldn't say no.

On my way to the store I saw a crowd of people eyeballing a huge hole in the mountainside. A pamphlet handed to me colored it as the famous Mammoth Cave with more miles of pathways than days in a year. Wanting an exciting and bold story to write home about, I got my courage up and walked right into the cave. A little boy with buck teeth and a spot of ringworm on his cheek stomped on my foot and screamed, "You cut in front of the line!" While I hopped up and down on my good foot, his mother yelled at me, "You've gotta buy a ticket, lame brain. And the line is way back there." Her thumb pushed backwards over her shoulder.

I slunk away to the sound of everyone laughing about my "weird eyes" and "crazy hair." Their spiteful snickers rolled over and under my feet, tripping me up so much I had to catch myself from falling in the dirt.

My legs were still shaking, and my breath remained shallow and quick, as I made my way over to the store. While sitting under a nearby tree, I tried to free myself from the grip fear had on me. I watched grownups and little kids go into the store empty handed and come out with all sorts of unfamiliar items peeking out of their pockets. I struggled not to stare, but I had never been in a general store, and I wanted to appear as normal as everyone else when I went in. I was scared that, just like the folks in town and at the cave, people in the store would look upon me as broken. I chewed on my fingernails, then folded and unfolded my money while I read every sign in the store's windows, and never tripped up on any of the words; course they were small words, not thought provoking like those in the books I read. (Just because I lived a simple life didn't mean I was without vital thoughts.) Still, my scaredy cat legs were about to send me running when Winthrow showed up.

"Whatcha doin' out here, B. Thankful?"

I don't know why, but hearing his manly voice made me sniffle. I tightened my lips and looked away to a crying little girl who had dropped her ice cream in the dirt. I sniffed again and my lips went loose, my well of tears overflowing.

"Ah, come on now." Winthrow took my hand, the calluses on his own, scratchy. "Let's go get those graham crackers for Nadine."

Once inside the general store, my questions were as plentiful as the unfamiliar items on the shelves.

"What are potato chips?" I asked, holding up a bag.

"Potato chips are sliced potatoes deep fried to a crisp." Little G said anything deep fried was worth a try.

"Is it okay to buy this bag?"

"Why sure, B. Thankful, why do you ask?"

"Because it's got Laura Scudder's name on it and I don't want to get in trouble for taking it." After Winthrow got done laughing, he promised me Laura Scudder wouldn't mind.

"And what's Coca Cola?" I asked, holding up a bottle.

"You don't know what Coca Cola is?"

"No, sir, I don't." I pulled on Winthrow's sleeve and whispered so no one else could hear. "I've never been in a general store."

Winthrow took me by the hand and led me up and down every single aisle in the store until he was exhausted by my curiosity. By then, I had filled my basket with potato chips (regular and barbecue), Coca Cola, Slim Jims, Laffy Taffy (I had to buy it for the name alone), a deck of cards with a color picture of Mammoth Cave National Park on the side without numbers, two post cards, some stamps, and a pair of sunglasses. I also bought a bucket of worms so I could go fishing with Winthrow in the morning. Just as I was about to pay for everything, I remembered why we came in.

"I'll be right back."

All on my own, I ran to the right aisle and picked up a box of Nabisco Honey Graham Crackers. Winthrow slapped his leg and laughed hard when he saw the box.

"Nadine would have kicked our butts if we came back without her graham crackers."

Outside, Winthrow pointed to a shady spot under a tree where we could sit a spell before going back to camp. He reached in the sack and pulled out a Slim Jim for himself, and two Coca Colas. I was at a loss as to what I should try first, but finally settled on potato chips. Their saltiness stuck in the corners of my mouth, and the grease made my lips slippery.

"Lip smacking good, aren't they?"

"Yes, sir, they are." I wiped the grease from my hand on the grass and set it on Winthrow's hand. "Thank you." Winthrow gave me a nod, but said nothing. We sipped the rest of our ice cold Coca Colas without trading small talk as we watched people come and go. As simple a time as that may sound to some, for me, it was like waking up and finding myself on Mars.

Back at the campsite, I gave Nadine the box of graham crackers and she gave me an all sides hug, which I learned, as the days went by, was one of her favorite things to do.

"Make sure to drop by for s'mores tonight. Mine are scrumptioulicious!" Nadine Wainwright asked me to *drop by*. Why, I would *drop by*.

As daylight found its way to the other side of the world, my first twilight away from home glowed around the edges of the park where little boys ran toy trucks through hand dug tunnels, red dirt and a forever memory packed under their fingernails. I found hope in the friendly exchanges of homespun remedies for sunburns and bee stings, for even I knew the outside world was not in a glorious mood. Just last spring that nice Reverend King was killed, and while we were picking the early harvest of our summer garden, poor Rose Kennedy lost another son. Outside that special place, those same folks may have walked right by one another, but that night in Mammoth Cave National Park, the very best in people found its way into the forest. The magic in the air was as warm as the glow from the fireflies.

Maybe some kind of magic had spun itself around me, too, or maybe it was the smell of down home cooking coming from the campfires that led me to set down my shy to the bone way, and take a stroll through the campground. Never in my life had I been in the company of so many strangers, and after my hurtful experience at the cave, it surprised me to find myself being invited to join in. I wasn't surprised, however, by the affection shaped by a pot of beans when a spoonful offered up for tasting won a sigh and a kiss, or how a man's hefty belly shook with appreciation over a prized potato salad and barbecued ribs; no surprise for me that corn on the cob boiled up in sugar water could give birth to corn kernel smiles; smiles so big, they made me smile, too.

By the time I made my way back to my campsite, I had sampled ribs, potato salad, corn on the cob, and pineapple upside down cake baked right over the fire in a cast iron Dutch oven. It was the first time I ever tasted pineapple, and it was sweet and sour at the same time. In addition to a full belly, I was sporting a shirt from Big Dave of Big Dave's Diner in Topeka, Kansas that read: WELL, BUTTER MY BUTT AND CALL ME A BISCUIT!

Nadine's burst of laughter rang loud and strong as I waddled over in her direction. "You look like a tick about ready to pop!" She was right. I was so full I had to unbutton my trousers.

"Well, I hope you saved room for one of Nadine's s'mores because they're the best in the whole damn world!" Winthrow's pumped up pride pushed out to the edges of the campground.

"Seriously, B. Thankful, if I only had one meal left I'd want one of Nadine's s'mores."

Winthrow's mention of a last meal made my ears perk up and my worry meter start to tick. Without being outright obvious, I looked to see if Winthrow or Nadine was waving one of those time markers Daddy talked about in my direction. Using a casual tone, I asked Winthrow and Nadine how they were feeling, and was happy to hear Nadine tell me they'd never felt better, except for Winthrow's occasional bout with piles. Winthrow shook his head and quickly changed the subject by firing off a round of questions at me that sprayed out like buckshot.

"What's a young girl like you doing on the road all alone? Who are your people? Where do you come from? Who taught you do drive that RV? Where are you headed?"

"Christ almighty, Winthrow, who do you think you are, Amos Burke?"

"Who's Amos Burke?" I asked.

Nadine stopped making s'mores and studied me the way Little G studied the chickens when they stopped laying eggs.

"Why, only the finest detective ever to live! And a millionaire to boot!" Nadine sighed.

"You know, on television," Winthrow added.

I shook my head *no,* and reared back when the shock on Nadine's face led her brisk charge in my direction. In three giant steps Nadine was nose-to-nose with me, her painted blue eyelids blinking off and on.

"You don't mean to tell me you've never seen television, do you?"

"I have never seen television." You'd a thought I told Nadine about Big G's vestigial third tit, that's how shocked she was.

"You don't know about *Ben Casey? Gilligan's Island? Batman? I Dream of Jeannie?*"

Nadine's eyes started hopping up and down as fast as a lizard crossing hot rocks, her disbelief stuck to his burning feet. *"The Big VALLEY? THE DICK VAN DYKE SHOW?* CHILD, WERE YOU RAISED BY WOLVES?"

"Nadine Wainwright, you're spending way too much time with Harvey Wallbanger!" Winthrow scolded.

I lowered my voice, hoping Nadine would do the same so the folks I just met, and who seemed to like me, wouldn't change their minds and think less of me because I'd never seen television.

"Not only have I never seen television, I've never been away from home, never been in a general store, and, although it may be hard to tell, I never drove an arvee before today, except during my lessons with Pride out on the property."

"So, what are you doing on the road all alone?" Winthrow asked.

Thinking it best not to tell them Jesus had sent me on a road trip or the last supper business, I told Nadine and Winthrow I was going to meet my Daddy in San Francisco by the Golden Gate Bridge.

"Is he in Alcatraz?" Nadine asked, but before I could answer, she hugged me full on, my face buried between her ample breasts.

"Mmmmph mmmpphh mmpppphhh."

"Not to change the subject, but really, you've never seen *Bewitched*?"

"Mmmmph." Nadine rocked me back and forth until Winthrow finally saved me from the clutch her bosom seemed to have on my face.

Nadine did her best to shake off the unthinkable, but every now and then she'd take a sidelong gander at me as she lined up the s'mores fixings just so: graham crackers, marshmallows, chocolate bars. With a clean snap, she broke the graham crackers in half and placed four squares of the chocolate bar on one half, then pulled out a long stick and loaded it up with marshmallows.

"This is the tricky part," Nadine said. "If you hold marshmallows too long over the flame, the marshmallows catch fire and they're ruined; too little time in the flame and they're useless. Step back and let me show you how this is done."

Prickly flames crackled within the circle of stones as Nadine turned the marshmallows until the white puffs began to blister and turn the same color as Jesus's hair (number 12-sienna brown). I worried she was going to set them afire, but Nadine was a pro and, just like Big G fixing jellied pig's feet, recognized the exact moment of perfection. Nadine pulled the puffed up marshmallows from the stick, their gooey insides stretching like string, placed them on top of each chocolate bar, and topped them off with the waiting graham crackers.

"Eat 'em while they're hot," Nadine said.

I bit into my very first s'more, and the crunch of the graham cracker mashed down the marshmallows, melted chocolate oozing out the sides onto my hands. In between the graham cracker on top and the one below, I tasted a little bit of Heaven. So awestruck by Nadine's s'mores, Winthrow leaned over and kissed her again and again, their puckered lips locking up as the sticky marshmallow cooled. Next thing I knew, they were throwing me a "good night" over their shoulders and hustling into their arvee.

"Good night," I called. "Thank you for the s'mores. I'll never forget them." *I'll never forget you.* That was the night I fell in love with Nadine and Winthrow Wainwright from Flamingo, Florida, which, according to Nadine, was located in the tip of the penis of the United States of America.

All of their smoochin' made me want to lie under my dream catcher and fall asleep while thinking about Pride's kiss, hoping it would lead me to a dream where Pride and I met up in a place where stars had yet to be born. Eager to start dreaming, I twisted the dining table around and it magically turned into my bed for the night. The soft sheets and pillows buried under the seats called to my exhausted body, which, after my first day on the road, was eager to untangle the knots in the fibers holding me together. When I rested my head upon the pillow, I heard a rustling sound. Inside the pillow case, I discovered a piece of paper with a drawing of Pride and me standing hand-in-hand, his words spiraling round and round us.

Dear B. Thankful, I hope your first day on the Good Red Road was filled with wonder. I'll see you in my dreams tonight and forever. Love, Pride

Pride's penmanship was firm and the curves of his letters knew exactly how what was being said should look. I let the perfect loop at the top of Pride's *L* in *Love* enfold me as I drifted off to sleep. Pride made his way through the web of my dream catcher and down the eagle's feathers.

I found Pride sitting in Little G's chair, his easy back and forth rocking, the only movement; a creak from the tired rung on the left side, the only sound. He opened his arms, and I climbed into his lap and rested my head on his chest. Pride laid his hand on my cheek and rocked me through my first night away from home.

I awoke to an early morning knock on my door and a friendly call from Nadine. "Yoohoo, B. Thankful, come on out and have breakfast with us. Winthrow's frying up potatoes, bacon, and eggs."

Next thing I knew, a redheaded Nadine was sitting behind the steering wheel, studying the pictures on the dashboard. Nadine flipped her hair over her shoulder and turned to me, her voice missing all of her silly way.

"Who's that?"

"My Little G and my Daddy."

I stuck my head back under the covers and held my breath while Nadine pondered the picture of me with Little G and Daddy. What would I do if Nadine Wainwright didn't embrace all of God's colors, only saw black or white; worse yet, chose one over the other? With such a hunger inside me for Momma love, I took to Nadine right away, and the fear I might lose her started rummaging around in my chest.

"Best not to tell Winthrow what I'm about to say because he's a man through and through—likes to shoot things, fish, drink beer, eat, make love, and fart—and he'd go jealous berserk if he found out I thought your daddy's one fine looking man."

I lifted the covers, my breath pushing out into the arvee, my smile and tears on the same side of happiness. Nadine wiped my cheeks with the tip of her sleeve and looked into my eyes as if she saw my whole life story there. Real Mommas can do that, you know.

"I can't imagine it's been easy for you, but I've never seen such pure love locked into a picture before. I knew you were special when I saw you fall out of your RV yesterday. Oh, I may flap my hands around a lot and act loud, but I'm listening and watching while I do it." Nadine gave me one of her full on hugs. "Now, come on, sweet thing, let's go eat."

"Before we go, can I ask you something, Nadine?"

"Ask me anything."

"Is your hair a different color today?"

"Yes, it is," she said, as she ran her fingers through her wavy red hair. "A girl's gotta do what a girl's gotta do to keep her man interested, and variety is the spice of life. Course, the drapes never match the carpet, but Winthrow doesn't seem to notice." Nadine's nature confused me, but she was more alive than any other human being I had ever met and I liked that.

Taken by my good fortune in finding such kind folks, I lingered at the Mammoth Cave National Park for three more days. Every morning, before Nadine and the sun rose, I'd meet up with Winthrow and we'd take his boat out on the water. On the very first day, he asked me why I was wearing my sunglasses, and I told him about the folks back home, ringworm boy, and the crowd at the cave.

"People can be so hurtful. Why, you've got the most beautiful eyes I've ever seen. But don't tell Nadine I said that. Being a woman through and through, she'd go crazy berserk with jealousy." Winthrow took my sunglasses from my face and placed them in my shirt pocket. "At least wait until the sun comes up."

We tricked so many fish into taking our bait that day, we invited Big Dave's brood to join us for a fish fry. When the last of the tall fish tales and recipes had been passed back and forth, and the other campers and Winthrow called it a night, Nadine set out two chairs by the fire so we could have a little "girl talk time." Maybe she saw their tiny faces in the flicker of the fire, for she never took her eyes off it, as she shared her heartbreaking story of loss.

"Winthrow blames himself, says his seed has gone bad bouncing up and down on the tractor, but that's not it. No, it's me. Seems those little buns just can't rise in my oven," she said, leaning on Harvey Wallbanger.

It didn't seem fair that Nadine, who I could sense would have made a perfect Momma, never got the chance to wrap all those hugs around her own child's shoulder. Nadine would have been the kind of Momma who cheered you on; ran a comb through your crazy hair; showed you how to put on lipstick, if you were so inclined; told you how wonderful it was to fall in love; shared the secrets of a wedding night and how babies were made—vital information every girl should have.

With a Momma like Nadine, I wouldn't have had to rely on secondhand facts I overheard when Onida told Bubbles Tulane, so nicknamed for his constant case of snot bubbles, women got pregnant when their husbands joined the military and went off to war.

Little did I know Onida's only proof rested on eavesdropping on the womenfolk in her family, where she learned Cousin Cornelius was born while his daddy was in the Navy, Baby Roy was born while his daddy, Tucker, was in the Army, and Onida, herself, was born while her daddy was in the penitentiary. Seeing Onida was two years older than me, I figured she had to be in the know about baby making, but then Bubbles Tulane let out a snort, not only spraying Onida with snot, but with his version of how babies were made.

"Nuh-uh," Bubbles said, wiping his nose on his sleeve. "Babies get borned by a man puttin' his diddle wand into a woman's hooha. Every fool knows that."

I had no idea what a diddle wand or a hooha might be, but the sound of those words made me laugh until I was rolling on the ground. That's why Onida, covered with Bubbles's snot, went red faced, turned on me, and called Momma and Daddy those awful names, and I got kicked out of school for punching her in the belly.

Nadine would have been the kind of Momma who, when I told her Onida's grip on where babies came from, would have told me the true facts, not summed it up like

Little G did to avoid answering the question. "All you need remember about babies is they're easier to get in than they are to get out," Little G said. End of conversation. That kind of no-brain answer is exactly why a girl like me needed a Momma like Nadine. She would have told me all about diddle wands and hoohas.

"You're exactly the kind of girl I would be proud to call my daughter," Nadine said. A passing shadow of doubt told me it was probably Harvey Wallbanger doing the talking. Nadine saw my disbelief, leaned out of her chair, and took me by my chin. "I've never given that gift to anyone. Please don't throw it in the fire."

"Okay, Mommadine. Okay." I can't say why I called her Mommadine, but Nadine took to crying so hard, black lines ran down her cheeks.

What with Nadine being so doggone honest, it was only right to tell her my whole story– how I wasn't conceived in love, how Momma died right before I was born (that took a while to explain), how Daddy adopted me, and how twenty-eight days ago he and Little G died, one right after the other, and left me an orphan. Then I told her all about Harmonia and Pride, how they saved me from my sorrow. And when I found my courage, I told Nadine about my gift and how Jesus sent me on this road trip. By the end of our storytelling, we were hugging on each other the way we could only imagine a Momma and daughter would do.

On my last night in the park, I wandered through the camps and said goodbye to all the folks I had met. Everybody had a "little something" they wanted to share with me. Big Dave's family sent me off with a hefty helping of their beloved Aunt Jenny's potato salad, more of Dave's ribs, and my very own pineapple upside down cake. At the

Wainwright campsite, Nadine, who had gone from red to brown hair, was busy frying chicken while Winthrow waited for me, hand on hip, eager to make sure the arvee was running just right before I left in the morning.

"Not that I would, but Nadine will worry herself sick tomorrow thinking about you and what might go wrong. I swear that woman could make a career out of worrying. Anyway, I want to do a system check with you so I don't have to listen to her blab all the way home."

"I appreciate that, Winthrow. More than you know." I kissed Winthrow Wainwright on his plump cheek and it turned red, red, red.

"Go on, now. That's enough," he said.

Winthrow went through his *be careful* list. I was to be careful of hitchhikers, and he better not find out I picked one up, and I was to watch out for kooks when I got to California. Winthrow said they didn't work and I'd recognize them by the flowers in their hair. He said they smoked marywanna, which made them loopy, danced all day, and believed in free love. I didn't know what marrywanna was, but wearing flowers in your hair, dancing all day, and being able to love the one you loved freely, sounded perfect.

"Winthrow, don't you believe in free love?" I asked.

Nadine laughed so hard she dropped a fried chicken wing in the sand. Winthrow got real busy checking under the hood of the arvee, where he harrumphed and huffed and changed the subject by calling to Nadine about a camera.

"Mercy, I nearly forgot." Nadine took to their arvee and came back with an armload of boxes.

"Now don't make a fuss, B. Thankful," she said, laying the boxes on the picnic table. "Winthrow and I want you to have this Polaroid camera and all this film. You can take pictures and develop them on the spot. It's magic. Watch."

Nadine called over to Big Dave and asked him to take two pictures of the three of us—one for them and one for me. Everybody cheered when our faces came into view. Then I took one of the entire group and it wasn't more than a minute later, I held them all in my hand.

"I've never received a gift like this. It's just way too—" Winthrow cut me off.

"B. Thankful, be just that, and say no more."

"I am thankful, Winthrow. Truly, I am."

The next morning, I rose up before anyone stirred and looked around for Livia, but she was nowhere to be found. With the hope she was trying to find me, I tied another lavender ribbon to a tree to let her know I had been there. From behind the tree, I watched as Winthrow and Nadine settled around their morning campfire and sipped their coffee. Winthrow slipped his arm around Nadine and pulled her into him.

"B. Thankful will be all right, Nadine. She's a strong young woman. No need to worry. She'll make it all the way to San Francisco just fine."

"But Winthrow, that child's never seen *Laugh-In*."

I slapped on a smile, and set out to say my final goodbye. Winthrow gave me a quick hug and told me not to eat too many potato chips or I'd get a big butt. Nadine and I traded addresses, and I promised to send postcards as I made my way across the country, but Nadine's look turned doubtful. I took her by the chin. "Please don't throw my promise into the fire."

Nadine pulled me to her and held on tight. "My baby girl," she said, over and over again into my wiry hair until Winthrow gently pulled her away.

Before I left, I gave Nadine a Banner Bar and suggested she use it the next time she made s'mores. In return, she treated me to a bag of marshmallows and a pack of graham crackers so I could do the same. *Remember me, for I will remember you.*

Twelve

Bobby Lee

A patch of bad weather thundered down all day, blurring the passing clouds caught in the windshield, the wipers sweeping my mindset from one side back to the other. So caught up in my way, I didn't even stop to sample the mile high butterscotch pie at Sweet Lorraine's Café, and the sign promised it was the world's best. I drove all day, and right through the midnight hour, with an unexpected loneliness sitting in the spoon of my throat, that little dip in your neck where emotions wait to be served up.

Until that cloud filled, starless night, there had been a certain rightness about my journey. And then, without a word of warning, all of God's road signs were gone, and I was lost. To add to my gloominess, a hissing sound was coming from under the hood of the arvee, pushing steam through its seams. I cast my hope for a helping hand around a solitary light shining in the distance, and coasted up to the front of the windowless building, peeling paint leaving behind bruised strips of plaster, SOS scrawled over the door in large black letters. Perhaps SOS stood for Save Our Souls and inside I'd find a nice preacher man who knew a thing or two about engines.

The footpath quaked as I drew near to the building, the language busting through the walls to the outside, brutal and peculiar. Little G once told me about Pentecostals and speaking in tongues, and while the rain pelted me as I stood under the bright light, I considered how I may have happened upon someone being rid of evil spirits. I knocked, but no one answered, so I pounded on the door until it flew open with such force I tumbled forward. Fast as a swollen river, I recognized it wasn't a holy place when I saw the man standing before me.

It was night, mind you, but he wore sunglasses, and must have been in an awful hurry when he left home, for there was no shirt underneath the black vest, and his chest and arms were covered with words and pictures. A cigarette sagged from the corner of his mouth, the sparks landing in a wiry beard that hung down over his bare belly onto grease covered pants. He held onto a bottle of something called Jack Daniel's as tight as Little G did to one of her long held opinions. All of that added up put the fear in me, but when he looked me up and down in a badly behaved way, that's when I knew for certain there was trouble in the air.

"I'm sorry," I said, trying to keep my voice from cracking. "I saw your SOS above the door and thought maybe you were a church." That bear of a man laughed so hard something shot out of his mouth onto the wet sidewalk. "I'll just be on my way," I squeaked, and started to back up to the arvee. But before I could make a getaway, he shoved his hairy hand through the door, grabbed me hard by my wrist, and pulled me inside.

"Notthofath. Heymotherfutherslookahere!"

Maybe he *was* speaking in tongues, for I didn't understand a word he said. Then he turned around and I saw the back of his vest. SOS didn't stand for Save Our Souls, it stood for Sons of Satan. Lord, help me.

Eleven lookalikes stacked up behind the first Son of Satan to see what the commotion was about, then began to circle me. One pushed up against me and flipped my hair with his rough hands, while another lifted the edge of my t-shirt. Wicked words I had never heard before, not even from Onida Bossier, bounced off the walls and landed at my feet. I know Daddy said a fist never solved anything, but I kept mine clenched white tight even though I was sure it couldn't save me. *Be fearless. Be fearless.*

While all of this was going on, blaring music punched at me, the singer's voice gravelly and fuming, her sorrow and anger squeezed into the same note when she wailed her man should break another piece of her heart. Another kind of wounded cry came from behind a door at the end of the hall, but this one didn't pierce my ears, it pierced my heart and memory.

Out looking for peace of mind in the woods one day, the tortured cries of a dying animal called to me. Maybe a coyote or bobcat had downed the fawn and for reasons unknown, left her beautiful self to die slowly without her momma. At first sight, the fawn's mangled neck sickened me, but when I looked into her eyes, the rest fell away, and I held her until she found her way to the other side. And I think that's what every creature wants when the end comes—just to be held.

A chain of cries silenced the Sons of Satan, leaving room for a childlike voice to whisper in my ear.

"That's my baby boy, Bobby Lee."

W-h-a-t-s-y-o-u-r-n-a-m-e? I tapped on my leg.

"Annabelle. Please help my boy."

I-l-l-d-o-m-y-b-e-s-t-A-n-n-a-b-e-l-l-e. Two steps forward and a rough hand grabbed my shoulder, his voice buttermilk thick.

"Where the fuck you goin'?"

"Why, I'm going in that room to help whoever's in there. You don't have a problem with that do you?" I wasn't being smart-alecky, but a ruckus worked its way through the crowd.

"Yeah, Turd, you gotta problem with that?"

Just as my future was about to take a sharp turn down a road of ruin, Livia flew through the door, landed on the top of my dripping hair, and spread her wings for all to see. Livia carried a holy dare under her wings that created a fearful awe in those on the wrong side of righteousness. And the way Livia wiped down my forehead with her wing, casting the rain into the Sons of Satan, it appeared we were setting up for a bar room brawl. Never taking their eyes off of Livia, everybody moved clear across the room. With Livia on my side, I opened my fist and dropped my concern to the sawdust covered floor.

When another scream came from behind the door to the back room, the man called Turd pushed through the crowd and pulled me aside. He yanked his dark glasses down, his bloodshot eyes sizing me up. When I didn't look away, he spit a wad of chew on the floor, just missing my shoe, but I didn't flinch.

"He's dyin'. He's shot up dope and backed more whiskey than ten men; still won't let us near him, still screams in pain. If you can do something to settle him down, free him of his suffering, we might let you leave here in one piece."

"Okay, Mister Turd. Okay."

My knock on the door was answered by a bottle crashing up against it with a warning inside. "Stay the fuck outta here!"

I jumped back from Bobby Lee's shattering anger, the Sons' hard laughter tumbling down behind me, bumping up against my already unsteady legs. Before I lost my nerve and ran from the building, I opened the door, ducked through, and quickly closed it behind me. Broken bottles were thrown around the room, their jagged edges as threatening as the mean sounding words carved into the walls. Cigarettes smoldered in piles next to a dirty mattress where Bobby Lee lay wounded; the bare yellow light overhead swayed back and forth across his hollow face, and over the crook of his arm—home to a patch of open sores. The word MONSTER ran down his right arm in blue-black ink while SONS OF SATAN raised hell on his left arm. With the harshness of his life carved into his skin, I found it sad Bobby Lee could never change his mind about the way of it. Sometimes life bends you, and other times it breaks you into a million pieces.

As if cornered by a fever dream when he opened his eyes and saw Livia, Bobby Lee pushed himself up against the wall.

"Oh, this is Livia, she's a mourning dove," I said, reaching up and stroking her wing. "She means you no harm, nor do I. My name is B. Thankful Childe-Lucknow and I'm pleased to meet you, Bobby Lee." I extended my hand in friendship, but Bobby Lee grabbed my arm, squeezed as hard as he could, and pulled me toward him until our noses were nearly touching. He smelled as bad as the cracked eggs I found tucked in the corner of the chicken coop after several days in the hot sun. I didn't want to offend him by retching, so I held my breath.

"How'd you know my name?"

"Your momma, Annabelle, told me."

"My momma's dead!" Bobby Lee shoved me hard and I landed on the floor, a sharp pain shooting through my sit bones, my held breath flying across the room. I couldn't tell if he was angry at his momma for dying, or if his dander was up because I reminded him. Either way, there didn't appear to be a whole lot of life left in Bobby Lee, so it was best I get on with it. My intent was to start out slow, but my question had a timing of its own.

"Are you scared of dying, Bobby Lee?"

"Hell no!" But he was. Just like the fawn, he was so scared he kicked at me as if I was the cause of his troubles. Weak as he was, though, even through a locked jaw and clenched teeth, his threat was clear.

"I don't know who you are, but I'm gonna give you a chance to walk out. If you don't..." Bobby Lee couldn't finish his warning, for his breathing went shallow.

"His heart broked when he's born," Annabelle said, her words small, not fully ripe.

Trying to find my way in with Bobby Lee so he'd stop kicking and trust me, I picked up an empty bottle and threw it at the door I came in by. I almost took to laughing when I saw a startled look fill up Bobby Lee's face, but it wasn't the time to think myself funny.

"I don't want your friends to think we're getting along." Bobby Lee tried not to laugh, but he did, until his wounded heart said *no more*.

When Little G was in her dying way, it seemed a heavenly sway led me to her picture box and recipes, then to the picture of Big G, who, when called upon, came down to guide me. Without a picture of Annabelle, I wasn't sure how to get her to come a calling inside me to help take her boy home.

"Bobby Lee..."

"Call me Monster. Bobby Lee died a long time ago."

"Okay. Monster, do you have a picture of your momma?"

Bobby Lee started to unbutton his shirt, and I became what Little G called "new bride nervous," and fixed my eyes upon my rain soaked shoes. Bobby Lee took note of my unease.

"Don't fret, little girl. You ain't my type."

When Bobby Lee pulled back his shirt on the left side, I could count his ribs; that's how skinny he was. But it wasn't his ribs Bobby wanted me to see. Drawn over his heart was a red rose, the center of the full bloom cradling the face of a young girl, her long golden hair woven into the petals of the rose, her brown eyes looking up to watch over her boy. Like that night in the kitchen with Big G, but as delicate as the early morning mist floating over the river back home, Annabelle came to roost inside of me.

Bobby Lee stared down at the rose covering his heart. "She was only fifteen, and I, only three, when she disappeared on the tracks. Yeah, that's right; my momma was only twelve years old when I was born." Bobby Lee challenged me with a hard stare, waiting for some sort of judgment to form in my eyes, but I had none and he seemed to recognize that. Without an ounce of pity for himself, or if there was it was tucked in a dark corner of a boxcar riding the rails, he went on.

"Down the road, when I was older, I learned there wasn't a relative around who'd take her in when she got pregnant; that's why she started hoppin' trains from town-to-town. I was born somewhere between Here and There, and there ain't even a piece of paper that says I was ever born."

The pain of memory, or Bobby Lee's weak heart, snatched him up and he passed out. Annabelle and I waited by his side until Bobby Lee's eyes flashed open, and, as if the natural rhythm of his storytelling, picked up right where he left off.

"The last day we were together we had a picnic. Bein' just a girl, Momma knew nothin' about cookin', but she had a trick up her sleeve, and all you need is one good trick. Whenever she wanted to calm me down, or put a smile on my face, Momma fed me graham crackers; fuckin' graham crackers. When Momma broke off those little bits and fed them to me I felt..." Same as the fawn when she finally gave herself over, Bobby Lee stitched his last words together with surrender. "...a love beyond anything I've ever known." But as soon as his words saw the light of day, Monster's twisted up mind, tight as a hanging rope, caught hold of Bobby Lee and shoved him aside.

"You tell anyone what I just said, I'll ki—" A loud banging on the door put a hitch in Bobby Lee's threat, which was a good thing, but, at the same time, I was afraid the angry pounding might send Annabelle rushing out of me. I rubbed on my right arm, hoping Annabelle could feel my intended comfort.

"Hey, bitch, what's goin' on in there?" Turd yelled out, the room behind him so quiet I could hear his liquored breath rubbing up against the door.

My Little G believed you had to meet ill-mannered people head on; of course, she was usually holding her shot-gun when she met them. Though not my way, I reached down into my womanly ancestry, who held no tolerance for mean speak, and hollered out a warning. "You better mind your manners, Turd!" I threw another bottle at the door for good measure. A harsh burst of laughter came from the other side.

Bobby Lee tilted his head and offered me a breakable smile as he tried to light a cigarette, but his hands were too shaky, the match unable to hold a flame. I took the cigarette and lit it for Bobby Lee. When the smoke hit my lungs, I choked and coughed.

"I don't know who you are, or what you're doin' here, but you're all right, girl. You're all right." Bobby Lee took a drag off the cigarette and blew smoke rings into the air. Before they floated away, one of the rings lassoed a memory and he went on with his story.

"The last time I saw my momma, she was runnin' alongside the train. She had just tossed me into the arms of another boxcar traveler and was about to jump in when she fell." The hurt of his memory was too much for Bobby Lee to hold; Monster furiously brushed it off.

"Fuck it. That's the way it happens. After Momma died, I was tossed into one orphanage after another, beaten and abused in ways a girl like you can't imagine, shouldn't imagine. If God didn't see fit to take care of me, I knew the devil would take me in, so I ran away and started my own family—the Sons of Satan."

I sucked in the air of sorrow floating between Bobby Lee and me, and looked inside myself for words of com-fort to offer him for the wrong doing he suffered, but the only words I could find had holes in them, and echoed back to me, hollow as the Mammoth Cave. Bobby Lee was right, I couldn't imagine the awful deeds he had suffered, for my family loved and protected me from the very world that devoured Bobby Lee and gave birth to Monster. But even though our childhoods were as different as night and day, Bobby Lee and I had one thing in common: we were patchwork pieces of the same quilt, connected by the thread of tragedy, for we never got to know our mommas. And that's a sad, sad song for any child to sing all their live long days.

After hearing her baby boy's story, Annabelle whispered her idea to me. I rose up, opened the door just a crack, and stuck my head out to the other side. When I called out to Turd, every Son of Satan set his sight on me, twelve bullying scowls locked into place. Turd shoved his way through the crowd, his big frame blocking the door. To my surprise, and Turd's, I grabbed hold of his beard and pulled its length through the narrow opening to my side of the door.

"Listen up, Turd. Monster said you've got twenty minutes to get my arvee to keep from spilling out steam. And don't you dare knock on this door until it's fixed, or there's gonna be trouble like you've never seen."

Turd tried to look in on Bobby, but I slammed the door in his face. When I saw the tip of his beard wedged in the door, I opened it fast and pushed it through to his side. I was so scared, I felt a little pee drop onto my underpants.

I turned to Bobby Lee and with as much *because I said so* in my voice as I could muster, told him we were going for a ride, just the two of us. Either too tired, or too near the end, he didn't put up a fuss.

"I don't want those guys to see me like this." Bobby Lee was afraid the Sons of Satan would see right through Monster's hard crust to the terror rattling his bones.

"Then let me do the talking," I said.

I was so up in myself, I believed I could carry out Annabelle's wish. In mind speak, like I had learned with Big G, I told Annabelle we were taking her little boy on one last picnic, and her giggle so tickled my ear, I had to rub on it. A knock on the door hushed Annabelle and brought me to quick attention. I opened it just a sliver and found Turd on the other side.

"Your rig's ready. Just needed some water." Turd acted as if I had stepped on his feelings, but I stayed headstrong.

"Lucky for you, 'cuz Monster and I are going for a ride. Just the two of us." When Turd pulled back at the idea, I locked my jaw and clenched my teeth.

"Don't make me go loco on you," I said, and slammed the door.

"Don't push it, little girl," Bobby Lee warned. "Don't push it."

The room turned bone chill silent when we stepped through the door. I had done my best to make Monster look like he was in charge by placing his Sons of Satan leather jacket over his shoulders, tucking a lit cigarette in the corner of his mouth, his bottle of whiskey in his pocket, and Livia on his shoulder. Monster had his arm thrown around my neck as if I was his new possession, but the burden of his weight pushing on me as we walked through the Sons told the true story. I watched as they parted and made way for Monster to pass. Under all their ink and leather, under all their burly male bluster, stood twelve men who, in their own way, loved the dying man leaning on me. And loving him so much scared them.

Once inside the arvee, out of earshot, a sharp cry of pain nearly split Bobby down the middle. A hefty dose of Little G's elixir calmed Bobby Lee and he fell asleep under my dream catcher.

"Sweet dreams, Bobby Lee. Sweet dreams."

I stepped on the gas and followed Livia's flight down the road. So frail a spirit, I forgot Annabelle was nesting inside me until I felt her leave, pale pink sparkles filling the air next to me. Annabelle wore a pair of tattered dungarees, a threadbare work shirt, scuffed leather boots, and a man's hat that hid most of her honey colored hair. Her gentle brown eyes, though having forgiven, could not deny what she had seen in her short life.

"Hey, Annabelle."

Annabelle looked at me curiously, then out the window at the passing scenery.

"What am I doin' here?" she asked.

Silly me, I figured maybe someone, not mentioning names as I glanced in the rearview mirror at my Last Supper painting, would have told Annabelle about the task at hand, but that didn't appear to be the case. Heck, I was new to this last supper business myself, and now I had to try and explain it all. Well, good luck to me. When I found my voice, I tried my hardest to make my words float cloud soft like Harmonia did.

"I believe you're here to take your Bobby Lee home." The tip top of the sun broke the horizon line, Annabelle's memory riding upon its rays.

"Oh, I 'member. My baby boy," she said. Twenty-two years had come and gone since that day along the tracks, but Bobby Lee was still her "baby boy."

"I kissed 'em. That's all. Just kissed 'em." Annabelle's words sparkled like stardust.

"Kissed what, Annabelle?" I asked, slowing for a curve in the road.

"Why, silly, the graham crackers. 'Fore I fed 'em to Bobby Lee, I kissed 'em so my love would always be inside my baby boy."

Oh, my, my, my. Right in the middle of that curve in the road, I had a sudden leap of understanding. Graham crackers kissed by his momma were to Bobby Lee what Banner Bars from Daddy were to me. Just because food wasn't stirred up in a pot or baked in an oven by the person who held you tender didn't mean it wasn't laced with the same eternal, loving intention: *Remember me, for I will remember you.*

God bless Nadine Wainwright. I had a pack of graham crackers in the cupboard just waiting to be kissed.

"Let's go have that picnic," I said.

We followed Livia down a long dirt road for several miles, mud splashing from under the tires into the tall grass along the edges, until we came to a grove of trees where drops of rain clung to the leaves like sparkling diamonds. A far off train called out long and low. In my rearview mirror, I saw the twelve black and silver motorcycles trailing behind, and saw Bobby Lee beginning to come around again. In a hushed tone, I told Annabelle it was time to come back inside of me. Haunting as the brush of fog against skin, I felt her return.

"Where are we?" my mind asked.

"Near the tracks where me and Bobby Lee had our last picnic."

"What are we doin' here?" Bobby Lee asked, looking out across the meadow.

"I thought we'd stop and rest awhile. I've got some blankets we can throw out under the trees. Rain's all gone and the sun seems determined to have its way."

Bobby Lee was so near gone, I mostly had to carry him over to the trees. As I set him on the blanket, a coughing jag gripped his lungs and I was afraid he was going to die before partaking of his last supper. A stab of panic flushed Bobby Lee as his time marker began to surface, not even the heaviness of the damp morning air able to weigh it down. Through air bubbles caught in his throat, Bobby Lee called out for a drink.

"Hold on, Bobby Lee. I'll get you some of my Little G's 'shine. That'll help."

I ran to the arvee and searched the cupboard for the graham crackers. Annabelle's hands worked quickly through my own to open the package. Together we pulled the graham crackers out one at a time, raised them to my lips and kissed them, Annabelle blessing each one with her petal soft love and cherry candy breath. I grabbed the bottle of 'shine and a glass and ran back to Bobby Lee.

I dropped down on the blanket, poured a shot of 'shine in the glass, and gave it to Bobby Lee. His hands took to trembling, most of the 'shine spilling down his front. After a few more tries, he dropped the glass and lay down on the blanket. Like a dry blowing wind, Bobby Lee's crying swept over me, stinging my eyes, as I lifted him up and rested him across my lap. I broke off a small piece of graham cracker and raised it up for him to see.

"It wouldn't be the same, little girl. But thanks anyway." Bobby Lee's voice sounded as if it was walking ahead of him toward the peaceful valley.

"Well, since I've got 'em, why not try 'em?" As I rested the graham cracker on his tongue, Annabelle's spirit shined through me for Bobby Lee to see. With my next breath, Annabelle floated from my body and lifted her baby boy from my embrace.

"Momma?" Bobby Lee asked. All the years of anger and fear scratched into his skin disappeared, his face turning childlike and innocent.

"I've missed you so much, Momma. Can we go home now?"

I walked away from the mother and child reunion and stood in the meadow near the railroad tracks. Time rode the clouds across the sky; a gentle breeze carrying the news moved through me. When I got back, I rested Bobby Lee's body across my lap, and recognized he was gone. I wrapped the picnic blanket around him to keep him feeling secure and, having learned a valuable lesson with Little G, immediately closed Bobby Lee's eyes, then laid him out nice and straight so his friends wouldn't have to bury him sitting up.

In the distance, the long, low call of another train came down the tracks. Cross my heart, on the other side of that field of dreams, Bobby Lee and his momma waved to me from a Heaven bound boxcar as it lumbered down the track. I waved back and took to running through the meadow toward the train, calling out, "I'm so glad I got to meet you, Bobby Lee. I'm sorry your life was so hard, but I can see you've been lifted up. Oh, Bobby Lee, you've earned your railroad wings!" My tears came quick and hot, my cheeks as slippery as the rain soaked grass.

The thunder of motorcycles shook the path beneath me as they drove by, the back of their jacket bearing their

Sons of Satan name: Turd, Stump, Hell Raiser, Typhoid, Scorpion, Blade, Clap, Sing-Sing, Mofo, Shadow, Twisted, and Pisser. One-by-one, they came to a stop, the sound of silence filling the meadow land.

"I'm sorry about your friend. I know you all loved him very much."

Turd was the first to walk over to where Bobby Lee's left behind body rested in peace. He tapped the bottom of Bobby Lee's boot with his own.

"Shit, Monster. Why'd you have to go and die?" On the sly, Turd slid his thick fingers under his sunglasses and mopped up his tears. "I say we bury him right here. I don't know why, but this was his favorite place." Turd turned to me. "Do you think that's a good idea?"

"I think it's a perfect idea, Turd."

Once they all agreed on Bobby Lee's resting place, Blade and Typhoid wanted to go back and rob the hardware store for shovels, but I convinced them to use the shovel in the arvee storage bin. They seemed disappointed, but didn't argue.

While Blade and Typhoid dug Bobby Lee's grave, I had Turd and Pisser (I know, I know) build a fire to heat up water to wash Bobby Lee's body. Never having groomed a body for crossing, I had to tell them what to do, and why I couldn't help. None of the Sons made jokes or carried on the way they had at the clubhouse, and I was grateful for the respect they showed their friend.

Suddenly, without warning, an uncontrollable tiredness knocked on my joints so firmly, I had to go inside and have a lie-down. Livia came to rest on my pillow as I slid down the ladder of sleep to the sound of a shovel digging into the ground, over and over again.

Jesus stood along the far edge of a beautiful lake, the colors so radiant I had to shade my eyes to look upon him for more than a glance. "B. Thankful, you are purity and light." As real as skipping stones, Jesus's words danced across the lake. I caught each one and put them in my pocket, where they rested on a bed of graham cracker crumbs.

The sun was long past a noontime sky when Turd woke me from my dream to tell me Bobby Lee was ready. Turd and Pisser had prepared Bobby Lee's body the best they knew how, even combed his hair, tucked his shirt into his pants, shined up his boots, and rested fifty-cent pieces on Bobby Lee's eyes to pay for his crossing.

"We polished the coins as best we could and put a couple more dollars in his back pocket, just in case he needs a shot of whiskey." Turd said.

"You did fine by your friend," I said.

From a distance, Bobby Lee's grave looked to be at least three times more than what was needed. Arriving at the edge of it, I discovered why. While I was catching skipping stones, Typhoid and Blade traveled back to the clubhouse to fetch Bobby Lee's motorcycle so it could be buried with him. "It's our way," Turd explained, as Hell Raiser and Scorpion lowered Bobby Lee into the ground next to his "ride."

Looking down on Bobby Lee's resting place, Sing-Sing hollered out, "Let's have a little sympathy for the devil!" The Sons were off singing about Lucifer being a man of wealth, how Jesus had his moment of doubt, and all that Pilate hand washing business. I had never heard such music, and mind you, at a funeral. My Big G rode hymns to Heaven, and Pride and Harmonia sang ancient Earth songs to lift my Daddy and Little G higher and higher. But then

I looked around at the Sons, hushed the words so only the sound of their purpose remained, and found it to be all the same. In their own way, the Sons were wishing their friend well on his ride home.

Turd handed me the shovel. "We want you to go first."

I was so touched by the honor and their acceptance of me, my tears took up where the rain left off. I blew my nose into the sleeve of my shirt. Turd put his bear of an arm around my shoulder.

"Ah, shit. Don't cry, little girl. Come on. I'll help you out."

My hand on his, we pushed the shovel into the pile of dirt, the sound of goodbye hitting Bobby Lee's body, painfully familiar. I passed the shovel to MoFo and watched as it made its way around the circle of Sons again and again, until Bobby Lee's grave ran an even plane.

"Did you know Bobby Lee's momma died when he was just three years old? She fell, right over there, along those tracks. This is the very spot where they had their last picnic. That's why he loved this place, Turd. You chose the perfect spot to lay your friend to rest."

Turd stroked his beard. "His name was Bobby Lee?"

While I shared the story of Bobby Lee and Annabelle, I pulled the leftover graham crackers from my pocket and broke them into twelve pieces. I shared a bit of graham cracker with each man, followed by a pull of Little G's 'shine.

"This is Bobby Lee's way of saying, *Remember me, for I will remember you.*"

After Clap partook of a graham cracker and a pull of Little G's 'shine, he lifted his head and howled, all the Sons joining in. I raised my face to the sky and howled along with them.

When the time came for me to leave, I shook each man's hand, looked him right in the eye, called him by name, and offered my own in return. It's all I ever wanted; maybe it's all they ever wanted too. I took a Polaroid picture of the Sons of Satan and taped it to the dashboard, their rugged faces eyeing me. I was just about to turn the key, ready to start the next leg of my road trip, when Turd called out to me.

"Hold up, B. Thankful. We want to take a picture of you for the clubhouse."

I stepped out with my Polaroid camera in hand, and the next thing I knew I was wearing a Sons of Satan black leather jacket that read MONSTER on the back and had a bottle of Jack Daniel's whiskey in my hand.

"Monster would want you to have his jacket," Turd said. "And the Jack Daniel's is from us, 'cuz, fuck, that rot gut shit you're drinkin' will kill you." Turd snapped my picture and we weren't half way through the moment of magic, when a stern mother voice called upon me.

I-w-i-l-l-t-e-l-l-h-i-m. I reached up and pulled on Turd's beard.

"Bartholomew Pinter, I don't know what the word *fuck* means, but your momma, Tanya, said you better clean up your mouth because she's waiting for you on the other side." As I strolled to the arvee, I threw Turd a wink over my shoulder and found his jaw hanging as loose as a used up udder.

In my rearview mirror, I watched as the flames of the fire rose higher and higher, heard their wild cries ride the rails alongside the memory of their good friend into the mystery as I headed down the road. The sign up ahead told me I was leaving Sweetwater, Missouri, not far from crossing into Oklahoma, but I hadn't gone three curves down the road when my head nodded back and forth, my eyes staying shut for more than just a blink. No way would I make it to the border that night.

I pulled into a turnout on the side of the road and set the brake. The minute I stopped long enough to catch up with myself, I found my stomach ached with hunger, but my brain was so tired it snapped tight as a fishing line tricked by an old log hiding under water, and it was all I could do to flip the table over and fall onto my bed. I rolled up blankets and pillows, pushed my back up against them, and pretended to be spooning with Little G, but there was no heart beating up against my back, no old lady arm pulling me in closer, closer still. There would be no campfires burning through the night, no storytelling or laughter running along the edges of the park, no Nadine calling out and knocking on my door, no Winthrow to take care of me, and no one to tell the story of my most incredible time with Annabelle and Bobby Lee, and the Sons of Satan. I ran my hand along the edge of my paint-by-number picture.

"Good night, Jesus. I hope I did right by Bobby Lee."

"Adam and Eve on a raft! Order up!" I called out.

The waitress, Hickory Smoke, came and took the plate away with one hand and grabbed a pot of coffee with the other. "Someone's here to see you," she said, on the fly.

Through the serving window, I saw Jesus sitting on a stool at the counter, swiveling side-to-side. I smoothed down my apron, and pulled off my hair net, red curls springing out of control. I picked up a pad and pencil and walked toward Jesus, reminding myself with every step to call him Mister Jesus. So as not to attract attention to him, I did my best to act cool and calm, but Jesus was the only one in the diner wearing a robe and sandals, so it may have been for naught.

"*Good morning, Je...Mister Jesus. Whatmightyoulikefor-breakfastthisfineday?*" *I was so nervous, my words came out as unnatural as a constipated poop. Jesus smiled at me and his gaze was so magnificent, I had to smile right back at him.*

"*B. Thankful, I'd like you to fix me breakfast.*"

Oh, I really didn't think that was a good idea, but I wasn't going to say no to Jesus. I was about to ask him what kind of food really lit him up, maybe something his momma made for him when he was a child, but Jesus read my simple thoughts before the asking took place.

"*Be fearless,*" *he said.*

"*Okay, Je...Mister Jesus. Okay.*"

On my way back to the kitchen, I tried to calm myself by taking into account it was a person's loving intention that created an everlasting tie, not the words and numbers in a recipe. I would fix Jesus's food with so much love it would eternally sing, "Remember me, for I will remember you."

I got right to work on the biscuits, sifting flour and baking powder with a pinch of salt, and adding a goodly portion of cold butter bits and cream. So as not to turn the biscuits to stones, I gently mixed it all together, rolled the dough out nice and thick, and made perfect little circles with a jelly jar. Into a hot oven the biscuits went, and I set out to fix the rest of the meal. I took the two nice trout filets Casper Lawton caught that morning and dusted them with flour and lots of black pepper. When they were as powdered as Little G's cheeks, I slipped them into a pan of brown butter, where they sizzled. In another frying pan, I cracked two eggs into hot oil deep enough to bathe them sunny side up.

When the biscuits came out of the oven as golden as Nadine's marshmallows, I split one in half and placed some of my strawberry jam on each side. I slid the eggs, their edges bubbly and crisp, on top of the biscuits, and laid the fried trout by their side.

Jesus saw me come out of the kitchen and tucked his napkin under his chin. I set the plate down in front of him and poured Jesus a cup of black, to-the-point coffee. Jesus took my hand and so much love came through his wounded palm I nearly fainted.

"Father, thank you for this gift of food and your child, B. Thankful Childe-Lucknow. Amen."

"Amen, Mister Jesus," I said. "Amen."

Jesus didn't hurry through his meal the way some people do. No, he'd take a bite, set down his fork, and then he'd close his eyes. Jesus had that "look," and I could tell he was pondering the way the flavors came together, how the richness of the egg yolks and the brown butter fish married with the sweetness of the strawberry jam. Jesus felt all my love for him in every bite, and by the look in his eyes when they met my own, I'd have to say my food had Jesus all lit up.

Without me even asking, Jesus answered my concern over Bobby Lee. "Some partings may seem too soon, but never doubt that you have 'lit up' those you have been chosen to serve. Like me, you were sent to—"

Jesus was about to give me the answer I had been waiting for my whole life when a light, so bold it caused me to shield my eyes, surrounded him. The light moved around and around, up and down.

My eyes opened and closed, opened and closed, and my dream catcher swayed from side-to-side. Heavy footsteps moved through the brush and crossed the gravel up to the arvee. My heartbeat quickened, my pulse raced. Something or someone outside was trying to break in and there was no one to call out to, no one to come and save me. A bright light came through the windshield, striking me in the face, and blinding me. I tried to sound as bold as Little G when warning trespassers.

"Who's there?" I shouted. "You better not wake up my husband or he'll shoot your toe off!" *Shoot your toe off?*

"You got a husband in there, B. Thankful?"

"Turd, is that you out there?" If it was Turd, I was gonna hug on him for not being a prowler and then give him a serious talking to for putting a bunch in my unders and pulling me away from Jesus, who was about to tell me why his Daddy picked me for such an important job. When you get that close to such a life changing answer and an ordinary flash of light runs off with it, all you've got left is an ill temper. I opened the door and glared down at Turd.

"I saw you pulled over here and wanted to make sure you were all right. Are you all right?" Turd stretched his neck inside. "Is that bird in here?"

"No, Livia's out right now. But don't think I couldn't take you down by myself if I had to."

"Oh, I don't doubt you could, but I mean no harm. I'm just feeling so down and lonely. Can I come in?"

Turd looked so forlorn, my anger with him for knocking on my dream time with Jesus dropped in the river where the unsuspecting trout had been swimming right before the eagle snatched him from the water.

"Sure. Come on in. I'm not going anywhere." My stomach growled so loud Turd took a backward step.

"Are you hungry, Turd?"

"Yeah, I could chow down some."

I pulled out Dave's barbecued ribs, Aunt Jenny's potato salad, and sliced off a big helping of pineapple upside down cake. When our stomachs were full, we climbed to the top of the arvee, where we rested under a web of stars. Through the shelter of darkness, the shiver of his manliness unseen, Turd could speak of love.

"Monster was my best friend, B. Thankful. I loved him like a brother. I don't know what I'm gonna do without him."

I reached through the darkness and took Turd's hand, and he wove his thick fingers through my own. "I know. I know." Oh, how I knew.

The sun shining through the trees brought me around to a new day. Rubbing my eyes to rid them of the call to go back to sleep, I found Turd had rolled all the way over to the edge of the roof, one leg hanging over the side. So afraid he'd fall to the ground if I spoke, I grabbed him by his belt before trying to wake him. Turd thrashed about, nearly taking both of us over the side before I could manage to allay his kicking and yelling.

"Jesus H. Christ, woman! You almost killed me! You're lucky I don't..." Before Turd could tear off another angry strip, I looked to Heaven. "My momma's not talkin' to you again is she?"

"No, but you better clean up your mouth, and if you use Jesus's name, it better be in prayer, Bartholomew Pinter."

Turd narrowed his eyes, so I narrowed mine. We stared at each other, weighing our options, and started laughing. I crawled over to Turd and put my arms around his neck and he gave me a big squeeze in return.

"Thank you for seeing me through the night," I said.

"Same to you, little girl. Same to you."

After breakfast, Turd made a quick inspection of the arvee and found everything A-okay. And then Turd did something that would change the flavor of my road trip forever—he showed me how to work the radio. Lo and behold, there was some grief stricken guy singing how he left his cake out in the rain and never having the recipe again. All that fuss over a cake?

"Here's how it goes," Turd said, as he turned down the radio. "You're gonna call me if anybody bothers you." Turd slipped his phone number into my hand. "I don't care where you are. Do you understand? There are twelve men who owe you for seein' to their friend. Once you're in with the Sons of Satan, you're in for life. We've got your back, little girl."

I called out my goodbye as I climbed behind the wheel, and headed down the Good Red Road. My hands were tapping to the beat of a song about a girl named Sunny when the music was shut down by a news flash, shattered words slipping through the screams.

"Chicago…conv….beaten…"

The shouting made my insides hurt so much, I had to turn off the radio. Having spent my life as an outsider, and sheltered by my Gs and Daddy from the harshness of the world, I could only hold little pieces of its makeup at a time; even then, the pieces had to be cool to the touch. But according to the radio, the world was on fire, blazing out of control, and it scared me. It scared me so much, I wanted to turn around and go home. Home, where I could sleep in my own bed and wake up to God's light as it came over the hills, eat pancakes with Harmonia and Pride, and swim in the river one last time before the icy layer of winter came to call.

Maybe if I had ignored Big G, Little G would have hung on; maybe if I hadn't come along with those graham crackers, Bobby Lee would have gotten better. Maybe… Maybe… Maybe…

"What in the name of..." I swerved off the road, threw open the door, jumped down, and ran to the foot of a sign so high up I had to bend all the way back to take in the whole of it. In the picture, a little girl with shiny brown hair, the ends flipping up like a perfect letter J, knelt by her bedside, head bowed, her prayer clasped hands resting on her lips. Through a window draped with lavender curtains, a Heavenly light shined down upon her, her prayer winding its way up into the light.

"Now I lay me down to sleep, I pray the Lord my soul to keep, but if the Lord my soul would take, send me off with a Banner Bar for goodness sake."

Floating above her bed was a Banner Bar, the gold wrapper sparkling, the lavender ribbon held up by two plump cherubs. Letters, as tall as a healthy fish is long, appeared in the bottom corner: *B. Thankful Childe-Lucknow.* And below that: *Winner of Banner Chocolate's 100*[th] *Anniversary Contest.*

"That's me!" I hollered, jumping up and down. "That's me!"

After a quick run to the arvee, I came back to where the sign stood and climbed the ladder leading up to the ledge. I sat with my head leaned up against the foot of the little girl's bed, my legs hanging over the edge. I unwrapped my Banner Bar, folded the gold wrapper into a square, and tied the lavender ribbon around it. I broke the first *B* off and let it rest on my tongue. Not having anyone to share my news with made the bitter sweetness of the chocolate more noticeable. That's when I heard my Daddy's voice.

"Congratulations, B. Thankful. I love you, daughter."

I-l-o-v-e-y-o-u-t-o-o-D-a-d-d-y.

I stayed up on the ledge and waved to the passing cars as I ate my Banner Bar. It didn't matter to me whether or not they knew I was the one who shaped the prayer. What mattered was, just as I was beginning to doubt my ability to serve those in need, God sent me a sign—one that said I was a winner. That's what mattered. Maybe my life would always be a series of doubts and signs from God saying otherwise. Most important part, I reckoned, was not to miss the signs. I broke off an *R* for *Remember*.

Next voice I heard was Little G reminding me again that time was a wastin'! As a joke, I thumbed out Y-o-u-a-r-e-n-o-t-t-h-e-b-o-s-s-o-f-m-e-a-n-y-m-o-r-e. No sooner had I finished my claim, I swear I heard lightning fast footsteps so close I thought for sure Little G would appear.

"I'm going! I'm going!" I called out as I hurried down the ladder. Before I left, I took a picture of the Banner Bar sign and added it to my collection.

When I turned the key, I was pleased to find the shouting on the radio had been swapped for a song about a beautiful morning and I was sure I could make it all the way to my next stop free of trouble.

Thirteen

Mister

It was dark and the air gauze thick with heat when I reached the finger pointing end of Oklahoma, the part that says *New Mexico this way.* Loud and proud I had been singing in duet about a Wichita lineman when my ear warmed up, unexpected.

"Pull over, please. My Mister is sitting there." I reached for the radio dial and turned the sound down all the way.

M-i-s-t-e-r? I tapped out on the steering wheel.

"Yes. I am his Missus."

I had no recall of her voice, the names unfamiliar to me, but I did as asked, for Missus spoke in unusually lovely notes that surely added up to a song I was meant to hear. I parked the arvee in an empty lot a couple of blocks away from where I spied her Mister and walked down the street in his direction, the air circling me tarnished by the mistrust of those passing by.

I looked into eyes, vacant as a moonless sky, as his outstretched hand, empty as a pocket with a hole in it, brushed against me. Misunderstanding, I took the man's opened hand, shook it, and offered my name. I offended him in some way, for he pulled it back, hurtful words hidden under his tongue breaking free and stinging my ears. So as not to appear ill mannered to the others, I kept my head down and my hands in my pockets until I reached the bus stop.

Up close, Mister's dandelion fluff of white hair called up all the wishes I had ever made as the twirling puffs flew up and away, but a strong wind that carried no doubt told me a thousand wishes hadn't mended Mister's life. Even with his head hanging near to his knees, I recognized he'd stand a solid six feet tall if you could take the curve of misfortune out of his spine. Mister took no notice of me when I sat down next to him, but the man whose hand I wrongly shook did.

"He no be talkin' to you. He talk to nobody. Every day he just be sittin' there waitin' for a ghost to come home. Besides, you a white girl." His hard edged words stunned me, and, as if a fool, left me open mouthed.

"Spare change?" the man asked. I stared at his empty palm.

"He is asking you for money," Missus explained.

The change from my purchases at the general store jingled in my pocket when I reached in. I counted out the money the way the clerk did. "One, two, three, four dollars, twenty-five, fifty, seventy-five, eighty-five, eighty-six, eighty-seven cents. Four dollars and eighty-seven cents." The man shrugged and drifted away.

Mister still paid me no mind when I sat down again, took no notice as I cast my eyes over his coffee with cream skin, and cheeks sprinkled with molasses colored freckles. Ordinarily, I would have introduced myself, but Mister didn't seem to be at home.

I-d-o-n-t-k-n-o-w-w-h-a-t-t-o-d-o-M-i-s-s-u-s, I tapped on the bench advertising a contest where the lucky winner would win seven cars—one for each day of the week—and a year's supply of Dr. Pepper.

"Attendez juste." Her words were as pretty as the petals of Little G's cabbage roses in full bloom, but I had no idea what they meant and was embarrassed I had to admit my ignorance.

W-h-a-t?

"Just wait," she said.

So *a ten day juice* I did. Silent, which was so hard for me to keep up, I sat on Mister's bench for two solid hours, all the feeling in my butt cheeks falling between the slats to the sidewalk below, until just after midnight when Mister up and walked away, the blanket of night folding up behind him.

"Let him be for now," his Missus said.

I dragged my bone tired body and mind, which was still trying to latch on to what anyone would do with seven cars, and made my way back to the arvee where I found Livia resting on the hood. Exhausted as I was, I still had to find a place to park for what was left of the night. No sooner had the thought come and gone, Livia flapped her wings.

"Okay, show me the way." Livia led me down a dark, narrow road in a park setting, no lights but those of the arvee pointing straight ahead to where the road ended, and peace and quiet took hold.

I dropped down on the bed cushions and took stock of my most recent events. My day started with high spirited discovery: the radio and music, a barn-sized sign with my name on it, and more towns with curious names like Non (where I stopped at Duvall's Drugstore and ordered my first tuna melt sandwich from a spin around stool). But at the end of the day, I landed in another world: a world with moonless sky stares and outstretched hands, a world where one man's hardship held him prisoner at a bus stop. That was a jam packed, up, then down, kind of day for a girl like me.

After I laid out some seed and cornbread crumbs for Livia's supper, I stripped off my clothes, and filled the sink to soak my unders and t-shirt. I didn't wear a brassiere like my Gs, for my breasts were small and didn't require any support to stay where planted. Little G thought it hilarious to corner me in the chicken coop, manure in one hand, the other raised high in promise that if I'd just let her rub some manure on my chest for a few weeks regular, I would have womanly breasts in no time. Curious, I almost let her do it one day until I recalled seeing Big G's vestigial third tit, and the memory of that oddity put me off the idea for good.

The shower water was as cool as the night air was hot, and I lingered under its spell until the sway of my tiredness began to bend me. By the time I climbed into bed, Livia was already nested on the windowsill next to Jesus and his apostles. I ran my hand over the crown of her head, a deep peace traveling through my hand into my body and mind.

Sleep came softly, but so many departed voices, eager to share their stories about a loved one left behind, found their way through the windows, that I tossed and turned, working hard to hear everything being said. Elders with dust covered stories swept into corners long ago and children with honeysuckle sweet voices came to call, but too many longed to be heard all at once. A sudden hush came over them, making room for one voice.

"Bonjour. It is time to wake up."

My wide yawn disagreed, and I slipped my head under my pillow to avoid an argument. Tssss, tssss, tssss, tssss. Quiet. Tssss, tssss, tssss, tssss. Quiet. Tssss, tssss, tssss, tssss. Quiet. Tssss, tssss, tssss, tssss.

"Is that you making that noise, Livia?" I peeked out from the underside of my pillow. The noise came around again. Tssss, tssss, tssss, tssss! I drew back the curtain. The tssss, tssss, tssss, tssss was the call of a sprinkler set out in the middle of…in the middle of…in the middle of a graveyard! What was I doing in a graveyard? Superstitious about such things, if still alive, my Gs would have thrown down the chicken bones to read what my future held after spending the night in such a place.

Livia flew out the window and stayed low to the ground until she came to rest upon a tombstone on the other side of a broken down fence rife with forlorn weeds. Eager as I was to follow Livia's line of flight, after a night of *just behind the eyes sleep* (that's what my Little G called it when you couldn't get all the way out of your daytime mind), I had to brew up some strong coffee to see me through the day, and seeing folks in the graveyard weren't going anywhere, I set down any hurry and took the time to fix some grits loaded up with Harmonia's wild clover honey, and then drank two cups of coffee.

Once the coffee made its way into my system my get up and go was on fire. Quick as lightning, I washed and put away my breakfast dishes, then scrubbed all my body parts. When I ran out the door to greet the new day, that old sprinkler caught my right leg by surprise, soaking my jeans, and turning my stride as lopsided as the single headlight on my Daddy's truck. Water bubbled up and over the sides of my red tennis shoes (a pair of hand me downs from Nadine, who thought their bold red color suited my "look"). Not wanting to hurt Nadine's feelings, I accepted her gift, even though Little G said only whores and clowns wore red shoes. Never having met a whore or a clown, I couldn't say if that was so, or if Little G was just yanking on my leg again. Besides, I did like their bold red color.

My weighing up the business of red shoes was cut short when I caught sight of hundreds of tombstones lined up like grocery items in the general store. With respect, I crossed through the tended graveyard, careful not to step where the bodies lay in eternal repose, as I read their markers. *Beloved mother..., dearest daddy..., soldier boy..., baby sister..., little angel called home..., rest in everlasting peace..., until we meet again.*

"Not that part of the cemetery, petite fille. Not even an empty coffin holding only the memory of me inside was allowed there."

M-i-s-s-u-s-i-s-t-h-a-t-y-o-u?

"Yes, B. Thankful. But ma chere, you call me Adamma."

H-o-w-d-o-y-o-u-k-n-o-w-m-y-n-a-m-e?

"Why, you are an ange de terre."

O-r-a-n-g-e-d-o-t-e-a-r?

"Earth angel."

Since I don't own the parts to be the kind of girl who's all up in herself and thinks she's the be-all and end-all, hearing such a kind remark turned my legs to runny peach pie filling, and down I went, landing between the tombstones of Cooper and Lottie Chatfield. As my mind lay in some faraway place, I measured out there was no way Adamma had met up with my Little G. If she had, Little G would've told her I was far from any kind of angel, and I'm sure she would have gone tattletale on me about that freezer business. My Little G had a hard time letting go of stories that had become tiresome to the told upon.

When I came to, Livia was sitting on my chest, her beak to my nose. "I'm all right, Livia. I'm all right." Once convinced I wasn't going to join Cooper and Lottie Chatfield for good, Livia waddled to the other side of the fence, the prickly weeds parting for her as the Red Sea parted for Moses.

I wasn't sure if the busted up fence was meant to keep some people in or some people out, and I certainly didn't mean to do any more damage, but I did when I pushed on the gate and it fell off its rusty hinges. Four of the five pickets crumbled to pieces and fell into weeds so brittle and high they hid the markers of those who rested there. I thought maybe I was standing in the graveyard for outlaws who were killed and nobody wanted to pretty up their graves, but two steps in, I tripped over the truth—a beat up board, paint peeled back, rusty nails daring me to pick it up. The letters were so worn, only their edges appeared, but their faded hard fact remained. C-O-L-O-R-E-D. I threw the no-good sign to the ground when the sting of a burning memory cuffed me back to a day when urgent whispers passed from my Gs to Daddy.

Big G stood guard on the porch, shotgun loaded, while Little G lifted the trapdoor beneath the rag rug near the fireplace, and Daddy took to a space no bigger than our Kenmore freezer. I wasn't allowed to go down to the river that day, forced by folks who didn't take to all of God's colors to stay tucked under the pleats of my Gs' strong wills and accurate aims. To soothe Daddy, I would settle close to him by stretching out on the rug, and pretend to work on my multiplication tables, but Daddy knew my signals. Two times two equaled I love you. Three times three equaled Daddy loves me. Even with all my multiplication love sliding down through the floorboards, it took Daddy countless days to come full into himself after such a flare up. But when his smile finally came around again, it turned my world right side up—until the next time.

Adamma's gentle voice brought me back around. *"I am three rows down, two over."*

One, two, three. One, two. I had to tug hard at the weeds to look upon Adamma's marker. *Adamma Baegne Tidewater–1933-1955.* Her inscription, meager as her time on earth, left me wanting more.

W-h-y-i-s-t-h-e-r-e-n-o-t-e-n-d-e-r-s-e-n-t-i-m-e-n-t-o-r-l-o-v-e-p-o-e-m-f-r-o-m-M-i-s-t-e-r-c-a-r-v-e-d-i-n-t-o-y-o-u-r-s-t-o-n-e?

"My maman and papa spend all their money to put my picture where my Mister could see me, but he has never been here."

With the edge of my t-shirt, I polished away the dirt on the glass. Though time had faded Adamma's picture, it couldn't take the shine off her loveliness. Adamma's wavy, black hair rested upon her shoulders, her midnight eyes shined confident, and her smile was full and certain. But there were those in the world too blind to see her beauty.

"I go to take care of maman. The, how you say…" Adamma pulled the reins of her story tight, looking for the word. *"…pneumonia was in her. They say she going to die. My Mister want to go to her, but I tell him he is needed here. I know the herbs and potions to heal her, so I go to maman and stay until she is well. Papa thinks I catch her fever because he sees me being sick. Once maman's eyes are clear, she sees the gift inside me.*

"I call my Mister the morning I am to leave and tell him I will be home in two days. I was so excited to tell him the good news, and to dance with him in the kitchen, his strong arms around me, singing that funny song—Hey, Good Lookin'."

I couldn't help but giggle as Adamma sang. Her foreigner accent jumbled up with a country tune gave birth to a whole new sound.

"Before we hang up, Mister asks in his sweet talking way if I will make my shrimp gumbo for him when I come home. How can I say no to my man whose words are creamy and sweet as honey butter?"

"But then..." Adamma took a deep breath, and my gut told me what was to follow was as fragile as a house of cards. I was right. And the house came tumbling down. *"...while I wait for the bus, everything go trés terriblement."* That had to be bad.

So blistering to the touch, I just couldn't hold Adamma's story. Fearful my heart would shatter again if I let her go on, I jammed my finger into my ear, and, trying to drown out the hurt, hummed a song I heard on the radio about a sunshine good day. Between one hum and the next, I gave myself over to the judgment of the man on the street with the hurtful words hidden under his tongue. He was right. I *was* just a white girl. What made Jesus think me cooking up a meal could mend Mister's long open wound? Heck, the world's long open wound?

Livia flew from Adamma's marker to my shoulder and pecked at my finger until I pulled it out of my ear.

"Jesus isn't asking you to mend the entire world, B. Thankful. Just take it one soul at a time, honey," Little G said, and there was no bossiness in her voice at all.

O-k-a-y-L-i-t-t-l-e-G.

I-m-l-i-s-t-e-n-i-n-g-A-d-a-m-m-a.

"Only my gold heart necklace with a picture of my Mister on one side and his Missus on the other was found. That's why my Mister be sitting and waiting all these years, why he doesn't visit

my grave. My Mister believes his Missus is still out there. Just lost." Adamma, her certain smile in place, stared up at me from her marker.

Coming to grips with what needed to be done, I tapped out that Adamma would have to teach me how to reach in and take hold of her Mister to help him cross over, tapped and tapped that do so, her spirit would have to come down from Heaven and nestle inside me. And then it happened. A sensation akin to a Banner Bar left in the noonday sun slipped under my skin and settled into my limbs, softening my gawky angles, and leaving me willowy. My lazy posture stirred from a long held slumber as Adamma's exotic elegance undid my everyday awkwardness, turning me divinely feminine, and wedging a puzzling desire in my bones.

Instead of heading directly to town as intended, I was drawn inside the arvee, where I found myself slipping out of my work clothes and into my lavender dress. I even took the time to tie a few ribbons in my hair and left my work boots behind altogether. Since I wasn't but a mile or so from town, I decided to walk, and what a walk it was. The sway of river reeds in the wind caught in my hips and moved me down the street in a slow motion way. The cool push of autumn came up through the cracks in the sidewalk and nipped at my toes. My arms glided back and forth with grace. My fingertips spoke of love to the flowers along the walkway. My shoulders pulled back and my chin rose up.

"I am here," Adamma said.

Since Mister wasn't the storytelling type, Adamma graciously obliged my curiosity around how they happened upon each other. Adamma Baegne lived on the bayou, where fresh caught shrimp were simmered in a spiced up sauce born from a red-brown roux, and sweet beignet were stolen like kisses; where the men cried *laissez les bon temps rouler* as the women danced under the moonlight with silver bells on their ankles and bright colored scarves on their heads. It was down in the square where Mister, who lived a world away in Oklahoma, first laid eyes on Adamma. And if her dancing was anything like the way she walked, well, no wonder Mister was hooked on first glance. With her hook set in place, all Adamma had to do was reel Mister in with an invite to dinner. Adamma laughed, recalling that night, said she wasn't sure if the sweat on Mister's brow was born under the hard edged stare of her papa or from the heat of her shrimp gumbo.

After dinner, as they sat alone on the porch swing and the embers of their eternal tie still smoldered in his belly, Mister made his move. With the stars bearing witness, Mister proclaimed the passion of Adamma's soul rested on every spoonful of gumbo that reached his mouth, and from that day forward he would carry her spirit inside him forever. When you know you're somebody's somebody, why waste any time? Three weeks later Adamma married Mister by the light of a full moon. And until her visit to help her momma, they were never a day apart.

Now it was time to reel Mister in again, but I had a snag pulling on the line: how to get Mister to trust me. Sly as it may sound, but for his own good, I was going to have to trick him if I wanted to get close. Right off, I knew what plan to use because I had used it once before.

It was early summer when I spied a lost coyote pup in the woods. I didn't mention it to Little G, for she would have tanned my hide if she caught wind I was thinking about feeding a wild animal. But sometimes I just have to do a thing because it's the right thing to do. Every day, I'd sneak down to the woods and put a bit of food out, hide behind a tree, and wait for the pup to come snatch it up. After a very long week, for time always passes slowly when you're waiting, I sat where the pup could see me. Day after day, I inched my way closer and closer until that great day when he let me pet him. I didn't want to keep the pup, only wanted to see him through until he found his way to his pack. That's what I wanted to do for Mister Tidewater, and when Adamma caught sight of her Mister, cheerless and slouched on the Dr. Pepper bench waiting for his Missus to come back to him, she agreed my plan was the right thing to do.

What happened next when I sat down near Mister was as much a surprise to me as it was to him. I crossed my legs in the most womanly fashion, rested my elbow on my knee, and placed my cheek in my hand. My eyes went dreamy and Adamma's sun-kissed chocolate way turned up.

"Bonjour," I said, but it sure wasn't my voice doing the talking. In mind speak I called out, *"Whoa! Wait a minute, Adamma. That didn't even sound like me. I think we might be in over my head here. What does bonejer mean, anyway?"*

"Good morning," she said.

"Okey dokey, I think you better skedaddle. I'll take over from here."

The minute Adamma skedaddled, she took her chocolate grace along with her and I went back to my own ham fisted self, my elbow slipping off my knee, the ribbons falling from my hair, landing over my eyes, and I took to stuttering letters that didn't even make up words. But Mister must have caught sight of Adamma's familiar before I turned into such a pitiful picture, for he held me tight with his eyes. That same rush of excitement I had when the coyote pup took his first nibble came over me, but Mister turned skittish and shuffled away. Well, that was the end of that. Best to let him be. As Adamma said before, "a ten day juice."

On my way back to the cemetery, I traded in the sway of Adamma's hips for the heft of a wheelbarrow filled with supplies and flowers from the hardware store. I had some wrongs to right.

When troubled or trapped in the hour of decision making over a tricky situation, Little G, firm in her belief that digging in the earth helped one dig deep into their soul at the same time, handed me a hoe and sent me to the garden. Little G was right. It felt good to pull at those ratty old weeds covering up the markers of people I hoped to meet some day. Joy cheered me on as I cleared away the dead wood on their graves and tucked in flowers here and there to sweeten their eternal dreams. Though late in the season, I planted gardenias around Adamma's headstone where the fragrant white flowers would rest above her right ear when a new summer came around. I hooked up a new hose to a water spout just waiting to be used, the tssss, tssss, tssss of the sprinkler carrying cool water to the other side of the fence, the parched earth sighing.

"Thank you, my earth angel, for caring for my friends and me."

M-y-p-l-e-a-s-u-r-e.

By the time the sun gathered the blanket of night around her, I had a fine stack of fence pickets, which I came to understand was built to keep some people out. When I finished, the only part left of the gate was a broken latch, and, as if a final warning, it pierced the palm of my hand when I reached for it. I tossed the latch, along with the C-O-L-O-R-E-D sign, into a hole I dug, and buried that old wound.

"That's our girl," my Gs said. *"That's our girl."*

After supper, I took to the top of the arvee with pen and paper. Maybe if I put Adamma's story on paper and shared it with Pride, who I knew would hold it in his heart, my skin would stop burning from the sting of such bold injustice. The stars were bright, the light of their songs falling from the sky and landing on the pages of my letter.

Maybe I'm not trying hard enough, or maybe it's just beyond my imagination's imagining, because I can't understand how or why such dreadful harm could befall anyone. Some of the sting fell from my skin as I placed the words one after the other on the blue lines of the page.

Maybe it helps if we cry for each other. I circled those words, swollen and smudged by my sorrow.

Since I didn't want my letter to only tell of sad doings, I told Pride about the Banner Bar sign with my name on it and the extraordinary music I heard on the radio.

Have you ever heard the song about Lucy? There are tangerine trees and marmalade skies where she lives, Pride. So far, I've not seen such trees or skies, but I'm going to keep looking. How are you faring, Pride? Are Beautiful Beulah and the hens behaving?

Love,

B. Thankful Childe-Lucknow

P.S. Don't forget to miss me.

I took my time writing the word *Love* because I wanted Pride to feel how special I meant it to be. Pride was *my* somebody, and I wanted him to know it. I switched off the flashlight, laid my head down, and gazed up at the stars until my eyes became heavy and I drifted away.

Hours before the sun had yet to rise, I woke up from a dream so bright I found its shadow resting next to me. In my dream, Pride was standing between two tangerine trees, his generous smile welcoming me. He reached down from a marmalade sky and rested his hand on my shoulder, its warmth and weight securing me. I was tempted to bring my dream back around to see what happened next, but jumped to when I saw Adamma sitting on the edge of my bed.

It was the first time I had seen Adamma and the exquisiteness of her spirit was as dazzling as a trip around the sun. Her wavy, black hair was so shiny, I'd swear if her midnight eyes hadn't held me like hypnotized prey, I'd've seen my reflection in the silky strands. Adamma kissed my one cheek, then the other, her touch awakening all the questions I had tucked there, but with the sun coming up in a couple of hours, bringing with it the hour when Mister would take to the bus stop, I knew there was no time to dillydally. Her graceful spirit immediately stirred up inside me again, and we set our sights on the immediate task at hand—getting Mister to take that first nibble.

Fortunately, Harmonia packed my cupboards with enough supplies to see me through a hard winter, and we found everything we needed to make Adamma's bayea. As a keepsake, I wanted to print the ingredients on a card like Little G used to do and asked Adamma if she would be so kind as to spell bayea for me. Being a good speller, I figured I was right on the money, and then Adamma tipped the change out of my hand. *"B-e-i-g-n-e-t."* Not even close.

Adamma moved through the tiny kitchen space and beignet making with such ease and grace, it felt like I had a lazy Sunday morning living inside me. We sifted the flour, salt and baking powder together in one bowl and in another, we mixed eggs, sugar, milk, a little oil, and then combined it all together to make a soft dough. When the pan of oil on the back burner bubbled up hot for deep frying, we rolled out the dough and cut it into circles with a knife. Adamma said she always used a knife, for using a jar would press down the edges, a proper rise suffering the consequence. We dropped the circles into the oil one at a time, the oil bubbling up and over the dough, the arvee filling with an aroma reminiscent of Big G's fritters. As much as that memory delighted me, the batch of beignet began turning brown and puffing up at the same time the sun started to raise its head; that time of day when Mister took to the bus stop to begin his daily dedication.

Once we sugar dusted the beignet, Adamma took her leave from me and I was back to myself. I splashed some water on my face, pulled on my overalls, grabbed the basket of beignet, and took off running to beat Mister to the bus stop. I ran through the cemetery, leaping over graves and dodging early morning sprinklers. I rounded corners and crossed streets toward town with the same speed Little G urged on me so I could outrun danger should it sneak up behind me. Out of breath when I reached the bus stop, and unsure how much precious time was left before Mister arrived, I placed the basket right next to where he waited for his Missus, then hightailed it back across the street. Adamma, who was still moving like a lazy Sunday morning, eventually caught up with me, and just moments later, Mister's sad, solitary figure came from around the corner.

So as not to frighten Mister with my eagerness to lend a hand during his time of need, I reached into my pocket for my dark glasses and put them in place. I pretended not to notice him by taking interest in the window display of the hardware store, but I wasn't sure how long I could fake being awed by sacks of fertilizer, hoes, and shovels. I did my best to stay quiet, but staying quiet doesn't come easy for me, especially when I'm excited.

The smell of the sweet beignet drifted under Mister's nose, and he lifted his head from his long held, hang dog commitment. Just like the lost coyote pup, Mister looked around with a hefty helping of suspicion, but some fresh baked memory that sat as close to his heart as his stomach wouldn't allow him to ignore the package. Mister unfolded the napkin with great care and looked upon the beignet the way I looked upon a Banner Bar. He gently placed a beignet in the palm of his left hand and cupped his right hand over the top, tenderly holding the sweet dough as if holiness resided within. He lingered in regard for the longest time, so long, my bones started to jangle and I finally cracked under the strain of my enthusiasm.

"Take a bite, Mister! Take a bite!"

I so took Mister by surprise I completely knocked the air out of him and the perfect round puff of sugary dough when it hit the sidewalk. Too late to hide. Even with my sunglasses in place, Mister recognized me from our first meeting. He took to looking at his shoes and then walked away in the direction from which he came.

I-m-s-o-r-r-y-A-d-a-m-m-a-I-d-i-d-n-t...

Before I could finish my apology, the finest thing happened. Mister took pause in the middle of the street, turned himself around, and fetched the basket. Mister never looked my way, but the same rush of excitement that climbed up my spine when the coyote pup took his first nibble was at it again. The bait had been taken.

Later in the day, I saw Mister back at the bus stop, the empty basket by his side. I kept my distance, lingering across the street while I sorted out my latest concern. Little G had my Daddy to turn to in times of need, Bobby Lee had the Sons of Satan watching over him, but Mister Tidewater was so alone. Who on earth would I look to for help?

Like summer thunder rolling across our fields back home, a shake and a boom made its way out the door of Pearly May's Kitchen, trumpeting the arrival of a woman wearing a black patch over her right eye and cheerfulness in her call.

"Soup's on! Come on in and break bread at my table. Let the warmth of a good meal fill your soul." She laughed and the sidewalk shimmied beneath me.

As burden worn as folks in the line appeared, she was just the opposite, smiling and calling every man and woman by name as she shook their hand, or gave them a welcoming pat on the back, and offering up an encouraging word. When she reached Mister, I stretched my neck out as far as I dared to hear what she had to say, though, more curious as to whether Mister had anything to say in return.

"Did your Missus make it home last night, Mister Tidewater?" Her question was the type a person asks even though they know the answer: a charitable gesture that says it's okay to want what you want. Mister shook his head from sorry side-to-side. And even though she knew *getting what he wanted* was impossible, she offered up a side dish of hope.

"Tomorrow," Her Kindness said. "Maybe tomorrow."

There was no doubt in my mind that good woman had jumped right out of Heaven and landed in the very spot God intended. When everyone in the line had been seen to, she turned, and her friendly thunder rolled in my direction.

"And who might you be?"

I looked over my shoulder, expecting to find another broken down soul on the side of the road for her to feed.

"You, with the red hair and bare feet. Sweet thing, do you need a meal?"

"No, ma'am. I'm just traveling through your lovely town."

She rotated her head, her one able eye taking in the boarded up storefronts, the line of down and out folks running the length of the street.

"Well, come on in and help me serve my friends some lunch." She wrapped her soft-as-a-feather-pillow arm around my shoulder and pulled me into her worn-sofa-cushion side.

"I'm Pearly May, and you are?"

"I'm B. Thankful Childe-Lucknow and I'm pleased to meet you, Miss Pearly May."

Pearly May pulled down on my dark glasses. "Hosanna Banana! Aren't you special with your two-toned eyes and a constant reminder for a name." At the mention of my eyes, I dropped my head in shame, but Pearly May's hand, rapid as a river current, silky as silt, raised my chin.

"I'll bet you see the world in the way of no other."

"I try my hardest to hold all I see with tenderness and enthusiasm."

Miss Pearly May chucked me under my chin. "We need more of that, B. Thankful. Come on. Let's go feed God's people."

Like our kitchen back home, Pearly May's Kitchen wasn't fancy, but sincere in its purpose. Tablecloths with red and white squares, perfect for playing checkers, covered the long tables graced by Coca Cola bottle vases holding daisies, and every place setting had a red napkin and silver-ware that didn't match but had been shined up real nice. A blackboard nailed to the wall read: TODAY'S SPECIAL: Corn Chowder, Buttermilk Biscuits, and Tapioca Pudding.

Pearly May came up behind me, slipped an apron over my head, and tied it firmly around my waist. She spun me around and smiled so wide her eye patch raised up a smidge.

"Well, you certainly look like you belong here."

After having that stranger dress me down when I ar-rived, added to the hard time I was having breaking ground with Mister, hearing Pearly May say I belonged staggered me. So taken by her kindness, I bent over, intending to act like I was tying my shoes while I wiped away my grate-ful tears, but found myself staring at my bare feet. Pearly May pretended not to notice my emotion dripping on my foot and steered me toward a soup kettle filled with creamy corn chowder. I filled the bowl of each customer (Pearly May called them customers even though no money traded hands), then Estelle Chudruddy expertly placed a warm, golden brown biscuit on a side plate, and Homer Jenkins finished off each tray by offering up a fine looking dish of tapioca pudding, and his blessing for the day.

When Mister stepped up to be served, I took a gamble at putting a smile on his face to go with his corn chow-der, but as soon as the words to the Hey, Good Lookin' song slipped under Mister's door of memory, his soup bowl crashed to the floor. I ran around to the other side to help and, before I could stop, stepped on a porcelain shard, blood trickling from the bottom of my foot. I froze up when I reached down to pull it out, and left a trail of blood behind me as I hopped on my good foot to the near-est chair.

Pearly May was clear across the room tending to the needs of her guests, but I thought for sure she would rush to my aid. I was wrong. It was Adamma's spirit who came to call within me and whisper pretty words to comfort me, but not a single word passed from Mister to me as he walked my way. Mister knelt before me, pulled the enemy from my foot, and then rested one hand over my eyes, the other on my wound. An electric shock ran through me, but not as bad as the time I stuck a knife down in the toaster to loosen a stuck piece of bread and touched the wires inside. That hurt like the dickens. After Mister tied the napkin I'd used for the beignet around my foot, he walked out the door to the bus stop.

"Thank you, Mister Tidewater," I called after him.

It was all my fault Mister lost out on one of Pearly May's fine meals, and though Pearly May was no ordinary apple, even so, I was sure she'd take my apron away, so I stripped it off, folded it up, and handed it to her along with my regret.

"Miss Pearly May, I'm so sorry, so very sorry. I just wanted to put a smile on Mister Tidewater's face with a song he used to sing to Adamma."

By the time my brain took notice that my mouth had come unhinged and, like a barn door in a storm, was flapping open...closed...open...closed, my yammering rushing in and out like the wind, Pearly May was sitting across from me. She moved her question across the checkerboard tablecloth and trapped me in the corner square.

"How do you know the name of Mister Tidewater's wife, B. Thankful?"

Until I could make up an answer, I acted like I was sitting in a state of recollection. "Well, I think...hmmm, uh, well, well..."

"Last I heard, a well was a hole in the ground," Pearly May said.

"Okay, but before I tell you, may I take some lunch over to Mister Tidewater? He's gone back to sitting at that old bus stop, and I'm hurting something awful for causing him to miss one of your fine meals."

Pearly May gave me the same sliver eyed look Little G used when she figured I was hoping if enough time passed she'd forget I owed her honest testimony.

"All right, but I expect you to keep your word and come back."

"Yes, ma'am."

I hobbled across the street and set down a tray with a bowl of corn chowder, two biscuits, a dish of tapioca pudding, and a Coca Cola bottle holding two perfect daisies on the bus stop bench. Poor Mister Tidewater had carried his woes a great distance, and as much as I wanted to pluck him from the center of his grief, I tethered my eagerness. I had already done enough harm with the best of intentions. As I limped my way across the street, I heard the clink of his silverware, but I didn't look back.

Pearly May was waiting for me at the table with an offering of lunch, but before she could king me with another question, I quickly filled my mouth with a hefty spoon of creamy corn chowder, my eyes welling up with gratitude when the sweetness of the corn and the salty bacon came to rest in my belly.

"Pearly May, this is the finest soup I have ever tasted."

Pearly May sucked on her teeth. "I've got all the time in the world, B. Thankful."

"How 'bout I finish my lunch first and then I'll—" Pearly May stepped on my words.

"Like I told you, I've got..." I broke in. "...all the time in the world."

"It's okay to tell her your story, B. That Pearly May's a good egg," Little G whispered in my ear.

"This could take awhile," I said. "I know, I know. You've got all the time in the world."

Same as that day with Pride when we started out under Momma's tree drinking lemonade, then made our way out to the orchard where I handed him peaches along with my story, I told the tale of B. Thankful Childe-Lucknow while Pearly May watched me close with her one eye. After I finished telling the part where my dead Big G came calling on me to help fix Little G's last supper, how that very same day Little G died, then hours later Daddy joined her, Pearly May set down a tray of dirty dishes and began to bawl.

"Oh, Miss Pearly May, don't cry. I'll be okay," I said, as I wiped away her one-eyed tears with the hem of her apron. "Do you want me to stop and just get to the story of Mister Tidewater and Adamma?"

"Heck, no!" she said, snapping up her tears. "It's like a movie script. And I love movies. Oh, that reminds me. *Funny Girl* is playing down at the Bijou. Meet me there tonight at six o'clock and I'll treat you to the movie and popcorn. Now, tell me more. I want to hear it all, B. Thankful."

We washed and dried all the dishes, put bright yellow cloths on the tables, and started putting the fixings together for the next day's lunch crowd while I told my story—right up to the part about Mister helping me with my foot. We were in the middle of cutting up vegetables when Pearly May told me to keep an eye on my wound. Figuring she was worried it might get infected, I assured her I had a box full of Little G's poultices and salves.

"No, darlin', it won't get infected." Pearly May put down the vegetable peeler and took all of me in, maybe checking to see if I was listening with both ears.

"You see, B. Thankful, Mister Tidewater holds the power in his hands. He helped heal countless folks in this neighborhood, but you're the first person I've seen him touch since Adamma went missing."

Little G once told me some people were given the gift to help others mend. By the laying on of hands they drew the fire from burns, the colic from newborns, helped a wound to heal, or spared a child from being stunted. I'll admit, even though I could hear voices of the departed, I thought she might be pulling my leg. My Little G was that kind of trickster. But now I knew better, and, of course, that kindled my curiosity.

"Pearly May, did you ever think to have Mister Tidewater lay his hands upon your..." I pulled my question up short when Little G cleared her throat the way she did when alive to tell me I was about to cross the *none of your business* line with my nosiness, but Pearly May had already stitched the asked and unasked together.

"No, B. Thankful, I never wanted Mister Tidewater to heal my eye. God gave me one eye for a reason and, lucky for me, it turned out to be the eye of hope. I might not see the world the way I do if I had a second eye pulling me off in another direction. We're alike in that way, you and I, and how we look upon the world—you with your tenderness and enthusiasm, and me with my hope.

"Ever since Adamma went missing, sorrow and shame, like jagged bookends, sit on either side of Mister Tidewater at that old bus stop. Day after day, they carve their names into that poor man's soul, but I have never given up hope,

B. Thankful. And after hearing your story, I believe another healing will take place. A healing that Mister Tidewater deserves."

It was near four o'clock when I left Pearly May's Kitchen, and though kind of her to offer me a place to stay above the dining room, I declined it for the pleasure I found in my bedtime in the arvee. It made me feel close to Pride to have his belongings around me, a certain comfort tucked in the corners of my sleep. But I did promise Pearly May I'd be back for the movie and again tomorrow to help serve lunch. Pearly May was so happy she hugged me for a really long, long time, her stomach, soft as Nadine's puffed up marshmallows, near to folding in half around me.

Wanting to look polished for my outing with Pearly May, I hopped in the shower and lathered up my body parts and washed my hair. My shoulders were sore from all my time working in the graveyard, and the puncture that old gate latch hollowed out in my palm still pained me some, but when I scrubbed my feet, I found the wound from the porcelain shard was healed, save the tiniest pink scar left behind as proof.

Good thing my foot was healed, because I lost track of time and had to run all the way to the Bijou where Pearly May was waiting for me at the entrance. Pearly May stood out from the crowd in her tent-sized dress covered with big red polka dots, her black, everyday eye patch replaced by a silky red one; and her silver hair, twisted round and round on the sides of her head, made me long for Little G's Sunday morning cinnamon buns.

"You look beautiful, Pearly May."

"My bunions are killin' me," she said when I took notice of her fuzzy red slippers.

Little G's outlook on folks who wore red shoes was still wedged in my brain, but even I knew better than to ask Pearly May if she ever spent time as a clown or a whore. Besides, my stomach was flip-flopping like a fish out of water, that's how twitchy I was about seeing my very first movie. I was happy I watched Pearly May go in first, so I didn't fuss when the man at the door tore my ticket in half and kept some for himself. Right off, I noticed a machine pop, pop, popping corn until the basket spilled over. A boy wearing a stiff white shirt, a black bowtie, and a friendly smile, scooped up the fat kernels of corn and dropped them into boxes that read POPCORN!–the word alone causing exclamation.

"Give me two popcorns, a box of Dots, and some of those ice cream bonbons, Scooter."

I checked the candy counter. No, no Banner Bars. The lights began to flicker and Pearly May let out such a high pitched squeal I almost dropped my box of popcorn.

"Hurry, B. Thankful, the previews are about to start. We don't want to miss those."

Even with only one eye to show her the way, Pearly May hustled through the darkness and down the aisle without hesitation. My uneasiness kept bumping into me in the darkness, turning me awkward as a three legged toad, one with the fits and starts of a full on laughing spell when Pearly May's ample rear end knocked off a lady's hat.

"Sorry, Leticia," she said, as she handed Leticia her hat. "I hope you don't mind sitting up close, B. Thankful. It makes me feel like I'm right there in the movie." Second row was that place.

I had just settled into my seat when the theater suddenly went from cave darkness to bright lights and action, music filling the entire space. Overcome by the newness of it all, I jumped up and turned to see where the musicians were sitting, the light from the movie projector shining in my eyes and casting my shadow upon the screen.

"Sit down in front, stupid!" someone yelled. A room full of laughter knocked me back into my seat, my excitement sliding off me onto the sticky floor along with a good deal of my popcorn.

Pearly May stood, her generous shadow filling the entire screen, her voice thundering through the theater. "Who said that?" When no one spoke up, Pearly May remained standing, placed her hands on her hips, two triangles of light breaking through to the screen. "If you want to see what's coming to the Bijou next week, you better offer up whoever called my friend stupid or I'll stand here all night. And my bunions are hurtin' big time, so this could turn ugly real fast."

Embarrassed by the fuss, I pulled on Pearly May's arm. "It's okay, Pearly May. Please sit down."

"No, B. Thankful, it's not okay, and you need to start standing up to anyone who treats you less than your wonderful self deserves."

A voice called out from the back of the theater. "It was Lucky Bodene, Pearly May. Now sit down."

"I'll see you after the movie, Lucky Bodene." Turning around, she knocked Leticia's hat off again. "Oops. Sorry, Leticia."

As if standing out and being called stupid wasn't reason enough for a quick exit, what happened next would have definitely been the end of my movie going adventure were it not for Pearly May's arm looped through my own. The most peculiar music, awful as the squawk of one of our chickens when she caught the wind of Little G's ax, pierced my ear drums, and suddenly the movie screen was filled with apes dressed up like human beings. When the apes started talking and beating on a poor, near to naked man, I tried to make a run for it, but Pearly May pulled me back into my seat.

"They're just actors wearing costumes, honey."

Not good enough for me. I kept my eyes shut tight and stuck my fingers in my ears until it was all over. When it was, I told Pearly May I was as certain as dung draws flies, I would never go to see that *PLANET OF THE APES* movie, and she laughed so hard she nearly choked on a bonbon.

The theater went dark and quiet, Pearly May sucking on that bonbon, the only sound. On the screen–3-2-1–A fancy lady in a leopard skin coat and hat to match walked with her back to the movie screen. She wore high heels and her butt wiggled just like the secretary's butt at the Mercantile Bank back home.

I could go on and on about the movie, but Pearly May said the worst thing a person could do was give away a movie's story line. But I will tell you this: we both cried when Fanny Brice sang about people needing people. And poor Pearly May was so broken up when Fanny sang about loving her man and how he'd never know, she stopped sucking on her bonbons. When the movie was over, THE END came up on the screen and the lights in the theater came back on. Pearly May snapped up her tears and barked out her warning to Lucky Bodene, but Lucky was long gone.

"B. Thankful, I've gotta run. I can't let Lucky get away. See you tomorrow?" she asked, rumbling down the aisle, taking Leticia's hat with her one last time.

"Yes, ma'am," I said.

Outside the Bijou, I caught sight of Mister sitting at the bus stop, that old lamp light turning him a cast of no color I ever saw in my paint-by-numbers. My nature, such as it is, wouldn't allow me to walk by him without having a go at putting a smile on his face. Like I said, sometimes I've got to do a thing because it's the right thing to do. I plopped down next to Mister, tucked my hands under my legs, and tried my best to remain still, but I was so wound up my legs started swinging back and forth.

"Evening, Mister Tidewater." I didn't expect an answer and one never came, but I just had to share my news.

"I know you're not the talkative type and that's okay, I don't mind doing the talking. Besides, I'm busting at my seams to tell you I just saw my very first movie. It was called *Funny Girl*, which is kind of funny because Fanny Brice, that was her name, didn't really have a funny life, she just play acted at funny when life was getting the best of her and she didn't want anyone to know how sad she was. When Fanny sang a song about people needing people, I've got to tell you, Mister Tidewater, I thought of you. Really, I did."

Right then would have been the perfect time for me to stop and take a breath, but something came over me and all the words to that song about people found a place to rest in my head. Before I could stop myself, I was up and singing to Mister, right there on the sidewalk. When I got to the part about how lovers were very special people, my voice dropped down low the way Fanny's did. For an instant, and I would be willing to take an oath, the corners of Mister's mouth turned right side up. My hand on the lamppost, I swirled round and round, singing about people needing people until I was breathless and dizzy, and dropped back down on the bench. I studied the colorful advertisement for the Dr. Pepper contest until my breath and I met up again.

"Mister Tidewater, what in the world would a person do with seven cars?"

Mister didn't say a word, but I recognized the voice coming from behind the bench.

"Who do you think you are comin' up here singin' and actin' a fool? Go on now and let that old man be."

The stranger's words stung me, and I knew from my own personal loss that a single sting can take all the life out of a person. Any other time, I would have hung my head down and apologized for being me, but down the street I saw Pearly May giving Lucky Bodene the what-for on my behalf. If I wasn't going to stand up for myself, why should Pearly May? Hands on my hips, teed off words on my lips, I turned mad as a wrongly shot pig and pushed the stranger up against the lamppost with my newfound mindset.

"Excuse me?" And trust me, I did not say "excuse me" in my usual *I'm sorry for being B. Thankful* kind of way. No, it definitely came up in a *Who do you think you're talking to?* manner of speaking.

"I don't rightly know what your problem is. I may be just a white girl to you, but my Daddy had the same color skin as you and Mister Tidewater. That's right. And for your information, I know a thing or two about how hard life can be for a person, no matter the color of their skin. For crying out loud, look at me. You don't think my crazy hair and my two-toned eyes mark me in a way that causes people to judge me, look down upon me? Did you ever think about that, sir? Hmmm? Well, did you? And not much more than a month ago I watched my Little G and my Daddy die one right after the other. How's that for hard luck?"

The stranger raised both his hands in the air. "Take it easy. No need to go sideways."

My insides near to calm again, I dropped my hands from my hips. "Well, I am truly sorry I had to holler at you," I said. I turned to walk away and caught sight of Pearly May mouthing to me the rest of what I was supposed to say. I made a quick u-turn. "However," I added, walking back to the stranger, "you were treating me less than my wonderful self deserves. Please see to it that doesn't happen again." I added that last part all on my own and couldn't believe how the words, when strung together with such resolve, made me feel taller than put forth by the notches on my bedroom door.

I took up my place on the bench next to Mister again. "Mister Tidewater, I'm so sorry you had to experience my irritation, and for bothering you with my over enthusiastic curiosity. You see, I thought I was sent to help you in some way, but I guess somebody made a mistake. I promise I won't bother you again. Cross my heart."

My lower lip started to quiver, but I told myself I would not cry. Mister reached out and took hold of my hand. We sat side-by-side in silence and watched hardship walk up and down the broken street. When the last bus of the day came and went without his Missus onboard, Mister let go of my hand and walked toward his hopeless life.

It was a long, lonely walk back to the arvee, and with every heavy step, I worked to figure out how I had gone wrong about my mission with Mister Tidewater. Even Bobby Lee, whose anger burned white hot, let me in after just a few hours of sitting with him. Why couldn't I get

Mister to trust me the way Bobby Lee and the lost coyote pup did?

When I opened the door to the arvee, I found Livia snoozing near my dream catcher, which hung as still as the night air. I placed my paint-by-number picture of Jesus next to me on my pillow, my drop-by-drop woefulness landing on the chalice (number 37-gold). I closed one eye and looked upon Jesus the way Pearly May might through her eye of hope, but the weight of my disappointment pulled it closed as a black smoke shadow moved across my dream mind.

"Down here, B. Thankful."

I recognized Jesus's voice calling to me and made my way through the darkness of the Bijou where I found him sitting in the second row enjoying a box of POPCORN! Jesus was eating popcorn!

"Nice to see you again, B. Thankful." Jesus reached into the sleeve of his shirt and pulled out a Banner Bar.

"Thank you, Jes...Mi...Mister Jesus." I was never gonna get that right.

"I thought we'd watch a movie together. How does that sound?"

What I really wanted to do was talk about Mister, to ask why I was failing at every turn, but Jesus appeared so happy to have a little time to himself, I didn't have the heart to burden him with my questions.

"Okay, Mister Jesus. I'd like that."

I offered Jesus some of my Banner Bar and he took a small piece and placed it in his mouth. I did the same. How about that? Jesus and I were sharing a Banner Bar and a movie.

The screen came to bright, colorful life and read:

MISTER
Starring—Mister Tidewater
Directed by
A blinding flash of white light filled the screen

I thought the projector had gone haywire when the screen filled with white light and said so to Jesus. Jesus laughed so hard while explaining his daddy's way of making himself known, I saw a tiny bit of Banner Bar chocolate stuck to his front teeth. As Jesus's laugh faded, the screen filled with the image of Pearly May standing in the heart of Pearly May's Kitchen. She looked exquisite, a queen in her blue satin dress with matching slippers, and a sparkling eye patch that twinkled the way stars do to let you know they're watching out for you.

Fancy cloths covered the tables lined with flowered china plates, sparkly knives and forks, and silver goblets so shiny Pearly May was practicing her smile in one. At the back of the hall, there was a dance floor just like the one Fanny Brice's momma had at her place, and the music playing was the kind Adamma was dancing to when Mister first laid his eyes upon her, the kind of music filled with mysterious power.

"B. Thankful, how are you doing in the kitchen?" Pearly May called.

In no hurry to see the big screen version of B. Thankful Childe-Lucknow, I covered my eyes. "Mister Jesus, please tell me I don't look like one of those dressed up apes."

"Open your eyes and see yourself, B. Thankful."

Since Jesus was treating me to the movie and a Banner Bar, and the fact he was Jesus, I made myself look at the screen. When I did, I saw I was dressed all in white—crisp white pants without a speck of dirt on them, white tennis shoes with no chicken poop or Beautiful Beulah's cow pies marking them, and a jacket that wasn't a hand-me-down with The Last Supper Catering Company *printed over the pocket in purple stitches. The rest of me: crazy red hair, and two-toned eyes, looked the same, but there was a shine coming off me I had never seen in the mirror.*

"Shrimp Gumbo is ready Pearly May," I called.

"Then let's open the door and feed God's people."

Through the magic of movie making, the door to Pearly May's Kitchen began to open all by itself and Mister Tidew…

Tssss. Quiet. Tssss. Quiet. Tssss.

"You've got to be kidding me!" I hollered when that doggone sprinkler ran off with my dream. I dropped my head back on the pillow and studied my dream catcher, looking for any leftover dream pieces. I closed my eyes and called on sleep to help me find the missing piece of my dream. Some time later, I woke to Livia nuzzling my cheek.

"Livia," I said, as I stroked the crown of her head, "I have a plan to help Mister find his way home."

At such an early hour, I was going to need some more strong coffee to get me through the long day ahead. Near the bottom of the coffee can, I found another note from Pride, but this one was so very different from the others. In this note, his words rubbed up against each other in a heated way and, like tender hands, lifted from the page and stroked my spine, giving birth to a fresh, new-fangled sensation. I tried to wipe the heat from cheeks, but they were aflame with a desire I could not name. As eager as I was to read his words again and again and again, I had to call on Adamma right away.

Before my message was fully tapped out, Adamma came to call on me. I told her all about my dream with Jesus and how it led me to a special idea for helping her

Mister. We made a long list of supplies, and headed off to share my revelation with Pearly May.

Pearly May didn't even hear me come through the door, that's how loud she was singing as she marched through the dining area, waving knives and ladles in the air.

"EYE ON THE TARGET…"

I ducked just in time when a knife flew from her hand in my direction. When I screamed, Pearly May screamed and clutched her heart. I was so tightly wound about sharing my idea, I didn't even notice the knife just missed my head, the blade buried in the wall, the handle flapping side-to-side, nor did I give Pearly May any time to compose herself.

"Pearly May, I have got to talk to you."

I chewed on my fingernails as I paced back and forth and laid out my plan, twisted at my hair while trying to remember everything I saw in my dream. Unbeknownst to Pearly May, Adamma sat on a chair near to where my inspiration took to soaring, my work boots scoring the floor, turn after turn. When I finished, I was drenched with excitement, and then Pearly May patted the seat next to her, same as my Daddy did when he had to tell me he'd be gone for a long spell. It's a cheerless pat you never forget.

"B. Thankful, there's nothing more I'd like to do than help you out with Mister Tidewater, but what you're talking about would cost way more money than Pearly May has to give. Looking at your list, times the number of people I feed lunch every day, well, you're looking at hundreds and hundreds of dollars, maybe more."

"Oh, Pearly May, I don't expect you to pay for it. Remember, I won the Banner Bar contest, and there's nothing I'd rather spend my money on. Besides, I promised my

Gs and Daddy I would make them proud of me, and they'll be twelve kinds of tickled I found a rightful way to spend it."

"Well, that's a horse of a different color! Now, it's going to take me awhile to get all of these ingredients together. Most of them aren't your everyday fare around these parts." My face wilted. "Oh, don't you fret, B. Thankful. Pearly May will get what you need." But would it be in time?

More than a week passed and we were still missing some of the ingredients, but during the wait, the new grass around the graves overtook the weeds, and the faces of the flowers I tucked here and there smiled back at me. Even Adamma's gardenias were blooming, their scent, as exotic as the woman herself, floating through the arvee window, and calling my name. That's when I looked up from my dishwashing and saw him there. Poor Mister was as lost as he could be as he searched for his Missus. He looked at the Polaroid picture of Adamma's marker I left at the bus stop, and then around the cemetery for the real thing.

I set down my dishwashing, made my way over to where Mister stood, and took his hand in mine. Sometimes walking without words crossing over from one person to the other can make time seem stretched out, but it didn't feel like that at all with Mister. Even so, my jaw bones were befuddled at being put on hold for such a long time and, sooner than not, my jaw was sure to come unhinged. Once I showed Mister where the memory of his Missus rested, I went back to the arvee before I broke my promise.

Mister's sad heartedness fell onto Adamma's lovely picture a drop at a time, but he did his best to wipe away the past so he might see her better. Watching him with my heart wide open, I weighed up how Mister loved his Missus through the seasons. Autumn–when the air painted the leaves orange and crimson, then gave itself over to the way of Winter–when the branches of the cherry trees lay bare until the herald of Spring–when the grass was newborn green and flowers shouted out their names–Lily, Violet, and Petunia—until they were spent by the heat of Summer–when vegetable gardens were abundant and cool streams called to Mister and his Missus. But then one day, the only somebody he was ever gonna love with his heart and soul for all of time never came home, and the brilliance of the colors and the shine of the sun turned to shadows.

Daddy once told me time hangs heavy on a man's heart when he clutches a notion so tight it becomes him. But if he can see his way to letting go of his grip on it, freedom comes a calling. For Mister's sake, I leaned on my Daddy's belief for both of us.

Mister checked his watch, the next bus due soon. He looked over his shoulder in my direction. I lowered my gaze and, as promised, kept my words under lock and key.

The next morning, I walked into Pearly May's Kitchen and she greeted me with a smile near as wide as her ample rear end. After ten long days of waiting, all of the must have items for Adamma's shrimp gumbo had finally been gathered together. That poor refrigerator was near to busting at the seams with sacks of vegetables, and crates of shrimp, while jars of fiery gumbo spices lined up on the counter, and, like me, waited to be of service. But first, we had to serve up that day's lunch to our customers: navy bean soup, cornbread, and baked apples.

All through the lunch hour, it was hard for me to stay focused on the task at hand–ladling up a bowl of soup and a smile–for my mind was wrapped around Mister, who, for a reason unknown to me, didn't pass through the line. When I spoke of my worry to Pearly May, she let me rub her eye patch, said it would bring me good luck.

After the lunch crowd had been served and the dining room readied for the next day, Pearly May handed over the keys to her kitchen and bid me a goodnight. While Adamma taught me how to make her shrimp gumbo, Pearly May would be over at the Bijou watching *Planet of the Apes*. Just thinking about those apes made my brain knot up, choking off a courteous goodbye. When Pearly May opened the door to leave, a breeze carrying the scent of gardenias marched through in slow time until Adamma's loveliness stood before me.

"My angel, Mister's time is very near."

The hour to help Mister was finally upon me, and the knuckles of doubt punched me right behind my knees. About to call on Jesus and ask if I might pass this cup for fear of calamity, out of the blue, I heard the backfire of Harmonia's motorcycle and her cry, "Be fearless!" I inhaled Harmonia's words and let them seep into the marrow of my bones.

"I'm ready, Adamma."

Adamma's beignet and Big G's fritters may have had something in common, but it was apples to oranges for sure when it came to how Adamma and Big G differed when using me to prepare their special dishes. Big G's movements were solid and swift. Adamma moved like cool music on a hot summer's day, no hurry held in the handle of the knife as we sliced through vegetables and peppers that made my eyes water with their vibrant heat. Even with Adamma's skilled hands working through me, it took a while for me to clean the slippery little shrimp, but once stripped, we stirred the shells up in some oil with onions and celery, a little chopped garlic, paprika (a spice near to the color of my hair), and bay leaves. As I added the bay leaves, I told Adamma about Harmonia Pennywhistle and what an expert she was when it came to herbs and spices. Once my story was blended with the ingredients in the pot, we added a goodly amount of water to the mix. When it came to a boil, Adamma gave me the signal to turn it down to a simmer.

It was when we started the red-brown roux that Adamma's cool movements turned hot and spicy. Again and again, Adamma encouraged me to slow down and *feel* the food we were fixing, not only with my soul, but my womanhood.

"Ma chere, to make a proper roux you must feel the flour give itself freely to the oil, feel how the oil, like a lover's arms, wraps itself around each bit of flour until they melt into each other and become one. You never want to rush such lovemaking. Imagine you are dancing with your man. Slowly he turns you around and around, and brings you back into his arms."

Adamma filled my hips with a life of their own as they followed her stirring motion, and I imagined I was dancing with Pride. Like I said, having Adamma's spirit inside me was nothing like Big G. For almost a full hour we stirred and stirred the roux, mindful of the flame, lowering it as needed.

"There, see how the flour and oil come together?"

"Uh-huh," was all my mind speak could muster. I was sweating in parts I didn't know could sweat and had to work extra hard to keep my attention full on the roux, not let my mind and special place wander off in the direction

of Pride's note of love. If I didn't keep the lovemaking of the oil and flour separate from how Pride's words flushed me so, I was certain I would burst into flames right in the middle of Pearly May's Kitchen.

"Now watch as the roux begins to deepen in color. This is the most important part. Not too much fiery lovemaking all at once or it will burn itself up."

When the time came to add the holy trinity (onions, green peppers, and celery), as well the hot peppers and all the spices, the roux bubbled and snapped until we added some of the shrimp stock to the pot.

"Watch as the flour releases the oil and it rises to the top. Slowly add some more of the shrimp stock."

While the rich red-brown stock simmered, we pulled the oil off the top, a spoonful at a time until the velvety sauce left behind was ready to welcome the shrimp. On the back burner, the pot of rice waited patiently to cozy up to Adamma's gumbo.

The windows of Pearly May's Kitchen were as steamed up as I was, but I could see someone trying to peek in. Thinking it might be Pearly May, I went to the window and cleared away a circle of steam to find it was Mister looking back at *us*. What with Mister showing up a day early and catching me in the act, the movie script written in my dream was no longer in apple pie order. I unlocked the door and offered Mister Tidewater entrance to Pearly May's Kitchen. Certain Mister would recognize his Missus within me if he looked too close, I kept my eyes downcast and did my best to walk like my usual self, but with Adamma hanging onto me, my hips swayed to and fro. With the flames of Adamma's womanhood swiveling my hips and nipping at my heels, I licked my lips and brushed away the sweat from my brow in a hot-blooded manner. Mister followed me behind the counter and looked into the pot of shrimp gumbo. He appeared rooted to a spot of memories floating within the red-brown roux and inhaled them one by one.

When Little G and my Daddy died, I held their faces in my hands, hoping to find a small piece of their being left behind that I might tuck in a pocket and carry with me forever. Looking for the same, Mister studied me, searching for the special somebody he had lost, yearning to find her close by. I held still and let him take a long, weathered look until he was ready to let go.

Once free from Mister Tidewater's gaze, I took two bowls and placed a goodly amount of rice at the bottom and spooned Adamma's shrimp gumbo over the top. As did the lost coyote pup, Mister followed on my heels to the table and sat across from me. I waited for him to taste the gumbo, but first Mister tucked his napkin under his chin and bowed his head. My old jaw bones started their jangling business, but I held to my promise and kept quiet.

When he was ready, Mister lifted the spoon to his mouth and rested the gumbo on his tongue. At that very moment, and I am not stretching the truth, music from the bay-ou filled the room. Adamma slipped from me and danced through the hall, the silver bells on her ankles jingling.

How could this be so? Mister's eyes asked when he took another taste. When Adamma danced right up behind him and peered over his shoulder, I waited for Mister to break out singing the Hey, Good Lookin' song, but he remained true to his wordless way. Mister took his time the way Jesus did, laying down his spoon between bites, savoring every memory held in each morsel. *Remember me, for I will remember you.*

After my first taste of Adamma's shrimp gumbo, I understood from top to bottom why Mister fell for her. Where Big G's jellied pig's feet were born of the earth, Adamma's shrimp gumbo was born of fire and passion.

The music in Pearly May's Kitchen turned slow, and though I had never danced with a stranger, I broke my silence and asked Mister Tidewater if he would do me the honor. Mister pushed himself up from the table to oblige me. He rested his right hand on the small of my back and held my right hand in his left hand about as high as a good-bye wave, which is not as high as a hello wave. When done properly, a hello wave is high over your head.

We waltzed up and down the aisles, slow to be sure, for Mister had used his get-up-and-go waiting all those years for his Missus. As we finished a full circle of the room, Adamma tapped me on the shoulder and cut in. With his Missus back in his arms, the curve of Mister's misfortune fell away, his spine straightened, and a half forgotten smile born of a moss covered memory lit up his face. The beauty of the love I witnessed needs no embroidery around the edges on my part and trying to make you understand what magic took place next would be like trying to capture moonlight in a jar.

I left Mister and Missus to catch up with each other the way I imagined Big G did with Little G, Annabelle with her Bobby Lee, and went about my business, a remnant of Adamma's exquisite spiciness tapping on my hips as I moved through the kitchen. Oh, how I looked forward to calling on my newfound womanly way one day.

Pushed by the force of habit was the only reason I could summon when Mister hurried through the door and across the street to the bus stop where he fell to the bench and looked at me from across the deserted street. *Must be some mistake,* crossed my mind when another bus headed down the street in Mister's direction. It was past midnight, no buses running until the next day at seven in the morning. When the bus came to a stop, I recognized the driver by his hair (number 12-sienna brown). The doors opened and there stood Missus, hand outstretched from her world into Mister's world. Mister handed me a slow, carefree smile as he took her hand.

The lamppost sparked and went dark. Only the stars, as thick as Adamma's gumbo, shined down to light my way as I hurried across the street and caught Mister's left behind body in my arms. With a gentle swiftness, Mister just slipped out of his body: no tussling or fretfulness, no visible pain spurring him on; at the last, no fear holding him back. In the center of his last breath, Mister simply let go of clutching a shadow, opened his hand to the sweetness of the seasons once again and, as my Daddy promised, freedom came a callin'.

I laid Mister Tidewater out on the bench, closed his eyes and covered him with the tablecloth still in my hand, then slipped off my apron to rest his head upon. As the bus pulled away from the bench, I ran alongside, my hand resting palm-to-palm with Mister's against the glass door, until I could go no farther and the taillights disappeared.

I knelt down by the bench where Mister's body lay. "You never did tell me what a person would do with seven cars. Now I'll never know."

I reached into my pocket for a tissue, but my hand came back holding a blue satin pouch with a perfect pearl button clasp. I ran the tip of my finger over the button, pressed the smooth satin to my cheek. Inside I found Mister's only keepsake—Adamma's heart shaped locket engraved with the letter *A*, a picture of Mister on one side and his Missus on the other. I placed Adamma's locket around my neck and heard the agreeable sound it made when it brushed up against my turquoise eagle. I closed my eyes and saw Mister and Missus riding the great eagle's wings beyond the clouds.

I wanted to hand the news of Mister's passing to Pearly May better than I had Little G's passing to Daddy, so as I crossed the street, I practiced over and over again. "Miss Pearly May, Mister Tidewater is dead as a…bought the…" No, those wouldn't do. If only I had the sweet lilt of Harmonia's voice, I just knew such disturbing news could be delivered and received as a bouquet.

I knocked and knocked, then called out Pearly May's name as well. Finally, Pearly May answered. Her hair was a fright, and without her eye patch I discovered there was a silver button sewn in the spot where an eyeball would feel at home. I collapsed into Pearly May's arms before I had the chance to hand her the bouquet. Like I said before, Pearly May was no ordinary apple, unless you consider the apple of God's eye ordinary.

"Take me to him, B. Thankful."

Pearly May took me by the hand, and we crossed the street to where Mister's body lay. The way his body rested upon the bench, all you could see of the advertisement for the Dr. Pepper contest were the words *Lucky Winner*. Pearly May stroked Mister Tidewater's brow as I shared how quickly and effortlessly he crossed over.

"I don't doubt God granted him a graceful final exit. Tender mercies abound, B. Thankful. Tender mercies abound."

I asked Pearly May if I could serve lunch to her customers in memory of Mister Tidewater, and she thought it a grand idea. I kissed her one cheek and then the other, the way Adamma kissed me when we first met. "I'll see you in a few hours," I said.

My time with Mister walked with me down the city street to the dirt road leading to Adamma's marker where Livia waited, her feathered, brown head resting on a gardenia, the sweet scent of nectar clinging to her wings when she landed on my shoulder. Livia cooed and then took flight, but stayed her course at a speed I could follow. A good ways down the road, I found myself near a stream where I laid down along the bank, stargazing and listening to the sounds around me. Mister's words, like diamonds and rubies flickering in the moonlight, made their way downstream, bending the reeds and sliding along the curve of my ear.

"Thank you for finding me."

M-y-p-l-e-a-s-u-r-e-M-i-s-t-e-r-T-i-d-e-w-a-t-e-r. M-y-p-l-e-a-s-u-r-e.

I skipped my bedtime altogether and met Pearly May before the sun came up. Recalling everything Adamma taught me, I made another hefty batch of her shrimp gumbo to add to the first. By lunchtime, the gumbo's fiery aroma had folks lined up clear around the block.

"Good lord, I've never seen this many people, B. Thankful. Do you think we can feed them all?"

I had my doubts at the start, but as the line of folks made their way through the door, I never reached the bottom of the gumbo pot, and the rice had a mind of its own, pearly bits peeking up at Esther Chudruddy whenever she lifted the lid. Lunch at Pearly May's Kitchen that day was like the miracle of the loaves and fishes—the gumbo and rice just kept multiplying.

The last customer I served was the gentleman I brought to task the night before. He lifted his tray and inhaled the fiery goodness of the gumbo. After his first bite, he shared his tarnished grin with me. "Maybe you not white after all."

Pearly May's Kitchen was packed with folks taking delight in Adamma's shrimp gumbo as stories of Mister Tidewater's healing powers made their way around the room. After lunch, they danced to the same Cajun music Adamma used to cast her spell on her man. Hearts were lifted and, though no longer present, the celebration of Mister Tidewater's life healed many folks that day. I have the Polaroid pictures to prove it. My favorite is the one of me with Pearly May, who, prankster that I didn't take her for, held up two fingers behind my head when Esther snapped the picture.

Exhausted and near to falling asleep, I sat down next to Pearly May and rested my head on her generous shoulder. I woke up sometime late in the night and found myself lying across Pearly May's soft lap, her arms cradling me as if I were a babe. The back and forth melody of her porch swing rocked me from here to there, here to there. Wrapped in the safety of her motherly embrace, I asked a question that since seeing *Funny Girl* had been circling my mind like a buzzard looking for leftovers.

"Pearly May, what did Mrs. Strakosh mean when she sang about a girl's incidentals? Are my incidentals bigger than two lentils?"

Pearly May's amusement bounced up and down, the porch swing groaning. "B. Thankful, your incidentals are perfect in size." She squeezed me tight. "You are a treasure, B. Thankful; a true treasure. Now go back to sleep, darlin'."

We buried Mister Tidewater on a Thursday morning, and what a heavenly day it turned out to be. Friendly clouds drifted across the sky as folks gathered at the cemetery, and though their season had come to pass, the flowers still shouted their names for all to hear, especially the Petunias.

Above, on a string of telephone wires, fat, round black-birds lined up like the whole notes across Little G's sheet music. They fluttered and traded places, held for a moment, and then winged their way up and down the wires as if they, too, were singing a loved one home that had fallen from the nest.

When the time came to lower Mister Tidewater into his grave, there was an awkward silence, something of import gone missing. Unsure of my place, I started out in a small voice.

"Hey, good lookin'..." A long, uncomfortable silence settled in at the foot of Mister's grave until Pearly May picked up where I left off, singing about a brand new recipe. Pretty soon everyone joined in with Pearly May. Eyes to Heaven, I listened to folks sing Mister back to his beginning, each adding their own flavor to the simmering musical pot. Some were still humming as they made their way out of the cemetery, arms around shoulders that hadn't been touched in a long while, eyes looking up rather than down and out.

With Mister laid to rest (by the way, the doctor said quick as his passing was, it was probably an aneurism that took Mister Tidewater), I was hoping to stay a spell, but it wasn't more than a few hours after we got back to Pearly May's Kitchen when I heard a call from far away.

Pearly May single-eyed me up close. "Is someone calling on you?"

"I believe so, Pearly May. I wish I could stay on and help you out, but my road trip for Jesus seems to have its own time schedule."

"Now, we're not going to say goodbye because I'm going to see you again. I've seen us walking down by a river, and when I see something with my eye of hope, it always comes to pass. I look forward to that day, B. Thankful."

Pearly May gathered me up in a featherbed embrace, and I savored her warmth the way I took pleasure in the last bite of a Banner Bar. When I finally pulled away, I saw her hopeful tears glistening on her cheek. It was then that it seemed to me my time with folks was a bit like dying—one minute I was there, the next, a memory. And hindsight being what it is, I got to thinking. When Little G and my Daddy died, a piece of me went with them. That same feeling came over me when Bobby Lee caught his train ride to the hereafter, and again when Mister took a seat on that final bus to home. How many more pieces of me could I do without before I, too, was all gone? I turned my hand over to see if I was becoming less, and my palm still bore the wound from the broken latch on the cemetery fence I tore down. If I was becoming less in one way, my wound told me I was becoming more in another. Maybe that's what dying is all about: becoming less to become more.

I posted the picture of Pearly May and me next to the Sons of Satan, kissed the tips of my fingers and touched the photo of me with my Daddy and Little G, and wagged my finger at a stern Big G looking back at me. I ran my hand along the edges of the picture of Winthrow and Nadine (who had brown hair that day), and took delight seeing the folks I met at the campground smiling back at me. How I wished I had a picture of Pride and Harmonia. Memories swept me up and away, and selfish though it may seem, I wanted them all with me, the gift of each by my side as I made my way deeper into the unknown world that lay before me.

Before leaving, I stopped to say goodbye to Mister and his Missus. When first I met Adamma, I figured the only thing we had in common was the way people looked upon us—like take away signs in arithmetic. But standing where they rested, I understood that together, nobody could keep us from adding up to something wonderful.

A cool breeze carrying the news of summer's passing and autumn's arrival, brushed my skin. An old bit of who I had been until then fell by the wayside, and a new bit of who I was becoming came to life.

Fourteen

Miss Hannah

elcome to the Land of Enchantment the sign read as I left the finger pointing end of Oklahoma and crossed the border. The farther I drove the back roads into New Mexico, the more the earth lifted up and the sky lowered, the closeness of the suntanned soil to the white puffy clouds above making me feel like the chocolate sandwiched between the graham crackers and marshmallows in one of Nadine's s'mores. But like the day after Little G and Daddy died, once again, life tricked me into thinking one thing, and then laid out a whole other story.

I was driving down the road listening to a song about a magic carpet ride, when, without a friendly word of warning, those big puffy marshmallow clouds rolling over the Land of Enchantment turned to black fists of twisted anger, and shot across the collapsed blue sky fast as a bullet from Little G's shotgun. Silver bolts of lightning split the air and stunned the tiny hairs on the back of my neck. Thunder hammered the sky. Wild and hungry for prey, the wind came howling down the road so fast and furious I didn't have time to pick and choose what needed to be done. From out of nowhere, that wind took aim and thrashed Pride's arvee with so much rage it flew backwards, spinning round and round, all my keepsakes, along with my paint-by-number picture of the Last Supper, flying around the arvee in slow motion, like pieces of a shattered dream. The kind of dream that leaves your pillow sweaty wet.

A burst brighter than the flash bulb on my Polaroid camera opened the sky, a violent downpour of rain and hail let loose by the thunderstorm. The parched ground, unable to drink up the rain that wouldn't take no for an answer, turned thick and swept across the road where a sign told me the town of Truth or Consequences lay just out of reach.

I held tight to the steering wheel as the arvee slid from the road into the mud slick land. Same as the predawn hour of the worst day of my life, the day I made my way to Harmonia's and fell into nothingness at her front porch, everything went dark when a wild punch to the side of Pride's arvee sent a jar of spiced peaches flying from the cupboard, hitting me above my right eye.

I don't know how much time passed before I came to, but the moon was staring me in the eye. I stared back with one eye, the other swollen shut. So this is how Pearly May saw the moon. I raised my muddied hand as best I could and moved the moon across the sky, a trail of stars following behind, but the moon and stars fell from the sky when darkness came to call again.

A small bite of light broke through the darkness. The opening grew larger and larger, the light expanding. I ran along the parched land through the opening, where I was greeted by a field of flowers so bright and unusual I couldn't even begin to guess what their paint-by-number calling would be.

Across the field, an umbrella of silver and gold cloth shaded a table where my Gs, my Daddy, Bobby Lee, Annabelle, and Mister and Adamma were sharing a picnic with Jesus. Daddy was wearing a summer sky smile and Little G appeared happy as a ripe peach. And no wonder, for when the lady with her back to me turned around, I saw it was Momma sitting between them, her head resting on my Daddy's shoulder. Bobby Lee sat right next to Jesus, and they were talking and laughing as if never a day in his life did Bobby Lee have a care. Adamma sat next to Annabelle with her arm around her shoulder in this most caring way, and Mister was chatting with Big G like there was no to-morrow. Maybe when you die, there is no tomorrow, just one long picnic perfect kind of day.

Livia flew over the meadow and rested on Jesus's shoulder. "I'm here, Livia!" I called. When Livia paid me no mind, I called out to the rest. "Over here, Daddy. Little G, it's me. Can't you hear me? Mister Jesus, remember me? I'm B. Thankful Childe-Lucknow. I'm being brave as brave can be out here on my own, but I'm broken down on the side of the road and I need help. Won't you come help me?" I took a running step forward and slammed into an unseeable wall. I knocked on the glass so hard, I was certain it would crack.

"I'm here! I'm here!" I cried, my fists pounding the air.

"Tere, tere, little vone." Her voice was warm as toast—crisp around the edges with a buttery soft center that left its moist mark on my heart.

A bright light overhead pained my eyes when I opened them; my head, heavy and thick, tried to make sense of words tucked inside a box, the lid opening and closing, cutting them in bits before they had their full say.

"Is...thi...pla...Hea...ven?"

"No, tis is not Heaven," the warm as toast voice said.

If I was dead and I wasn't in Heaven, there was only one other place I could be and, believe me, a thousand chapters telling the story of my misdeeds ran through my aching brain.

"Am...I...in h-e-l-l?" Out of habit, my thumb tapped along.

"No, sveet angel, you are in te hospital in Trut or Conseqvences. Ve had an accident, but you are safe now."

"What about Pride's arvee?" Pain blazed through my right eye when I lifted my head.

A hand stoked with kindness rested on my shoulder; the other caressed my face with a cool cloth. "It is fine, just fine." I traced the numbers on her arm with my good eye, but the darkness came to call again, as did the days and nights where I stayed wrapped in a soundless slumber until Jesus walked in through the darkness.

Jesus wore a long white coat over his everyday Jesus clothes. He pulled up a chair and sat next to my bed. "Hello, B. Thankful."

My feelings had been stepped on when Jesus didn't call back to me when I hollered out I was broken down by the side of the road, and I was hurt that he took his sweet time before leaving that fancy picnic to come see how I was doing, especially after all I had done for him. His overlooking my generosity made me want to call a halt to this last supper, road trip business.

"You always have a choice, B. Thankful."

I should have known to tether my thinking around Jesus. Still, their picnic looked so perfect and everyone so joyous, I couldn't let go of it and stayed firm to my uppity way when Jesus asked how I was feeling.

"I'm fine," I said, the way you do when you feel you have been wronged by someone.

Generous as a summer day is long, Jesus overlooked my rudeness and ran his hand over my forehead. All the love he carried in his hands filled me up and I just couldn't stay mad.

"I'm sorry, Mister Jesus. I was so scared there wasn't anyone to come help me out."

"You must learn to see angels in the eyes of others, B. Thankful. You don't think I do all of this on my own, do you?"

Well, as a matter of fact, I heard tell he did, but I didn't mention it to Jesus; thought it best to chew on the idea of what he said for awhile.

Jesus was nowhere to be found the bright morning I came all the way back from standing at the drop edge of yonder to find myself lying in a strange room. Like a rabbit on the run from Little G, my heart went wild when I found bars on either side of the bed, penning me in. *Don't panic. Stay calm. Be fearless.* Trying to calm myself went from tip-to-toe haywire when I discovered a bag hanging from a pole next to the bed, and followed the line down to a needle stuck in my arm! *Do something!*

Just as I was about to pull on the line and make a run for it, the door to the room swung open and in walked a man dressed all in white with *Dr. R. Juarez* stitched over a pocket that held a shiny black pen. If Nadine were to tell you about him, she would say he was one gorgeous hunk of man, and then she'd warn you not to tell Winthrow because he'd go jealous berserk. Even with a banged up eye, leaving me with only one to make a judgment call, I would have agreed with Nadine. Like all the walnut colored folks I met along the blue line highways of New Mexico, *Dr. R. Juarez* was quick to share a smile, and I had never seen such perfect teeth, except the four on Big G's upper bridge, which, if rightly remembered, was sitting in a shoe polish tin in Little G's top dresser drawer. As I said before, my family lived by an accepted wisdom of *Waste not, want not*, and, no doubt, Little G was in that very frame of mind when she buried Big G without her upper bridge. I never noticed it missing when Big G came a calling to help me with the jellied pig's feet. I mention that because, when alive, if she forgot to put her bridge in, or if Little G was feeling ornery and hid it, Big G had a lisp that tickled Little G to no end. And now that my Gs are residing on the other side of the Pearly Gates, I can admit that one day when they went hunting and Big G left her teeth behind, boredom got the best of me and I took a crack at putting her bridge in my mouth. Turned out that was a flawed idea. When I couldn't get Big G's bridge to budge, I panicked and wedged a butter knife between her false teeth and my own, gave a twist, and out it flew. From then on, Big G was bewildered as to why her bridge never fit quite right. "Well, welcome back, B. Thankful. I'm Dr. Juarez."

The oh so handsome doctor took my hand in his, held onto my wrist, and looked at his watch. *Tick. Tick. Tick.* He smiled. *Sparkle. Sparkle. Sparkle.* He shined a light in my eyes, my right one still sensitive to the brightness. With a touch so gentle it came with only a hint of pain, *Dr. R. Juarez* removed the stitches above my eyebrow, and once he pulled the needle out of my arm—which hurt worse than a pinch under the arm from Little G—my sense of freedom came back to me.

"You've been in and out of consciousness, but you're fine now. You may be a little weak when you get out of bed, so be careful. I'll send someone in shortly with a food tray for you." *Dr. R. Juarez* patted my shoulder and went to the other side of the curtain, which split my room in two.

"Emma, I need to talk to you in my office." Although I couldn't see the doctor, I could tell by the sound of his voice, there was no sparkle.

"I vill be right back," I heard her say. "I'm going to talk to te doctor."

Not wanting *Dr. R. Juarez,* or the nice lady, to know I had been listening in, I closed my eyes and pretended to be asleep when they walked by my bed and out the door. When it was safe, I stretched my neck to see what I could see on the other side of the curtain. On a bedside table sat a record player in a zippered case, records by its side, and a small black velvet box, just the right size to hold one special keepsake. But it was the picture, time worn around the edges, of a tall, kind looking woman with a fire burning in her eyes, and two same-as-same little girls standing in front of her, that called to me.

Even my dire medical condition couldn't keep my need to know from climbing out of bed and taking a look see at who was lying in the bed next to me. *Dr. R. Juarez* was right—so weak from being bedridden, not to mention the wallop my forehead took from that jar of flying peaches, my legs went newborn calf wobbly on me and I had to grab on to the side rail of her bed. I took a second look, then a third, and, just in case my eyes were playing tricks on me, blinked hard to make sure I was seeing proper. If I held a mirror up to myself, the face looking back at me wouldn't be any more exact than the sleeping lady was to Miss Emma. Her outstretched arm lay atop the covers, and I saw she had a number written in the same spot Miss Emma did. As stumped as I was by those numbers, I was more curious whether or not she was Miss Emma's twin. The only thing I knew about twins was the double yolk kind, which Little G considered good luck.

Looking near to gone, it appeared Miss Emma's looka-like had run out of luck; so, like that day down by the river, I prayed that there was magic waiting in the wings.

My very favorite butterfly is the Great Spangled Fritillary for its striking markings and because I so like the sound of the word Fritillary and the way my nose wrinkles up when I say it. When I was a little girl, and didn't know any better, I caught a Great Spangled Fritillary butterfly and placed Penny (that's what I named her) in a jar. I put clover in the bottom of the jar for Penny's bed and punched holes in the lid so she could breathe. Until that day, the only thing I ever kept in a jar was my Daddy's voice. Daddy would put his mouth to the jar and say, "I love B. Thankful Childe-Lucknow," over and over until he could say no more; then, quick as a wink, I'd cap his love for me inside. On those empty days when my Daddy was gone a great dis-tance, I would unscrew the lid, hold the jar near to my ear, and listen to my Daddy's love brush up against the curve of my ear until he came back to me. Like my Daddy's voice, I wanted to keep Penny close by so I had a friend to tell my secrets when the house went dark and quiet. That night, I put Penny's jar on the pine table next to my bed, and we watched the fireflies line the trees outside and imitate the stars with their winking way.

Next morning, I found Penny lying lifeless at the bot-tom of her jar. Crying, I ran to Little G and showed her my tragedy. Up until then, and for good reason, Little G had no idea what I had done. Little G never looked up from basting her fried eggs, her voice hard as an overcooked yolk.

"It's a crime to hold something down from its natural state, B. Thankful. It's wrong. Just wrong. How would you like it if someone thought they owned you and kept you in a jar? Now, go bury that butterfly and think about what I said."

You didn't have to boil the fat off Little G's words to get to the meat of her opinion. Wasn't it bad enough I killed Penny?

I grabbed the shovel from the barn and headed down to Daddy's favorite spot along the river, where magic filled the air. In Daddy's spot, the old saying *wishing doesn't make it so* sank to the bottom of the river and anything was possible. Maybe it was already written somewhere as so, but I'd like to think my wishing for it had a part in what took place. Not that it would mean I was more special for the giving, but because it would mean there really was someone out there listening. That would be the best magic of all.

I dug a hole and did as Little G told me to do—I let the thought of being held down when you were meant to fly push hard on me, and I felt the same hurt that tore me open when people made fun of me for my eyes, my hair, or the cloth I was cut from. If Little G was right (and I'd be the last to tell her she wasn't, unless I was walking away and talking under my breath) then maybe even butterflies were cut from the same cloth as people. If that was true, my hurting Penny was the same as hurting Daddy or my Gs, a realization as painful as the bite of a meat bee.

I let my apology spin with the threads of the lid as I opened the jar. When I reached in to take Penny from her wilted clover bed, she startled me when her frail wings began to flutter ever so slightly. I held Penny in my hand and whispered words of encouragement, told her she could fly away and spend her days flitting from flower to flower, but Penny couldn't fly away. It was all Penny could do to breathe in and out, in and out. I placed Penny on a Black Eyed Susan, the most joyful flower along the river, and sat down a short distance away. From the corner of my eye, I caught sight of another Great Spangled Fritillary. She flew up to the Black Eyed Susan and rested right next to Penny, her perfect wing brushing up against her frail friend. It's okay if you don't believe what happened next. I might not either had I not witnessed it. With true grit, the Great Spangled Fritillary worked her way under Penny until Penny was settled on her back. As they raised up some, then fell back, raised up, fell back, I tossed my wish up to Heaven.

"You can do it! You can do it!" I cheered. At long last, the magic settled onto the wings of Penny's friend and together they flew from the flower. *Small. Smaller. Gone.*

I don't know how long Penny lived, but I do know there was another willing to carry Penny to a better life. That's what Miss Emma's lookalike reminded me of–a tattered Great Spangled Fritillary who needed help to fly away.

A time marker floated above her bed with what appeared to be a shadow of the same by its side. When I saw more than one time marker, I blinked my eyes to be sure, but my wounded right eye was tuckered out and went blurry. And then, as suddenly as that thunderstorm split the sky, her eyes flew open. Through a veil, from some place far, far away, she looked at me with the same look my Daddy had in his final moment–with eyes cast to a future I wasn't ready to catch sight of. Miraculous as that was, the surprise of her eyelids flipping up muddled my wits and sent me shuffling back to my bed.

"Hannah," was all I heard in the curve of my ear, but after so much silence, it was a welcome start.

I climbed into my bed and, rendered childlike, pulled the sheets over me; sheets absent the scent of Little G's hands, hands she always rubbed with lavender before tucking my pillows in their cases so I'd have sweet dreams. In that way, Little G always confounded me—so tough in her everydayness, so soft when no one was looking.

I-s-o-m-i-s-s-y-o-u-L-i-t-t-l-e-G, I tapped on the scratchy sheets.

Rain tapped against the window. *Let me in. Let me in.* The day I met Livia, she tapped against Daddy's window in the same *let me in* way. Where was Livia? Did seeing Livia with Jesus in my dream mean the storm killed her? That sorrowful possibility broke me wide open. I was still mopping up my tears when Miss Emma came back into the room with the perfect doctor by her side. Miss Emma disappeared behind the curtain while *Dr. R. Juarez* approached my bed.

"You're going to be able to go home in a couple of days, B. Thankful. Who should we contact to come pick you up?"

I told *Dr. R. Juarez* the to-the-point story: dead Daddy, Little G the same, how I was an orphan. I did my best to clear the worry lined up on the good doctor's forehead by telling him I had Pride and Harmonia waiting for me at home. No, we didn't have a phone, but I'd be fine given a little time to rest up, and I could do that on the side of the road in Pride's arvee. I didn't tell him about my road trip for Jesus 'cuz that would have just opened up a can of worms not worth fishing with. The other truth I couldn't share with *Dr. R. Juarez* was that until Miss Hannah was set free one last time, I'd be staying put.

From the other side of the curtain I heard Miss Emma speaking to Miss Hannah. Although her words were foreign to me, I knew Miss Hannah found comfort there, for like the cicadas, we recognize the song of our loved ones even when we're far, far away.

It wasn't but a few minutes later, a nice young lady wearing a striped pink and white bib dress, white fold over socks, and pink tennis shoes walked into the room. A river bed of freckles running across her cheeks and disappearing into her short, brown hair bobbed up and down as she chewed a wad of gum. From my side of her thick glasses, her eyes were so large she looked surprised, or like someone with one heck of an idea. Looking even closer, I saw there was a certain just-around-the-corner wisdom shining off her.

"I'm Dee Corum," she said, then laughed as if her name was a hoot. The jokey part of my brain must have been bruised in the accident, because I didn't get the funny side of her name.

Miss Dee blew a pink bubble the size of a ripe tomato and snapped it back. Pop! With a push of a button, she raised my bed up, straightened my blankets, fluffed my pillows, and then, as if I were a child, she tucked a napkin under my chin. With fingernails painted as pink as her gum and lightning quick talk that held no quiet spaces where a breath would fit right in, Miss Dee introduced me to my lunch.

"Okay right here you've got your tuna salad on toast and a carton of milk with a bendy straw in case you're too weak to hold your head up for very long Say howdy to this nice lime Jell-O I'll be back later to pick up your tray."

On her way out, Miss Dee made a sudden stop and showed the same keen awareness I used in the woods when I saw the brush had been tamped down, the path disturbed by intruders. She gave the room the once over from corner to corner until she found the grievance.

"Who turned off the TV Why it's time for General Hospital Perfect TV watching with your lunch Don't you just love Dr. Steve Hardy and poor Nurse Jessie Brewer Her May-December marriage to Dr. Phil Brewer is never gonna work out."

Before I had a chance to tell her I'd never seen television, Miss Dee turned on a teevee sitting up high on the wall. Next thing I knew she was scooting me over and lying in my bed, her mouth in slack jaw awe of Dr. Steve Hardy (who was nowhere near as fine looking as *Dr. R. Juarez*). So wrapped up in her in teevee world, Miss Dee's mind went missing, for she tucked her gum under the edge of my food tray and helped herself to my lunch. She started with the lime Jell-O and had just struck up a friendship with my tuna salad on toast when the television screen went blank for a few blinks.

"Commercial," Miss Dee said, a patch of tuna salad stuck in the corner of her mouth.

Just about the time Miss Dee was suckin' down the last of my milk, I caught a glimpse of Miss Emma and told Dee Corum a little white lie—one that spoke of feeling tired and not very hungry after all.

"Okay you rest up I'll be back later to take you for a walk so you can get your strength back." Miss Dee left with a full stomach and my empty lunch tray.

I was pleased when Miss Emma turned off the television and pulled back the curtain that hid Miss Hannah from my view. It made me feel welcomed.

"Hello, Miss Emma. My name is B. Thankful Childe-Lucknow."

I extended my hand in friendship and, unlike the gentleman on the street who stared me down, Miss Emma accepted my offering. Because she didn't shake my hand crazy up and down like some folks do, I noticed right off two of Miss Emma's fingers were missing on her left hand—the pointy one Little G used when she dressed me down for one of my come apart ideas, and the finger Little G told me would find a resting place in her garden if she ever saw it standing up alone and pointed in her direction, though she never said why. Eager as I was to learn how Miss Emma lost her fingers, even I knew it was too soon to ask such a forward question; timing was all off, too, for when Miss Hannah gave up a pale moan, Miss Emma turned all her attention to her sister. I followed Miss Emma back to Miss Hannah's bedside, where she spoke to her with words born in a far off land.

Just because I didn't ask about her fingers, didn't mean I was sharp-witted enough to hold back on my other questions.

"Miss Emma, is Miss Hannah your twin? Did your momma put those numbers on you to tell one apart from the other? Where are you from? I love the sound of your words—crispy around the edges, but buttery in the center, like toast. Do you have toast where you come from? What do you talk to Miss Hannah about during the night? What's wrong with her? Why does she open her eyes? How do you feed—" Before I could finish my most important question of all, Little G grabbed me by my breath and gave a twist. O-u-c-h!

"You know my Hannah?"

Uh-oh. Miss Emma seemed so kind, I hated to fib, but I wasn't sure how much to share about Miss Hannah's time marker, so fib I did.

"Uh, I saw her name on her chart. I apologize for peeking."

I touched my forehead and put on a show of lightheadedness to buy a little time while I sent up an urgent request for Jesus to please keep me from becoming a fulltime liar. No need for Jesus to take time out of his busy day, for Miss Emma's potent gaze alone backed me into a truth telling corner. I had all the words in place, but all my practice in how to deliver sorrowful news in the way of Harmonia Pennywhistle stayed wedged in the corner.

"Miss Emma, Jesus sent me here to prepare Miss Hannah's last supper." My delivery sounded as indifferent as rain on a picnic.

It was obvious by the stunned look on Miss Emma's face some kind of good manners schooling to help a body do this part of the job would have been a fine idea. (Right then and there, I took it upon myself to start a notebook with important information. First item: *How to Maintain Good Manners While Delivering What Could Be Considered Really Bad News*.) Miss Emma held me to a standstill with the same fire in her eyes I saw in the picture of her momma. I hadn't been considered with such interest since my first meeting with Harmonia; so much so, my bum eye turned as agitated as our old washer when the load went lopsided. Fearful Miss Emma would send me back to my side of the room and draw the curtain, I made fast with a request for forgiveness.

"I'm sorry I fibbed about peeking at Miss Hannah's chart, and I should have told you the truth about Jesus sending me to fix Miss Hannah's last supper from the very start. And I'm sorry, too, for asking so many questions. I tend to become a bit overenthusiastic with my curiosity. Please believe I meant no harm, Miss Emma."

Miss Emma walked over to the phonograph sitting in the corner of the room, took the record out of its paper holder, and placed it on the phonograph. Very carefully, she set the arm down on the record, and the fury of the rainstorm found its way inside. Miss Emma led me to the side of Miss Hannah's bed and, as if nothing was amiss, introduced us.

"Hannah, tis is our new friend, B. Tankful. It vas her car ve hit in te storm. B. Tankful, tis is my Hannah." Miss Emma called me friend, and I liked the fit of the word.

"The pleasure is mine, Miss Hannah." Taking Miss Hannah's hand in my own, I recognized the coolness of her skin placed her somewhere between here and Heaven. She was also missing the very same fingers as Miss Emma, but on her right hand. Painful as it was, I kept my questions tucked inside my cheek, saving them for another time.

"You vant to know vhat I say to Hannah in te dark hours?"

"Oh, yes."

"Tonight, you vill come sit vit us."

Just as things were getting good, Dee Corum's gum popping pushed its way through the door. "Time for your walk," Dee said.

Since I had already cut off one too many slices of lying pie in a single morning, I made no more excuses and went with Miss Dee. We weren't but a stone's throw from my room when a complete stranger called out, "Woo-hoo, girly! That's what I'm talkin' about!"

Dee Corum looked behind me and pulled the back of my gown closed and tied it up so my hind end wasn't peeking out. "Shame on you Harlan Nutbush!" she scolded, then to me behind her hand, "Harlan Nutbush is a dirty old man with a hernia problem Pay him no mind B. Thankful and I'm sorry I didn't notice your derriere was exposed before we left the room." The farther down the hall we walked, the more dairyairs I saw peeking out of loose nightgowns. I minded my own and said nothing until Miss Dee pointed out a backside so furry you'd a thought he sat on a nest of squirrels. I tried not to laugh because it pained my eye, but I failed miserably.

There was a break in the drumming of rain and Dee Corum led me outside to a stunted patch of sunlight. "I really need a smoke You don't mind do you?" Little G told me if she ever caught me smoking a cigarette, her broom would come into contact with my behind; said those tobacco people were as bad as the coal mining bastards.

Without my getting nosey and asking a hail storm of questions, Dee Corum...Dee Corum. It was right then the jokey part of my brain woke up and I got the humor behind her name, but I didn't get to share my eye-opener, for Miss Dee was on a newsworthy mission, a mission with no time for stillness between her words, and so important, she didn't draw a room-for-me-to-say-something breath until it was all delivered.

"Did you know Emma and Hannah were traveling across the good old US of A on their way to San Francisco when they slammed into your RV Of course you don't you've been down for the count They were going to a reunion for some of the Holocaust survivors they saved I don't know all the details but one of the nurses told me on the hush-hush that Hannah and Emma were part of the German Resistance I really don't know anything about that organization I know a little bit about the Shriners 'cuz they put on the circus every year in the fall and I personally belong to the Candy Stripers a volunteer organization working in hospitals You know passing out magazines fluffing up pillows serving lunch just shedding a little joy in a person's life in case they die My specialty is TV watching with the patients They seem to like it Anyway whenever those Nazi fellas came around hunting for Jewish folks Hannah and Emma would play piano for them You know to throw them off track and then one day they got caught hiding their Jewish friends under the house To punish them the Nazis cut off some of their fingers and then hauled them to Ravensbruck One of those concentration camps."

Miss Dee snapped and yapped at such a high speed, my brain caught fire from the tragedy of it all and I fainted.

It was a sweltering summer afternoon, and I was about midway through Volume H of my encyclopedia lesson when I came across the word *Holocaust*. When Little G found me crying at the kitchen table, unable to partake of the fresh strawberry ice cream in front of me, she turned the pages and had me read about Winslow Homer instead. The painting next to Winslow Homer's name held two boys sitting in a green pasture under a white cloud sky. Little G had no answer to give when I asked how the world could have been so designed that dreadfulness and beauty were only several pages apart, so she set free from my lessons. I ran down to the river and stood with the wildflowers, looked upon the creatures roaming the low brush, those who flew above me. I dove into the river and floated on my back in its cool palm. Winslow Homer's painting filled the sky, those two boys sitting side-by-side.

Lying with my head on the sidewalk in that peaceful place, faraway from a world on fire, I pretended those Nazis saw Winslow Homer's painting of those two friends and understood its meaning; pretended Miss Emma's and Miss Hannah's suffering never happened, the same way I made believe hatred would never again find its way down our road, and never again would my Daddy have to hide under the floorboards; pretended, as always, that when I went down by the river my momma was lying at the water's edge, sun shining on her face, calling out my name to come lie down next to her, just the two of us soaking up happiness bit by bit, our giggles skimming the surface of the river until they fell to the bottom where they would multiply, and one day rise up to greet a passerby.

The hard concrete pushed against my cheek. As I raised my head, an old bit of who I had been stayed stuck to the pavement, and a new bit of who I was becoming lifted me up.

Once Dee Corum propped me back up on the bench, I recognized she had never stopped talking. "...so anyhow Emma and Hannah sort of have their own language They used it to escape from those Nazis right before they were to I can't say it B Thankful it's just too awful Poor Hannah got really sick the day they were gonna sneak away I don't know all the details but that same nurse told me Emma carried Hannah on her back for miles and miles hiding out for weeks and nearly starving to death until America or Russia or somebody came in and busted up the Nazis But here's the very best part of their story Those two women didn't let missing a couple of fingers stop them from playing piano No sir they just sit side by side and Emma plays with her right hand while Hannah plays with her left Well until Hannah went topsy-turvy And now here's the really weird part of the story Those Nazis used to say..." At this very spot, Miss Dee's voice turned as sharp as peanut brittle points. "'Tell us te truth or tere vill be conseqvences!'" Then she returned to her good-natured self. "And where did Hannah go topsy-turvy?" Miss Dee was on the answer before the dot under the question mark was dry. "Why right outside Truth or Consequences when the storm slammed their car into your RV Downright eerie isn't it B Thankful?"

Dee Corum grabbed her first gulp of air since starting her story, took the last draw on her cigarette, and then stubbed it out with her pink tennis shoe. She remained as quiet as she'd been talkative while she cleaned her glasses with the edge of her Candy Striper skirt.

"What do you mean by topsy-turvy, Miss Dee?"

"Right in the middle of the storm Hannah had a really bad stroke while she was driving It's kind of like she's already dead but her brain just hasn't read the mail It's a wonder she's still breathing."

Since I only had my small slice of life to compare with such goings on, I put my question to Miss Dee the only way I knew how. "You mean like when my Little G would take her ax to one of our chickens, its surprised head hanging from her hand, and even though truly dead, its body still ran around the yard as if nothing out of the ordinary had just taken place?"

Dee Corum popped a big pink bubble. "Exactly."

Seeing we were outside, I asked if I might take a look at Pride's arvee. There was a good sized dent in the side, but according to Miss Dee it was still drivable. Inside, every-thing was jumbled up and one of the cupboard doors was torn off its hinges. I gathered up my favorite belongings, grabbed a few jars of canned goods, and a Banner Bar to take back to my room. There were no telltale signs that Livia had been there, and her absence tugged hard on me. I tied a lavender ribbon to the antenna and then knelt down right there in the parking lot, black pebbles pushing into my knees, and prayed for her to come back to me.

By the time I made it back to my room, I was dog-tired. I placed my pictures and painting on the table next to my bed and hung my dream catcher on the side. When I put everything else in the drawer, I found my eagle neck-lace and Adamma's gold heart, and placed them around my neck where they belonged.

Once settled into bed, I fell, without pause, into a sound sleep and didn't rouse again until hours later when my dinner, which didn't look any friendlier than lunch, was delivered. I pushed the mushy carrots from side-to-side and cast my taste buds back to Little G's just plucked carrots and how she would bring them to tenderness in a bit of brown butter. In the middle of a pleasure filled sigh, Miss Emma pulled me back with an invite to come join them.

Miss Emma's long white hair was pulled back and braided, her gray eyes not as fiery in the dimly lit room. She wore a crisp white shirt, the cuffs held together by sil-ver buttons, and black pants, full in the leg, hung from her waist with such familiarity there was no doubt they were made just for her. Her shoes appeared more of a slipper and were as shiny as a crow's feather.

Underdressed in my gray hospital gown, I stood up straight as could be and made right sure my gown was tied up secure in the back so as not to offend. I took to licking my palms and having a go at my hair, trying, without success, to tame it. I sat down in the chair near Miss Hannah's bed, Miss Emma taking to the edge of it, and, holding her sister's hand, rubbed Miss Hannah's fingers as if her own. Lush musical notes drifted through the room to Miss Hannah's bed, stroking her skin with their beauty, and tucking her in.

Outside the window, the telltale colors of autumn were showing off while the moon and sun talked about trading places. A low-slung cast of red over the desert set all aflame as Miss Emma lightly tapped the keys of her story. I appreciated her slow, merciful tempo, one allowing me time to ready myself for all she had to say. Miss Emma didn't speak about the terrible wrongs done to them while they were in prison; no, it seemed more important she share with me how and why the women passed on recipes, the telling still so sacred it was wrapped in hushed reverence.

"During te long, dark hours, ve vould huddle next to each oter for comfort. Names called out in te morning, but no longer answered to by day's end, vould be remembered in te darkness and tear at our hearts. To brave te loss and sorrow, and to honor our lives as vonce lived, ve vould share our much loved recipes. Ve cherished how a dish vas made and held strong to our vay vhen someone argued a little less of tis, a pinch more of tat, vould be better. Only in te dark vas it safe to disagree.

"Vorking in te kitchen, I traded food for scraps of paper and bits of pencils to write down Mutter's recipe for roasted chicken and potatoes and sewed it in te hem of my jacket. On days vhen I felt all vas lost, days vhen I believed

Hannah and I vould perish, I vould run my hand along te hem. It gave me hope."

The thought of Miss Emma's barely there pencils bearing witness to a cherished recipe on bits and pieces of paper broke me and lifted me at the same time. I asked Miss Emma if it was okay to write down the recipe, for I could think of no better testament for the hope of a tomorrow.

Miss Emma leaned into Miss Hannah and stroked her brow, wiping away any remnants of forgetfulness, and reminding her, she told me, that they were two minds with single thoughts, two hearts that lived as one.

"Remember vhen Mutter vould make te roasted chicken for our birtday, Hannah?" Miss Emma turned to me. "All year long Mutter vould save her pennies. On te morning of our birtday Mutter vould valk into town to see te butcher and buy te plumpest roasting chicken he had to offer."

"Didn't you have chickens on your farm, Miss Emma?"

"Ja, but Hannah vas a very smart little girl, vit a gentle heart. To keep te chickens safe, she named tem all, so vhenever Mutter vould tink about killing vone, Hannah vould cry 'nicht Gertrude,' or 'nicht Adeline.' Not even during te bleakest times, vhen food vas scarce, or te year Papa died and tere vere no pennies, did Mutter ever harm Hannah's chickens."

No way would my Little G have spared Gertrude or Adeline if she got really hungry for some fried chicken, but it's for sure she would have honored them by name when saying grace over their crispy thighs.

Miss Emma placed her arms around her twin, pulling her in close as close could be, the way I always imagined it would be if I had a sister to tell my stories.

"And te roasted garlic, Hannah. Do you remember how ve vould stand at te table and vatch as Mutter took her time rubbing it under te skin of te chicken?" Without taking her eyes off her twin, Miss Emma spoke to me. "Vonce te chicken vas coated vit oil and salt, it vas ready for roasting. Next to te chicken, Mutter vould place te potatoes—kleine segnungen, she called tem—small blessings."

Maybe it was all Miss Emma's mouth-watering talk about chicken (one of my Little G's favorites), for lo and behold, right in the middle of Miss Emma's story, Little G sidled up to the curve of my ear and without offering up an *Excuse me*, started talking right over Miss Emma.

"Their momma, Sophia, says whenever Emma and Hannah tried to make her roasted chicken, they always added too much salt. Pay no mind to whatever amount Emma tells you. Their momma loves them with all her heart, but says they were meant to feed the world with their music, not their cookin'. And don't fret, B. Thankful, Sophia will be with you when the time comes to prepare Hannah's last supper."

With one ear pulled in the direction of Little G doling out advice, and the other trained on Miss Emma's storytelling, I glanced at my painting of the Last Supper, looking to Jesus for help, but he was too busy breaking bread with his friends. Dangerous an act as it was, I had no other choice but to s-h-u-s-h Little G so I might hear all Miss Emma had to say.

"Mutter vould take te chicken from te oven vhen te skin vas crisp and serve us slices of te tender meat. Te skin vould crackle under our bite, te juice and fat of te bird coating our tongues. And te kleine segnungen vere crisp on te outside from te chicken fat, and soft on te inside. Vit every bite ve could feel our mutter's love." Miss Emma turned to me. "Can you really fix a roasted chicken and potatoes just like our Mutter for my Hannah?"

"Yes, ma'am. I believe I can."

But before I started, I had a question I couldn't keep tucked in my cheek any longer, and it had nothing to do with roasted chicken. The newborn bit of me that pulled me up from the sidewalk after I fainted that morning, the new bit that wanted some answers to hard questions, was about to speak its first words. I went to Miss Emma, knelt down, and took her hand into my own.

"Were you ever angry with God, Miss Emma?"

Miss Emma didn't hesitate one iota. "Oh, ja. Every day I raised up my vounded hand and called out my anger. How dare God vatch te suffering of so many innocent people and not stop it. And ten vone day, vit my fist shoved in te clouds, Mutter reached down from Heaven, opened my hand, and vhispered into my palm te vords from our childhood."

"'Gott ist nicht im Himmel,' she vould say, dismissing te sky. 'Nein. Gott ist in Ihrem Herzen,' she vould remind us as she touched our hearts.

"I pulled my fist from te sky tat day and rested my hand over my broken heart. If Mutter vas right, God vas suffering, too. Vit tat understanding came te most difficult lesson on a day I vill never forget."

Outside, the moon rose as Miss Emma's sorrow fell from the corner of her eyes. Through her tears, she looked at me straight on, and I knew whatever words were to follow would be etched in my brain for eternity.

"Ve are alvays free to choose, B. Tankful. I chose to set down te veight of my anger vit te people who tried to strip us of our dignity so I could lift up my Hannah and carry her to freedom. You see, B. Tankful, I could not carry both."

Miss Emma's words sounded kindly, but I had a bee in my bonnet and couldn't get the buzzing out of my head.

"But if God is inside all of us, wasn't God inside the men who did you such harm?"

Miss Emma's words were clear of all trappings. "Ja, but fearful of tose who vere different, tey *chose* to turn teir hearts to stone, no room for God or te light to shine in or out. Te light is everyting, B. Tankful. Tere is hope in te light."

Goodness sakes alive, Miss Emma took all the hatred heaped upon her for helping her Jewish friends and wove it into a state of grace. With the same courage my Daddy's wisdom called upon, she let go of her anger so freedom could come calling, and looked upon it all like Pearly May through her eye of hope.

Miss Hannah let out a long, thick sigh and lingered a good while before taking in her next breath.

"Oh, my Hannah, ve have been togeter all our lives, not a day apart, not even in Ravensbruck. And now…" Miss Emma slipped into silence.

I started to feel fidgety, and that always turned out bad; then I harkened back to Mister and how I promised not to bother him with my talkative way. I practiced being silent with Miss Emma and waited my turn while her good bye notes filled the room.

While I lingered on the border line of hushed and yammering, I wrote in my notebook how names and words could double-cross you into thinking there was goodness in their meaning, only to find out later how badly they tricked you. Take Ravensbrook (my spelling may be a bit off): the beginning sound of the word called up the great black bird of mystery and magic, while its tail end reminded me of the brooks meandering off on their own from the river back home. By the sound alone, I would have thought it to be a lovely place. As I wrote my piece about words tricking you, Little G came calling again and, like her momma, got right to the point. Well, tried to get right to the point, but her way of speech held as much stop and go as our old radio.

"When Emma and Hannah were children and...their words... were so full—slow down, Sophia, I'm new at this—of sorrow they leaned...into each other, their momma took a sliver.... Sliver? Sliver doesn't make any sense, Sophia. Oh, silver. She'd take a silver salt spoon from...a felt-lined box...where...she kept...great grandma's silver. Sophia dipped the spoon into the salt...placed the salt...on their tongues. 'This is life,' she said. The bitterness soured their faces...something, something...and tears would flow down their cheeks. What's that next part? Sophia, my hearing is no better up here than it was down there. Say again. Okay. Once they had fried...no, not fried...cried...once they cried all of their tears, their momma would take....a spoon and place a dollop of... money—no, not money...honey on their tongues. 'This is life,' she would say. The sweat...strike that...sweet honey made Hannah and Emma smile. 'What the tongue tastes, the heart feels,' their momma would say."

Little G's voice went so quiet I could barely hear her. *"Just between you and me, B. Thankful, this turning a word from one language into another is yanking on my brain, so don't go all berserk with a truckload of questions I don't have the answers to."*

"Excuse me, Miss Emma. I'll be right back," I said, and slipped to the other side of the curtain.

Of course I had questions for Little G. The one at the top of the list was: if Sophia doesn't speak English and your ears are as dead as you are, just how am I supposed to understand what she's saying when it comes time for us to fix Hannah's last supper? Next on the list: how will I fix a first-rate last supper for her little girl without her help? And finally: do you spell Momma in their language M-o-o-t-e-r? But in the end, I didn't ask any questions, only punched out, F-i-n-e, on the sheets. I locked my eyeballs in place to keep them from rolling around in my head at the thought of how this was going to turn out with my Little G involved.

Since it seemed landing in Heaven was no guarantee of having all the answers—and that certainly gave me pause for concern—the decision-making was in my care. Somehow, I needed to prove to Miss Emma I wasn't like those double-crossing Nazis with a no-good trick up my sleeve. I opened the drawer and pulled out one of the provisions I took from the arvee. I set the jar on Miss Hannah's swivel-around tray, unfastened the canning ring, and lifted the lid. Piecing together Little G's version of Miss Sophia's story the best I could, I placed a bit of salt from the packet on Miss Hannah's dinner tray on a spoon, and placed some of Harmonia's wild clover honey on my spoon. I tapped Miss Emma on her shoulder.

"This is life," I said, and placed the salt on her tongue. The bitterness pulled the corners of Miss Emma's mouth down, and a frown creased Miss Hannah's forehead at the very same time.

"This is life," I said, and placed a bit of Harmonia's wild clover honey on her tongue. "What the tongue tastes, the heart feels." The sweetness of the honey lifted the corners of Miss Emma's downturned mouth, and when a full-on smile crossed Miss Hannah's topsy-turvy face, I dropped the spoon to the floor.

"Vhat my tongue tastes, Hannah's tongue tastes. Vhat my heart feels, Hannah's heart feels. And so it goes from Hannah to me."

And there was the answer to the most important question of all. Miss Emma would do the actual partaking of Miss Hannah's last supper and, through her, Miss Hannah would taste every bite of her momma's eternal love. But if Miss Emma was right and she felt everything Miss Hannah did, was she feeling less than her full self, too? I was about to ask that very question, but Miss Emma had one of her own.

"But how do you know about te bitter and te sveet, B. Tankful? I do not remember sharing it vit you."

You'd a thought by then I was used to telling my story about hearing the voices of departed loved ones, and how her momma would use me to fix Miss Hannah's last supper to render a peaceful crossing, but the idea still sounded out of this world even to me. And with all the two-timing lies and spitefulness they had suffered, my feelings wouldn't have been wronged had she doubted my story. But wouldn't you know, after my tale had been told, she leaned on her hope one more time.

I covered Miss Emma with the extra blanket and placed my arm around her exhausted shoulder. With all the Momma love I could call up from that faraway, someday place and time with my name on it, I whispered, "Lay your head down, Miss Emma. I'll hold on to you through the night. Let my arms remind you there is a tomorrow, and maybe it will be forever picnic perfect." The last thing I saw before my own eyes filled with the call to sleep was my dream catcher hanging from my hospital bed.

Pride was sitting in Little G's chair on the porch, rocking slow and easy, same as Little G used to do when she was end-of-day tuckered out. It felt as natural as my own heartbeat to climb into Pride's lap, place my arms around his neck, and rest my head on his broad chest, his heartbeat welcoming me home. Before my nerve fell between the slats of the porch, I told Pride about the accident, the dent to his arvee, the jar of peaches hitting me in the head, and the out of my mind time in the hospital.

"Even in a place and time I can't name, I missed you. That's how much I love you, Pride."

I shared how I met my lookalike friends and the hardship of their lives, the shelter of Pride's embrace giving me the courage to speak out loud what had been running circles in my mind.

"Miss Emma said the people who did them wrong were fearful of those who were different and chose to turn their own hearts to stone, leaving no room for God's light to shine in or out. For the life of me, I can't figure out why they would do that, nor can I hit upon what's in their thinking I can't find in my own. I wish I could take folks with hearts of stone by the hand and lead them down to Daddy's spot along the river. In the stillness, they would hear the ancient stories running from upstream to down and they would realize we're all cut from the same cloth, realize we all come from the same place. I'm certain they'd feel the magic that allowed Penny's butterfly friend to lift her up and carry her to freedom. When you feel such powerful magic, your heart opens so wide, life can never be the same." I raised Pride's hand to my face and laid my cheek to his palm. Smoke and apples.

"On my road trip for Jesus I've heard songs about being up on the roof, under the boardwalk; I've even heard a song about people living in a yellow submarine and, for sure, that song got me mulling over the how and why, but none can compare to the piano music of my lookalike friends. The first time I heard their music, it grabbed hold of me with a firm grip. The keys at one end seemed to be angry with the keys at the other end, an argument they couldn't seem to patch up. And then, the sound of danger spread across the

black and white keys, calling to mind the threats that raged our fields, forcing Daddy to run and hide under the house.

"But tonight, oh, Pride, tonight as I sat with Miss Hannah and Miss Emma and learned about food talk, the music from the record player was filled with warm sunshine. The notes rolled over Winslow Homer's green pasture, and the white keys tapped at his blue sky, while the black keys laid my hope for understanding at my feet. As the very last note closed in on itself, all of my familiar disappeared and, just like your painting, I found myself standing in a night sky, where thousands of stars holding all the secrets of the whole wide world whisked by me, just waiting for me to grab them by their shimmering tails.

"If you wait for me, I promise to find my way back to you and share all the tokens of tenderness I've filled my pockets with here on the Good Red Road. When I think of you, I see you through forever eyes and the two of us are walking down a forever road."

I kissed Pride, then walked to the edge of my dream and called back, "Pride, are you dreaming about me at this very same moment?"

I woke and watched dawn nibble at the stars until the sky was awash in blue. My left hand still held onto Miss Emma, but my right hand was clenched, a secret held inside. I opened my hand and Pride's voice floated by.

"Yes, I am."

My dream was still circling overhead when a loud, spun out moan from Miss Hannah shook me to my core, and woke Miss Emma. *Dr. R. Juarez* raced into the room to her bedside. Miss Hannah's time marker had risen nearly all the way to the top during the night.

I tapped out an urgent message to Little G to find Sophia and come help me out, but there was no answer. Dee Corum bustled into the room with breakfast trays and a gum snapping, "Good morning all..." Before Miss Dee could continue, I quickly placed a period on the end of her sentence by grabbing hold of her arm, and leading her out of the room.

"Miss Dee, I need you to be very quiet while I tell you something. I don't have time to tell you my whole story, so you're just going to have to trust me and do what I ask."

Miss Dee was worse than me when it came to keeping the lid down on her chatter. "You mean the whole truth and nothing but the truth so help you God like the episode last week on General Hospital where that no good attorney was trying to make Dr. Steve Hardy—"

To my surprise, and Dee Corum's, I placed my hand over her mouth. More to my surprise, I went Big G post-card conversation.

"I need a plump roasting chicken, cooking oil, salt, some small blessings, I mean potatoes, and I need a place to cook." Dee Corum's oversized eyes bobbed all over the place. "It's got to be today, Miss Dee. Can you help me?"

I removed my hand from her mouth, my palm, bubble gum sticky. Miss Dee tapped her foot the same way Little G tapped hers when she waited for me to find a gone astray story I wanted to share.

Unable to find any homeless words, I asked, "What?"

"Wouldn't you like some garlic to go with Sophia's roasted chicken and kleine segnungen?" Snap! Pop!

"I completely forgot about the garlic. Wait a minute! How do you know about the garlic? Whoa! How do you know about Miss Sophia and klina klinger zignoo?"

Dee Corum smiled, her large eyes sparkling, her riverbed of freckles full of life. That just-around-the-corner wisdom shining off of her earlier made its way clear around the block, and she toyed with me.

"I don't have time to tell you my whole story so you're just going to have to trust me." Dee Corum laughed, put her arm around me, leaned her head next to mine, took one deep breath, and said, "I can get you all the food supplies you need Ham usually finishes preparing dinner around four o'clock I know he'll let you use the kitchen Ham Dibble will do anything I ask him to." Dee Corum snapped her gum and gave me a wink, the tips of her eyelashes sparkling with mischief.

Jesus told me to be on the lookout for angels, said I'd be able to recognize them by their eyes. It was for certain you couldn't overlook Miss Dee's eyes behind those thick old glasses, but would a real angel smoke cigarettes, chew gum, and carry on with a cook named Ham Dibble? I certainly did hope so.

When I walked into the room, *Dr. R. Juarez's* hand was resting on Miss Emma's shoulder, and I recognized it as the kind of touch you want to push away from for the bad news it held. A cloud of dread hovered over Miss Emma as she held her sister. What must it be like to watch yourself fade away on the other side of where you sit? I didn't share the birth bubble inside my momma with anybody, but I could well imagine if you spent all your time floating together in a warm sea of love, how easier said than done it would be to stand by your lonesome one day; and according to *Dr. R. Juarez,* that day was today.

There was still no word from Little G, so I gave it another try. U-R-G-E-N-T!

L-i-t-t-l-e-G-b-r-i-n-g-M-i-s-s-S-o-p-h-i-a-t-o-t-h-e-c-a-f-e-t-e-r-i-a-t-o-n-i-g-h-t!

When I had no luck in reaching Little G, the hand of doubt reached out and grabbed hold of me, a sudden worry claiming my whole self. In the past, I had had time to get to know the nature of the spirit who would use me to prepare their loved one's last supper. Without having the chance to become friendly with Miss Sophia, I fretted about whether or not I would be able to prepare the final taste of understanding that would lead Miss Hannah to a peaceful crossing. Without that precious time together, would I be able to give rise to the extraordinary means necessary to recreate the meal that, above all other events, crossed the hands of time from one world to another? But even had we been given the time, there was another mountain to climb. I couldn't understand Miss Sophia's language. And then the hand of doubt slapped me hard, right in the face, with a question that shook me to my core: What if you fail?

The thought I might let down my new friends so frazzled me, I took to the shower, hoping if I rubbed hard enough, I would rid myself of any old bits of worry and doubt that might be clinging to me. I scrubbed myself with soap until my skin was shiny and pink, let the hot water run over the crown of my head, and prayed it would open me to a new way of thinking. But when I finished with my shower and looked in the mirror, I saw my mop of red hair, wilder than ever, couldn't even be contained within its edges, the cut over my black and blue eye looked irritated, and I had lost so much weight since leaving home, my freshly washed pants and t-shirt hung loose on me. Add all that together and I equaled a ragged looking mess. How could I expect Miss Sophia to trust such a sight?

Just when I needed time to stand still so I could figure out the sticky situation I found myself in, it went spinning out of control. I was sure I had just caught dawn nibbling at the stars, but by the time I got back to my room, twilight was already tugging on the hem of the sun.

Careful, the way you should always come upon a nest of baby birds while their momma's out hunting worms, and you're just too curious not to look—even though you had been told a dozen times that very same day to mind your own and keep the ladder away from the nest—that's the kind of careful I drew upon as I moved to Miss Hannah's bedside. Same as the night with my Daddy and Little G, I found another hatchling about to fall from the nest. Or was she about to fly?

Miss Dee peeked into the room and gave me the *good to go* sign and I touched Miss Emma on her shoulder with as much kindheartedness as my fingertips could hold.

"Miss Emma, I'm going to go and prepare Miss Hannah's last supper now."

Miss Emma never took her eyes from her sister as she reached her hand around her back and took hold of mine. "Danke." I knew that word meant thank you in Miss Emma's language from a song I heard on the radio.

"My pleasure, Miss Emma. My pleasure."

The overhead lights in the hospital kitchen had been turned off, only a bit of light coming from under a hood over the stove. Miss Dee was true to her promise: Ham had laid out everything I needed on the work table—the only missing ingredients were Little G and Miss Sophia. I tapped out another message to Little G warning her I was running out of time. I waited and waited. No answer. Tap-tap-tap. Tick, tick, tick.

The light over the stove flickered, then went out, then came back on just as suddenly, and there stood my Little G and a lady I took to be Miss Sophia.

"We're here, B. Thankful. Sorry. We took a wrong turn back there at Santa Fe." Little G stepped back and took me in from top to bottom.

"For a while I wasn't so sure you weren't comin' up for a fulltime visit the way you kept circling the drain the last few days. I'm glad to see you're feeling better, B. Why, even with that cut over your eye, you're more beautiful than ever."

My prickly mood at their lateness fell away, and it was my turn to give Little G the once over. Her hair was as pretty as the night I prepared her body, but the grip of glue I squeezed between her lips was gone and Little G would make the most of it to give orders while visiting. I could hear her know-it-all two cents jingling in her pocket, but I didn't give her the chance to spend it. Dead or alive, to talk to my Little G from outside the edge of good behavior was risky, but I had been called upon by a higher power than Little G to prepare Miss Hannah's last supper, to recreate an eternal soul connection for her peaceful crossing, and we were both running out of time, so I called it like I saw it.

"Little G, Miss Hannah's time marker is too near the top for this back-and-forth-she-said-then-you-say business. I need Miss Sophia to take her place inside me right now, before it's too late."

Miffed by my bossiness, Little G gave me a hard *I'll show you* stare followed by her stubborn *zip of the lips, twist of the key* threat.

"Oh, now, Little G, don't make me haul you over the coals, because I will if I have to."

My Little G laughed, and, truth be told, I believe she was proud of my newfound boldness.

After Little G spoke to Miss Sophia with her same stop and go delivery of words as before, Miss Sophia moved toward me. Since I didn't own the words to put across my very best of intentions, I kept very still and my face full open so Miss Sophia could see my aim to soothe her daughter was one hundred percent pure. I opened my hands and extended my arms the way I had seen Jesus do. A welcoming motion that also says: This is who I am. I am holding no secrets from you.

Miss Sophia took my hands in hers, and though she was near in size to Big G, I didn't go through the same *too long on the watermelon vine* feeling, nor did my limbs turn *divinely feminine* as they did with Adamma. When Miss Sophia came to call inside me, the Earth climbed up through the soles of my feet, the smell of fertile soil warmed by the sun lingered inside my nose, and the sound of clothes on the line pushed back at the breeze—*slap, slap, slap.*

"Now remember…" I never did hear the end of Little G's what's what, her voice shoved aside when a sizeable wind wrapped around me and carried us through a long, dark tunnel.

Miss Sophia and I stood as one in her kitchen from a time long ago. From the window I saw unfussy blouses hanging on the clothes line, sleeves waving in the breeze at two little girls swinging from a tree as old as time. Chickens ran carefree through the yard, and their own Beautiful Beulah munched on grass wherever she pleased. Unexpected, it was, how a place from another time, and clear around the world from all I knew, could feel so like home. Miss Sophia couldn't speak my language, but by a means I had no clutch on, she took me back to the very first making of the meal that kept her little girls eternally connected to their momma.

As if we were expected, a wooden work table was covered with the necessary ingredients, and we wasted no time getting to work. The outside parchment pages of its story fell away as we rubbed a full head of garlic between my palms. Once ready, we placed the garlic in a lidded container, where its new story waited to be told. The creak of the stove door and the heat from the crackling fire licking at my face were simple and true.

While the garlic roasted, we made quick work of any stray feathers found on the plump chicken, bathed the bird in a basin of cold water to get rid of any dirt hiding between this and that, and then patted the outside and inside dry. Skillful hands slid under the skin where the breasts resided, lifting it ever so gently from the flesh.

When we opened the door to the wood stove, the scent of roasted garlic filled the room and I marveled at the small miracle—how the garlic came into the world the way it always did, raw and bold, then given a little time and attention, turned into a new version of its old self, sweeter and more yielding. The back of a spoon and years of know how turned the roasted garlic cloves into a smooth paste, and supple fingertips worked through me to rub the paste under the skin, into the flesh of the bird.

We coated the chicken with oil, and then fetched a small bowl with blue and white flowers from the cupboard. Salt was scattered over the bird and, like new fallen snow too soon in the season for the staying, it was here then gone. Potatoes, scrubbed clean and sliced one into four, were placed around the chicken resting in a cast iron pan; a pan that had served up countless meals, but none so special. We added more wood to the oven's embers, placed the chicken inside, and waited for that moment when it all reached perfection; waited for the meal that would one day be written on a scrap of paper, and sewn into the hem of a jacket in the hope of a tomorrow. Remember me, for I will remember you.

The same wind that delivered us came rushing through the front door of their humble home and carried us back through the tunnel. Little G's voice snapped me back from around the world and a time gone by.

"Boy, B. Thankful, that trip through the tunnel did a number on your hair." Little G giggled and held up a shiny frying pan. My hair stuck straight up, same way Little G's did the time I took our Electrolux vacuum to her hair while she napped.

"Seriously, how are you doing, B. Thankful?

"I'm a little dizzy. Did I faint?" The clock's hands ticked their final warning.

"Little G, Miss Sophia showed me how to fix her baby girl's last supper, but I lost so much time in the showing, I'll never have enough time for the doing. I can't let Miss Hannah down. I just can't." I was about to fall over the cliff edge of panic, when Little G raised her pointer finger to my quivering lips.

"G-child of mine, hush now. You've not failed. Look here. You fixed up a fine last supper for Miss Hannah."

Little G was right. It was all there on the cafeteria counter—a roasted chicken, its brown skin, glistening, and the garlic pairing up with the bird in a friendly way. The potatoes were just as Miss Emma described them—crisp on the outside and soft on the inside. It was such a modest meal, but bound with so much love, the retelling of its making alone saw Miss Sophia's daughters through the darkest hours of their lives.

Together, Miss Sophia and I rolled the food cart carrying Miss Hannah's last supper to her room. When we got there, the curtain was drawn around Miss Hannah's bed, and I prayed I wasn't too late. I peered around the curtain where a harvest moon cast its memorable light upon the sisters. Miss Hannah's gray hospital gown had been replaced by a full-length crimson dress, and her silver hair lay loose around her shoulders. No other prettification was necessary. Miss Emma wore her hair in the same fashion, and the exact same gown, the velvet folds swaying back and forth as she walked toward me.

Standing in the middle of such an extraordinary event, one that would never come again, an idea for a keepsake flashed before me, and when shared with Miss Emma, she agreed it was a wonderful idea.

Rushing around the curtain, for time was still ticking by, I found Miss Sophia and Little G sitting on my bed, holding hands. I opened the drawer where I stashed the provisions I took from the arvee, pulled out what I needed, and hurried back to my friends.

Miss Emma was sitting beside Miss Hannah, a loving arm around her sister. Perfect. A minute later, I held a picture of my friends wearing their lovely red gowns. Miss Hannah's eyes were closed, but sometimes that happens under the best conditions, what with the flash so surprisingly bright. I set the picture right next to the one of Miss Sophia with her two little girls.

I lifted the lid from Miss Hannah's last supper, and their momma's perfectly roasted chicken surrounded by small blessings lay before them. Certain up until that night Miss Emma's *How could this be so?* wondering had been bound in anguish, I was grateful when the *How could this be so?* look in her eyes expressed joyful amazement. In the end, the hope held in the light came to pass. The moment was without equal, and determined as I was to show my respect through silence, there was a very important question I just had to ask.

"Breast, thigh, or leg for Miss Hannah?" I saw the curtain move just a tad, my Little G wanting to get at me for asking such a dim question, but she held her place.

"Mutter alvays treated us to slices of te breast vhere te garlic had married vit te meat."

I carved several slices from the chicken, placed them neatly on a plate, and laid the potatoes by their side. Miss Hannah's topsy-turvy head turned slightly in the direction of the food. Perhaps it was a part of her vital nature (the kind of mark you're born with that rises up of its own doing—like my tenderness and enthusiasm for life). You just can't keep a feature like that down when something draws on the truest part of you.

Miss Emma sliced off a piece of the roasted chicken and raised it to her mouth. "Vhat my tongue tastes, Hannah's tongue tastes."

All their waiting was laid to rest with Miss Emma's very first bite of chicken. A bite of one of the potatoes brought a sigh, perhaps carrying with it the memory of a day long ago in a faraway land where the clothes on the line waved at the breeze, where two little girls played piano, and their momma's love was all they needed. How powerful love is. How powerful indeed.

"Oh, Hannah, isn't it vonderful? Te chicken is so tender, te garlic like butter, and te salt, just right. Ve never got te salt right. And te potatoes are exactly like Mutter's kleine segnungen."

Miss Hannah opened her eyes, and a smile crossed her face as she looked beyond Miss Emma to where her momma stood. Miss Hannah's time had come. Her time marker and its shadow cast from the light of the moon were just a few breaths from the top. Miss Emma climbed onto the bed and placed her sister in her arms, two long-stemmed crimson roses lying together. Miss Sophia lay down on the other side of Miss Hannah so her daughter was embraced by Miss Emma in the *here* and her momma in the *after*.

I was down by the river with my Daddy when Big G helped Little G to pass, and stepped away when Annabelle held her wounded child, Bobby Lee. Until that night in Truth or Consequences, New Mexico, I had never witnessed a mother and child reunion. My own momma died before I was born, and I'm not a Momma yet, but that up ahead part of me is certain it must be an honor beyond compare to welcome your little girl into this world and to hold her hand when she leaves it.

The record went round and round, velvety petals falling from the piano keys. Whispers of love born in their far off land passed from one side of Miss Hannah and then the other.

Miss Emma in the here. "Nimm mich mit." Miss Sophia in the after. "Komm zu mir, meine Tochter."

Miss Hannah took a long breath in and decided to keep it for her bridge crossing, her head falling to her momma's shoulder. Gone she was. Miss Emma reached out and placed her own goodbye in the palm of my hand.

"Vhat Hannah feels, I feel. Vhere Hannah goes, I go." Miss Emma released what was left of her sister's in-breath and crossed the bridge with her. Two time markers had been rising all along. Miss Emma would never have to spend a day apart from her beloved Hannah. Ever.

When Bobby Lee died, I called out my good luck wishes as his train carried him away with his momma. I ran alongside the bus and did the same when Mister took a seat next to his Missus. But I could only watch out the window and wave a silent goodbye as Miss Hannah and Miss Emma walked with an arm around the other's waist, could only watch as they crossed the bridge where a gathering of women welcomed them home.

When they reached the other side, they turned and waved back to me; their wounded hands, healed; those awful numbers scratched into their arms, fallen away. Like beautiful Penny, they had been set free. I closed the eyes of my friends and kissed their cheeks.

"So glad I met you. I promise to tell your story."

I stayed by their bedside, a beam of moonlight rocking me in its blue arms.

"I love you, B. Thankful. Always have, always will." Like morning mist along the river back home, Little G's voice lifted up and floated away.

Not much more than a day is long had passed since I met Miss Emma and Miss Hannah, but they took a piece of me with them when they died. All a person has to do is hook you with one first-rate story about their life, and by the end of the telling you will love that person as if you had known them your whole life. That's how it was for me with Miss Emma, and so it goes with Miss Hannah. Short as our time was together, I would forever hold the blessing of knowing my lookalike friends in a special corner of my heart.

I found Dee Corum coming out of a room with an empty dinner tray. When she saw me, she smiled so wide I could see her pink bubble gum, and her lightning fast way with words reached me before she did.

"I came back to watch *Laugh-In* with old Harlan Nutbush He gets the biggest kick out of Goldie Hawn in her bikini What is it B. Thankful?"

This was my first opportunity to practice *How to Maintain Good Manners While Delivering What Could Be Considered Really Bad News:* 1) Choose your words carefully; 2) Deliver them slow and easy; 3) Make eye contact, but don't stare; 4) Don't make any sudden moves.

My first attempt may have sounded more slow-witted than slow and easy, but I worked on proper eye contact with Dee Corum, making sure I didn't linger to the point of strangeness, and I made no sudden moves. News delivered best as I could, Dee Corum placed her arm around my waist in a big sister way, the way Miss Hannah and Miss Emma sat while they played piano, and led me back to my room.

Miss Hannah and Miss Emma were placed in their very own sleeping bag for their airplane ride. I had no silver dollars to rest upon their eyes as payment for their crossing but found a humble offering at the bottom of my trouser pocket to pay their way–four pieces of Bazooka Bubble Gum.

Dr. R. Juarez, his sparkly smile tinged with sadness, handed me a note he found tucked under the record player. Miss Emma handed down to me their zip-up record player, all of their music, the photograph of them with Miss Sophia, and the little black velvet box. But how did Miss Emma know she would be crossing the bridge with her sister? Pearly May would say it was one of God's tender mercies. I say, may such wonders never cease.

To keep the memory of Miss Emma and Miss Hannah close by, I put one of their records on the player, and placed their Polaroid picture next to my paint-by-number Last Supper. Along with Jesus and his friends, they watched as I carefully carried the black velvet box over to my bed. I didn't look inside right away, wanting to savor the moment the way I did the last bittersweet bite of a Banner Bar. I held the box in my hands the way Mister held that single beignet, as if holiness resided within, while I tried to imagine what it could possibly hold. When I lifted the lid, I found the hope Miss Emma had tucked inside the hem of her jacket to see her through those awful days and nights—the recipe for Miss Sophia's roasted chicken and potatoes written on a barely there scrap of paper.

There is hope in the light, Miss Emma told me. I will carry the light in honor of Miss Hannah and Miss Emma, and all those women standing on the other side of the bridge.

When I laid my head down on my pillow, I found the smell of lavender from my Little G's hands lingering there, but no Little G to hold me through the hollow night. I opened the drawer next to my bed, pulled out my Banner Bar, and waited, but Daddy didn't come to call either. A sharp lonesomeness settled in my chest.

The door to my room opened, the waxy light from the hallway shining in. Miss Dee crawled onto my bed the way a sister would, and lay facing me. In the dark hours that remained, I shared my Banner Bar and the Ritual of the Five Senses with Dee Corum.

Like Winthrow's checklist for the arvee, *Dr. R. Juarez* marked all the boxes on my chart A-okay the next morning. Once inside the arvee, I found Ham and Miss Dee had tidied it all up and fixed the broken cupboard door. I pasted the picture of Miss Hannah and Miss Emma next to my pictures of friends and family, then hung my dream catcher in place alongside my paint-by-number Last Supper. Just in case Livia was still alive and longing to find me, I tied another purple ribbon to a tree, its leaves wearing the blush of autumn.

Miss Dee and I hugged and kissed goodbye, and took a picture of us pinky promising that we would write to each other. As I drove away from the hospital, I looked in the rearview mirror one last time and saw a pink bubble so large it seemed to be sitting on Dee Corum's shoulders.

Fifteen

———◆———

I came to a place in the road where I could turn to the right, or to the left. If I turned to the right, I was homeward bound, the cocoon comfort of my home and Pride's open arms waiting for my return. The last time I saw Jesus, he told me I always had a choice, which I took to mean there would be no hard feelings on his part if I saw fit to head home. Maybe Jesus said that bit about choice because he knew how much I missed Harmonia Pennywhistle's cloud drifting voice and her mysterious way of knowing the truth, or how it tugged on me that it had been so many weeks since I laid flowers at my Gs' and Daddy's graves, and told them my latest story. If that was Jesus's thinking, he was right. I did pine for my simple way of life and the heartbeat of the familiar—being lulled to sleep by the sounds of night and called to a new day by the song of the sparrow; the early morning groans coming from our old plank floor, as if I had stepped on a tender wound in my hurry to get to Beautiful Beulah before udder stutter set in; the way the autumn light slanted through bare trees, coming to rest for a spell on the kitchen counter where a fresh-from-the-oven pumpkin pie might be cooling; my walks down to the river where wonder gathered me in its arms and we listened to the sound of water lapping against shore, upstream stories floating downstream—and the list goes on. Heck, I even missed those pesky chickens. And it was all waiting for me. All I had to do was turn to the right.

Not as understanding as Jesus, the fellow in the truck behind me honked and honked, but I kept my foot on the brake pedal, and signaled for him to go around. A decision as sizeable as the one I was about to make could not be hurried.

I looked to my left, down the road that would take me farther out into an unknown world. Since leaving home, I had driven thousands of miles on back roads, some as narrow as the self righteous thinking of the town folks I left behind, or thought I left behind. Out in the world, I learned hard stares and harsh judgment weren't the private property of the town I left behind, for I had met up with a number of folks who felt a girl like me was trespassing where she didn't belong. But in the midst of the mean spiritedness and hard edges of the world, I also discovered there is deep rooted love in the strangest of places: a campground where I met Nadine and Winthrow Wainwright, and then there was the ramshackle building where I came upon the Sons of Satan. (All a person had to do was scrub away their hard ways with understanding, and add a little 'shine, to find the soft underbelly of their love.) After my time with the Sons, I came upon Pearly May's Kitchen and Miss Pearly May, the woman who made the earth shimmy with her laugh and served up her single-eyed vision of hope alongside the finest corn chowder I ever tasted. And who'd a thunk I'd ever meet a cigarette smoking, gum popping, earth angel in a place called Truth or Consequences, New

Mexico? Just when I couldn't imagine being more blessed, Dee Corum came along and showed me what sisterly love looked like. This I know for sure from my road trip for Jesus: if you're willing to keep your heart open and let the light shine in and out, you'll find love wherever you go.

I waved another stream of honking cars on their way as I reflected upon the pictures of my newfound friends looking back at me. Pride was right about the Good Red Road. I found every person I'd been sent to fix a last supper, and at every stop there were both heavenly and earthly folks who rallied around me when my doubt and fear reared up. In their own special way, each one helped me to shed the old bits of me that had to die so the new bits of who I'm becoming could be born. Oh, I'll always be B. Thankful Childe-Lucknow—the girl with red corkscrew hair, two-toned eyes, who hears voices of the departed. But now, with their heavenly help, and God's gift to me, I'm the girl they can call upon to prepare a fine last supper for their dying loved one. A supper that says, *Remember me, for I will remember you.* And that's one bit of me that I hope never falls away, because I know there's a bushel of folks out in the world who deserve a fine last supper, and whose stories are waiting to be told. And if this is the favor Little G told me God was going to ask of me one day, well, I'm happy to oblige Jesus's Daddy.

I turned the key and the engine hummed. On the radio, a fine gospel choir sang about the bright morning when life was over, how they would fly away to a land on God's celestial shore where joy never ends. Like old friends come to call, their hallelujahs rode the late October breeze through my window, lifting my spirit higher and higher.

Rays of heavenly light burst through the cracks between the clouds until the brightest ray of all bounced off the hood of the arvee. That's when I saw her. Livia rode down that ray of light through the window, landed on my shoulder, and stroked my cheek with her feather soft wing. I took Livia in my hands, and we studied each other the way long absent friends will do, and I cast myself back to the very first day we met, the day my life changed forever.

I checked the rearview mirror and caught sight of my paint-by-number Last Supper. There's no need for me to tell anything but the truth at this stage of my story and, hard as it may be for you to believe, please do when I tell you, Jesus winked at me.

With my choice set in place, I slipped on my sunglasses, flipped on my turn signal, stepped on the gas, and headed down the road.

3382495R00146

Printed in Great Britain
by Amazon.co.uk, Ltd.,
Marston Gate.